Tom's heart twisted with want.

Unfamiliar and conflicting. He shouldn't want May Anderson again. But here she was, standing in front of him, looking so beautiful and feeling so real. He tried to keep up the pretense of their little game, but the closer he drew into her, the less and less he was thinking about anyone else.

"I was actually wondering if we could go out sometime."

"Really?" May asked, breathless, and he wondered if she was still pretending.

"Yeah." He had an urge to laugh. "Just the two of us. Candles. Wine. Music."

"I'd like that. I'd like that very much."

With every word, her lips breathed against his. When had they gotten so close? Why did he want to lean in and close the space between them? Why did he want nothing more than to throw the past away and start over with the one person who'd made that very thing so impossible?

Did he...? Did he still feel something for her?

Praise for Alys Murray

"A feel-good summer novel."

Sweet Pea Summer

ALSO BY ALYS MURRAY

The Magnolia Sisters

Sweet Pea Summer

ALYS MURRAY

FOREVER

NEW YORK   BOSTON

Forever
Hachette Book Group
1290 Avenue of the Americas, New York, NY 10104
read-forever.com
twitter.com/readforeverpub

Originally published in 2020 by Bookouture. An imprint of Storyfire Ltd. Carmelite House, 50 Victoria Embankment, London EC4Y 0DZ

Forever Mass Market Edition: December 2023

Forever is an imprint of Grand Central Publishing. The Forever name and logo are trademarks of Hachette Book Group, Inc.

The publisher is not responsible for websites (or their content) that are not owned by the publisher.

The Hachette Speakers Bureau provides a wide range of authors for speaking events. To find out more, go to hachettespeakersbureau.com or email HachetteSpeakers@hbgusa.com.

ISBNs: 978-1-5387-4045-3 (trade paperback); 978-1-5387-5746-8 (mass market)

Printed in the United States of America

OPM

10 9 8 7 6 5 4 3 2 1

To Dad and Nicole –

who taught me that there truly is someone for everyone.

Prologue

In the small town of Hillsboro, California, rumors were like honey. Sweet. Addictive. And, once stained, impossible to get out except with a good, long, painful scrubbing.

Rumors could explain a great many things in a small town. Rumors could explain how a grandfather putting presents beneath the tree became a bona fide Santa Claus sighting. Rumors could explain how Mary Blake won Homecoming Queen over Linda Ashby when everyone claimed they'd voted for Linda. The happy tale of Emmy Bowen and her courthouse marriage—six months after she met the door-to-door vacuum salesman—grew into a scandal of epic proportions, and the rumors about the possible reasons for their quick nuptials didn't quiet down even after their marriage lasted for twenty-one years and counting. Rumors could also explain how a high school breakup forever changed the lives of the two people involved.

There were rumors about Thomas Riley, also greatly exaggerated. On his seventh birthday, he'd gotten a baseball as one of his top-tier presents, promptly and accidentally broken a window with it, and ran away before anyone could see that he was the one who'd done it. That story—small as it was—grew into a black mark of shame on him, an original sin to which everyone pointed whenever another story about his "misdeeds" sprang up. *Oh, remember Tom Riley? The one who broke the mayor's window all those years ago? Well, he's at it again...* Tom eventually found it too difficult to fight his reputation. By the time he'd reached high school, he'd surrendered to their perception of him. They'd called him a rebel, an outcast. And that's what he became.

Inside, he was this one thing—a good, hard-working kid who'd gotten a bad rap, who let them have their rumors so he could keep his head down, study hard, and one day get out of this place—while on the outside, he gave everyone what they wanted. A quiet loner who everyone could perpetually assume was up to no good. But one person had seen through the mask. And despite the sensational rumors that he was a bad influence, luring her away from all that was good and right and honorable, Tom Riley loved her with everything that he had.

And those two teenagers had a plan.

It had been their plan for most of their life together—*on the night we graduate high school, we're packing up the truck and running away from this place forever.*

Only...now that the night was here, Amelia "May" Anderson couldn't go through with it. She was too scared, plain and simple. Scared of a future away from her home. Scared of the great, wide, open world offering out its hand to her. Scared of the warm-smiling boy with the keys in his pocket. So, she left him.

The truth was that May Anderson left Tom Riley. You've got to remember that, because no one else in Hillsboro did.

Standing beside his gassed-up truck, her bright eyes fading in the moonlight, she told him she wouldn't be joining him on the adventure they'd always been planning, that she couldn't trust him—the town's resident reckless playboy, the renegade everyone said was no good—with her future. He tried to fight for her, tried to convince her that their fairy tale wasn't ending; it was just beginning. That he couldn't bear knowing that she believed the same lies and whispers everyone else did. The protests fell on deaf ears as she collected her suitcase and left him behind.

She didn't tell anyone what happened that night. Ashamed of the truth, she only said *we broke up*, before locking herself in her room and refusing to talk to or see anyone.

But by the time she resurfaced weeks later, that one little sentence—*we broke up*—had grown into its own mythology. *We've all been right about him, you know. He left her and broke her heart, shattered her entire life. He really was the cold, heartless troublemaker we all thought he was. Poor May. Poor thing.*

May didn't correct the rumors.

Chapter One

May

As Amelia "May" Anderson awkwardly slunk into the downward dog pose, she couldn't help but wonder how she'd gotten here. Willingly doing yoga on the back porch of her ex-boyfriend's ex-fiancée's house.

Well, willingly might have been a stretch. And, to be fair, she knew *exactly* how she got here, at least literally. One minute, she was having a very nice, very boozy lunch with her sisters and their friend, Annie Martin—the ex-boyfriend's ex-fiancée in question—washing down hash browns and fried, sugared dough balls with long sips of mostly-champagne mimosas, when Annie said, "Hey! We should all *totally* do yoga together."

May was a nice enough person, and even though she had absolutely no intention of ever actually doing the yoga, she enthusiastically agreed that yes, at some point in the future, they should absolutely do yoga together.

But she thought it was like when you saw an old friend from high school and promised to "meet for coffee to catch up," where both of you fully knew you'd never actually do that. After all, May wasn't exactly the yoga type, and Annie knew it. The most exercise she liked to do was walking from her shop on the square down to the coffee shop, then back with an iced coffee in one hand and a cinnamon bun in the other. At the very least, she hoped Annie would just forget about it.

Unfortunately, May kind of forgot that her new friend didn't do anything by halves and she could occasionally be a bit oblivious to even the most direct of social cues. Or, maybe Annie just liked to feign obliviousness, using that ditzy, wide-eyed exterior as a way to get people to do exactly what she wanted them to.

Whatever the truth may have been, May somehow ended up here, stretching her muscles to the point of exhaustion while supposedly "soothing" instructions from a nearby laptop talked them through the paces of a sun salutation. Her sisters had somehow managed to weasel their way out of this morning's sunrise session, leaving May and Annie totally alone out here on the fog-wrapped porch. For a few years now, May had run a small gifts and sundries shop on the main square of Hillsboro, a store she stocked with plenty of kitschy goods and even homemade treats and candles made from the products of the bees she cultivated at home. The shop wouldn't open for another few hours yet—sunrise yoga was *positively perfect* for working women, according to Annie—but in this moment, she wished she'd suddenly changed her shop to a 24-hour schedule.

When she thought too hard about it, the entire thing radiated with weirdness. It didn't feel weird, but she recognized it probably should have been. After all, her host and friend *was* briefly engaged to her ex-boyfriend. And Annie's older brother was currently dating May's older sister, Harper. Their being friends should have been fifty shades of weird, but instead...it was kind of nice.

When they'd first met, May had hated her. It had surprised her, the intensity of it. But it had felt like the pretty girl from out of town was stealing everything—the man she'd once loved *and* the friendship of her sister. Then, once all of that was behind them, May discovered a true friend in Annie. Despite her online performance as a shallow influencer, the woman was enduringly kind and thoughtful, smart and warm. Her bubbly effervescence brightened up May's down-to-earth, casual vibe, and the two of them seemed to understand each other in a way no one else in town did. Their short history was complicated, sure, and maybe not one many people would have been willing to overlook, but somehow, once they started talking, they realized that they just *got* each other.

Truth be told, they were both a strange brand of lonely, the kind you really only found in a small town. Surrounded by people but close to barely any of them. Known by so many folks but *understood* by none of them.

May had *thought* that Annie understood her, anyway, before this whole yoga thing happened. Now she wasn't so sure. Anyone who really understood her would have known that crouching on a yoga mat before sunrise in the early-summer breeze wasn't something she was going to enjoy.

Almost half an hour into this particular brand of torture—one that left Annie with a healthy, golden glow and May with a red, puffy face from the focus and exertion—she finally found her voice to speak, whispering as though the recorded instructor on the screen at the far end of the porch could hear them.

"So … where you come from, people do this for fun?"

Annie's smile didn't take away from the soft focus of her eyes as she moved into a warrior pose. May tried to copy her but couldn't quite manage it with the same grace. "For fun and for focus, yes. It's a good way to center yourself."

"I think I lost my center about twenty minutes ago when I fell on my rear trying to get my leg behind my head. I don't think twisting myself in knots all over again is going to help me find it any time soon."

The warrior pose, with its bent legs and outstretched arms, wasn't exactly the best example of twisting herself in knots, but May's screaming, stretched muscles didn't care. If this was what people in Los Angeles did for fun, she was glad to have been raised farther up the California map in Hillsboro, where their idea of fun was creek splashing and bonfires.

Besides, she couldn't imagine anywhere in Los Angeles with a view like the one Annie had here, on the deck of the home she and her brother shared. From up here, it was possible to drink in an entire valley's worth of greenery, of towering trees and winding vines, to catch the sight of silvered dew sparkling like gemstones in the beginnings of sunshine. In the distance, May could hear the barking of Monster, Annie's dog, just as easily as she could hear the chirping of early-rising hummingbirds and the last hiss of mist as it dissipated into the morning.

Despite the warmth of the summer sun just beginning to creep up behind the Mayacamas Mountains in the distance, a chill fluttered on the tail ends of the breeze, playing with the light hem of her overlong exercise shirt. May suppressed a shiver. Summers in Northern California were always like this, a magical mixture of warmth and cold, of light and shadow. Usually she found it absolutely enchanting. Today it reminded her why she didn't usually get out of bed before sunrise unless it was strictly necessary. Somehow, though, the cold didn't bother Annie, with her perfect, strappy sports bra and biking shorts.

"You know," Annie whispered, "yoga is supposed to be done in a meditative state."

"Is that code for silently?"

"Yes."

May smirked as she bent into the next pose, another relatively simple one that still managed to make her feel like a newborn deer struggling to stand for the first time.

May shook her head, as much as she could without losing her balance. "You like to talk even more than I do. How do you manage to stay quiet for this long?"

Annie's voice floated along, like mist over a pond. May could never imagine being that serene. How a woman who'd just canceled her big Instagram-celebrity wedding and dropped her whirlwind-romanced-fiancé could be so calm and so sure, May couldn't even begin to guess. "Being quiet for one hour a day is the *reason* I'm so talkative."

"Then this should definitely be outlawed."

That broke through Annie's perfect tranquility. With a gasp of mock outrage, she dropped her pose and tugged at her friend's hoodie. "How dare you!"

Laughter tickled at May's ribs, which would have been great if they weren't already sore from all of the stretching. Ducking out of the way of Annie's surprising reach, she tried to focus back on the small screen before them, with its sleek, white, recorded yoga studio and the high-ponytailed blonde who coaxed them through the end of their paces.

"Aaand…Deep breath iiin…Deep breath ouuut.…" Placing her hands in a prayer pose at the base of her torso, May tried her best to obey. "Relax. And go in peace, my friends."

More like pieces, May thought to herself, but she didn't dare say it out loud. Needling her friend about sunrise yoga would only get her so far. And besides, the last thing she wanted was to seem too weak to do a half-hour's worth of core-engaging poses.

"There," Annie said, relaxing her small, lithe body and smirking triumphantly. As always, things seemed to come as easily to her in real life as they looked in her social media feeds. "See? That wasn't so bad, was it?"

May reached for the water bottle in her bag, careful to take small steps so as not to agitate the newfound tightness in her calves. "You know those videos of puppies walking around in booties? Where they suddenly don't know how to walk?"

"Yeah."

"That's how I feel."

"Very funny." Annie shook her head and tucked her millennial pink yoga mat under her arm. "It's not that bad. And it's good for you. You know what *else* is good for you?"

The muscles in May's stomach tightened. Any time Annie got a knowing, excitable note in her tone of voice, she knew she was in for some meddling trouble. With her older brother head-over-heels in love with May's older sister, Harper, Annie had been itching for *something* to do here in Hillsboro besides her surprisingly profitable Instagram modeling...and if her current oh-so excited tone was any indication, May was about to be that next something.

No way. May wasn't going to fall into that trap. She was happy enough without friendly meddling, thank you very much. Eager for a distraction, May ripped a freshly jarred container of honey from her bag and presented it to her friend. She didn't know much, but she knew one thing: there wasn't a person in the world who knew how to resist the siren's call of the honey she cultivated on the family farm. These jars were *actually* meant to grace the shelves of her small shop in town—tourists to Hillsboro, California, couldn't get enough of her honey and her honey-treats, like the sweet candies and natural beeswax soaps she made from scratch—but she'd give up the sale if it meant distracting Annie from her scheming.

"Oh!" Annie's face brightened, and she clutched the jar to her chest. "You're a lifesaver! I was running out! Come on inside. I'll get us a couple of glasses of water and put this away. Sorry the house is a mess."

With an apologetic duck of her head and without waiting for May to agree to coming inside, the perky blonde practically flounced through the back screen door, waving for May to follow her. Since arguing with Annie was always out of the question, May shouldered her bag, collected her yoga mat, and did as she was instructed.

Usually, though, when Annie said something about the messy state of her house, it was because a crumb or an Amazon shipping box hadn't yet been tidied up, barely even visible to the naked eye or to her Instagram photo feed. Most visitors to her home learned to just roll their eyes and ignore her apologies. This time, though...

This time, when May stepped through the door, it looked like an aging copy of *Tiger Beat* had thrown up everywhere. Giant MTV and VH1 logos crammed themselves in the corner. Boxes upon boxes labeled *Batman Cereal* and *neon glow sticks* rested in towering stacks beneath the wide, open windows. An outfit that looked strikingly close to Madonna's "Like a Virgin" outfit hung in a dry-cleaning bag over the doorway to the pantry, apparently waiting to be carried up to someone's closet.

May's stomach twisted again. This had all the makings of a party...or someone having a fire sale on their fallout shelter from 1984. *Please*, May prayed, *let it be that instead of a party.*

"What is all of this?" she asked, trying to keep her voice bright.

As Annie skirted around the kitchen counter and started pouring them both fruit-infused water from a pitcher in her fridge, she pointedly didn't answer the question put to her. "What are you doing this weekend?"

"I'm never doing anything. That's kind of my thing."

"Right," Annie agreed, handing over a towering glass of water, her eyes adopting that motherly, slightly holier-than-thou concern she wore so well. "And it's bad for your health."

"I just saw Dr. Forester. He says I'm healthy as a horse."

"Your *body* might be. But your heart? What's going on in there, hm?"

Questions like this, May always expected when she was at home. Her mother and her sisters, and even her father, were *always* trying to pry into her personal life, picking at the scabs of her healed-over broken heart, trying to get her to pretend as if the past never happened. She didn't expect it from Annie, especially considering that they now *both* shared that same past.

She might have asked Annie how her heart was doing. After all, *she* was the one who'd ended an engagement and decided to split her life between the bustling metropolis of Hollywood and the little hamlet of Hillsboro. But May bit her tongue. Mostly.

"Is this the kind of third degree all of your guests can expect when they come over?" she snarked, helping herself to a handful of pink candies from a bowl on the kitchen counter. A perk of Annie being a wellness nut with thousands of followers hanging on her every word about which pair of yoga pants to buy was that she did have *very* good taste in snacks.

"No, just the ones I like very much. Listen. I'm having a party this weekend. Food. Drinks. Friends. Music. And real, honest-to-goodness human contact. Even some of my friends from L.A. are coming. Are you in?"

"I'd love to, but I'm incredibly busy right now."

Annie scoffed with a toss of her perfect ponytail. "You *just* said you never do anything."

"Right. Like parties. I don't do parties. I'm incredibly busy *not* going to parties."

"Come on!" Annie said, her voice on that precarious, teetering edge between begging and whining that only a girl as pretty as her could pull off. "It's eighties themed! I'll have a replica of *The Golden Girls* couch in the living room, and it's the perfect excuse to dress up as Kelly Kapowski."

May shrugged and finished off her glass of water. *You can't let Annie nicely bully you into going to a party. You just can't.* "I was always more of a Claire Standish girl myself."

"See? There you go. Get a pink shirt, a brown skirt, and a serious pout and you'll fit right in."

The familiar sting of uncertainty—and suspicion—radiated from the tips of May's fingertips all the way down to her toes. There was something else going on here. This wasn't just about a party. She narrowed her eyes at her friend, who set about preparing one of those sickening green-juice smoothies that she promoted online.

"Why do you want me to go so badly?"

When Annie responded, her voice was high and tight. An easy tell. "Maybe because you're my friend? Who throws a party and doesn't want their friends to come?"

"There's got to be something else. Spill."

Tension tugged at Annie's lips as May pressed her finger down on the blender's *OFF* button, keeping her from finishing her smoothie-making process.

"Okay. There *is* something else. So, there's this guy—"

"No," May groaned, releasing the blender. The last thing she needed—or wanted—was some man coming in and screwing up her life. She'd done perfectly well on her own for the last eight years since high school, and there was no way she was going to welcome the chaos that a man would bring into her world.

Lonely was good. Lonely was safe.

"Oh, come on! You don't even know anything about him!"

"I don't need to know about him because I *know* that I don't want to be going out with *anyone*! It's not my thing."

Annie started the blender, filling the air with the sharp song of blades slashing through ice and kale. With all of the rattling inside of her heart right now, May felt like she might as well have been in that blender, too. "What *is* your thing, then? What beats an Annie Martin party?"

"Long nights at home with my cat, my bees, and my British murder mystery shows. Just the way I like it."

That was…well, it was mostly true, at least. May did love her bees and her pet cat Bermondsey and her endless supply of British television. She liked the safety of her little life; she liked never having to risk heartache or pain by putting herself in anyone else's hands. But wow, when she said it out loud it sounded so…quiet. Chaos was frightening; there were too many uncontrollable variables. Her little life promised safety. Peace. Protection. That's why she clung to it so greedily.

There were times when she did wish for more, when cold, lonely nights seeped into her bones until she thought she'd never shake off the chill.

Still. A safe life was better than an exciting one. And a safe life meant no more wild house parties and definitely no more falling in love. She'd had enough of that for a lifetime.

Annie killed the blender, her face crumpling. Her body went slack against the clean marble countertop. "Please, May. Ever since the thing with Tom…I mean, it was all amicable and stuff, but…I'd really like to have just one night where everything's okay. Where I get a little taste of normal again."

"And matchmaking is normal for you?"

"It's my favorite thing," Annie said, as though she was confiding some great secret. "And it worked on your sister and my brother, didn't it?"

May laughed. She couldn't help it. No one other than Annie could have seen those two falling for each other, especially considering how much they'd hated each other at the beginning. "I don't think you match-made them."

"That's the mark of a good matchmaker, isn't it? So seamless and natural that they think they're falling in love all on their own."

There wasn't going to be getting out of this, was there? Annie had an answer for everything. Leaning against the counter, May helped herself to another handful of candy, chewing on the sweet stuff as she considered a compromise.

"Fine. I'll make a deal with you. I will go to your party as long as you don't try to, you know, set me up."

A squeal that could have broken the sound barrier stabbed through the air. Deafening, but at least Annie didn't look like an abandoned puppy anymore. "Deal! But if you *happen* to meet someone—"

"Then I'll give you full credit."

"Excellent! Now, should I put you down for sunrise yoga next week, too?"

Chapter Two

Tom

Once, when he was younger and less inclined to listen to anything any adult ever said about anything, Tom Riley was forced to spend an entire Saturday with his father and grandmother, listening to the two of them explain the family business. Now, at twenty-six years old, he'd forgotten lots of the lessons he'd learned that day, but he could still remember the way his back ached as he reached hour four of sitting atop a wine crate, the makeshift school desk he'd been using during this extensive lecture. He could still remember the smell of the tannic alcohol all around them, could still feel the slightest taste of wine on his tongue as his grandmother let him taste—and then immediately spit out—their family's various varietals.

And he could still remember, clear as day, one lesson that stuck with him through the rest of his life. *The reality of wine is twofold. There is making wine. And there is selling wine. And if you can't do one half of that right, then it doesn't matter how good you are at the other half.*

Tom didn't really understand that premise when he was

twelve. After all, he'd eaten enough fast-food hamburgers to know that they, at least, were good at the selling half and not so much the making half of *their* business.

Now, though, as Tom stood behind the bar of the Barn Door Winery tasting room, staring at a barren space where customers should have been, he felt his grandmother's wisdom rattle around inside of him like a lost cork in an empty wine cask.

Turned out, Tom was really good at making wine. When he'd left Hillsboro after high school, he'd gone to travel the world and learn the finer points of that particular business. The problem was…no matter how good his wine was now, he wasn't any good at selling it.

Or, rather, he had a feeling he'd be good at selling it if he could get anyone in town to actually, you know, drop by so that he *could* sell it to them.

Not that he would ever let anyone see him sweat. This town, for all of the qualities that had made his family stay here for generations, wasn't exactly the most forgiving kind, and he felt that every single day when he was forced to stand guard in the tasting room, just on the off-chance that someone might wander in.

This morning, he'd made his usual rounds checking the progress of the vines all around the family's sprawling property, dreading the moment when he'd, once again, be stuck inside. Settling onto his stool behind the bar, he picked up his latest read from the library—a biography on John June Lewis, a winemaker Tom admired—and readied himself for a long afternoon of flipping pages and little human interaction.

The pages blurred in front of his eyes, though, when the sound of an approaching car reached his ears. He paused, turned down the soft, ambient music playing throughout the tasting room, and listened again. Had it been his imagination?

"Tom! Thomas Riley!"

Nope. Not his imagination. His stomach turned at the sound of his ex-fiancée's voice as it pierced the walls of the small tasting room, though the fact that she was his ex-fiancée had nothing to do with it. During their brief engagement, Tom had done everything to keep Annie Martin from coming over to the vineyard and the adjoining tasting room, because he couldn't stand the thought of her seeing what a failure he was and how desperate he was for any kind of business.

Annie had a big heart; she was one of the best people he'd ever known. He couldn't handle her pity, just like he couldn't handle the thought of her trying to use her resources to help him. He'd always dreamed of building a marriage of equals, a union of partners. He didn't want her thinking he was some failure who wouldn't have anything to offer her or that she would be spending the rest of her life trying to bail him out.

Over the year since they broke their engagement, though, their friendship grew stronger than it ever had been before, and Tom found it impossible to ask Annie to stay away from the vineyard. She'd taken it upon herself to visit whenever she had some free time, and though she never expressed any kind of pity for the always-empty shop, she did always end up leaving with a few bottles of wine and olive oil, claiming that she wanted to keep the cellar stocked. Tom was halfway convinced that there was a room in the Martin house full of abandoned Barn Door wine bottles, but as long as she never turned those big, blue eyes on him with pity, he figured he could handle that.

Besides...no matter how proud he was, Annie was one of the few people in this town who actually did buy the wine. Sometimes, at the intersection of personal values and commerce, Tom found himself turning away from his pride and his values and toward whatever he had to do to keep the lights on. In this case, taking money from Annie.

Sliding his book beneath the bar, Tom straightened as the door above the tasting room clanged to life, announcing Annie's entrance. She swanned in like a theater star making a grand entrance to thunderous applause, despite the fact that she was fully kitted out in nothing but athleisure wear and oversized sunglasses.

"Tom!" she crowed, throwing one free hand over her heart as she approached the bar. "I'm so glad I found you."

When he was eighteen years old, Tom graduated high school and drove away from this town with only what he could fit in the back of his pickup truck. The woman he'd meant to go with—May Anderson—hadn't joined him, so the haunting emptiness of that seat sent him everywhere from the apple orchards of upstate New York to the Champagne Valley of France.

It had turned out to be a good thing, though. Instead of exploring the world with a woman who didn't want him, Tom had spent the years away from the vineyard learning and growing into a stronger, better man. He'd worked the lands of France until he knew every vine and every layer of soil. He'd tinkered with cross-breeding plant species and earned awards and made something of himself. And finally, when his parents decided it was time to retire and see a little bit of the world for themselves, he scrimped and saved every penny to come back home, to buy their shares and help his grandmother continue running it. That had been two years ago. He hadn't expected to come home some kind of hero or anything—after all, Hillsboro wasn't too quick to forgive anyone who up and left the town—but he hadn't expected the way the people seemed to actively hate him.

The way they blamed him for May Anderson's broken heart.

At first he was surprised about the rumors that had festered in his time away. But he'd taken it all in his stride, trusting that, sooner or later, May would come and visit him, explain what had happened, and help him to clear the air with everyone in town.

He thought he'd been honorable, keeping his head down and waiting for her to make things right. He'd used the time to help with the vineyard, to take all he'd learned during his travels and create some of the most special wine in the entire country. It was easy to ignore the whispers when he was so busy. Easy to ignore May.

But time passed. Wine aged. So did Tom and May. And one day, Tom realized that he'd been waiting for May to do something she was never going to do. He realized that she hadn't changed from the scared eighteen-year-old who'd chosen Hillsboro over him.

For years now, he'd kept her secret, never telling anyone that *she'd* actually been the one to dump him and break his heart. And for years, he'd let the people of Hillsboro trample all over him, convinced that if he just smiled broadly enough, just acted polite enough to everyone he saw, just pretended as if he *wasn't* the eighteen-year-old kid they still thought he was, then maybe they would open their hearts back up to him again.

He was used to fake smiles and stilted conversation. To trying too hard and getting nowhere. To pretending to be everything he wasn't. When Annie was around, for a few brief, shining moments, he felt the knots he'd tied himself into to please and appease everyone slacken. It was nice having a friend.

"What do you mean *find me*? I'm always here. I never go anywhere else."

Annie chuckled and pulled out one of the barstools. "Can I sit here?"

"I don't know. I'm not sure there's enough room, not with all of these customers around."

"It *is* a little quiet today," she agreed, gently as she could. After a brief glance at the menu—not that she needed it; she probably knew the whole list by heart—she said, "Could I get a glass of the rosé, please?"

"Coming right up."

Tom poured her a glass and an accompanying water. When Annie came in here, she didn't do the usual tasting slate that tourists or strangers—on the rare occasions that they came in—asked for. She liked heavy pours and long conversations about anything *but* wine. She took a long sip from her glass and sighed contentedly.

"This is so good. I don't know how these aren't flying off of the shelves. You should really let me do a post about this place—"

"I can't afford you."

One post on Annie's Instagram feed went for more money than he made in half a month. Considering that the marketing budget for the entire wine label settled at only a couple thousand dollars a quarter, he just couldn't make it work.

Annie protested, as she had the other dozen times they'd gone through this same conversation. "I'd do it pro bono."

"We don't—"

"Don't take charity," Annie scoffed and rolled her eyes. "I know. I know. But if there *happened* to be a picture online of me that *happened* to prominently display this wine bottle, then—"

"Then I would call you out for such blatant product placement and probably report you to the FTC for failing to disclose an advertisement." Tom's fingers itched to pour himself a glass of wine, but if he didn't want pity from her, he definitely didn't want it from himself. Self-pity was even more pathetic. He sniffed and pointed her toward a stack of flyers resting on the bar top. "Besides, with the Northwest Food and Wine Festival coming up, we're going to find our audience. I'm not worried."

Untrue. He was extremely worried. Everything was riding on this big festival—which would be filled to the brim with wine critics and buyers from all across the country—to turn their fortunes around. If anything went wrong, even the slightest thing...Barn Door might not be able to survive.

"So..." Tom said after a moment of silence that told him Annie didn't believe he was calm about this any more than he did. "What do you want?"

Annie had the audacity to look scandalized over her glass of rosé. "Thomas Riley! You think I need a reason to come here and talk to my friend?"

"I know you're not here for the wine and the company. Spit it out."

Tom and Annie hadn't been together long. Their whirlwind, long-distance courtship had thundered into a whirlwind, abrupt engagement when she pulled him aside on a starlit night and said, calm as can be, "We should get married, right?" The engagement had lasted all of a few months, but despite their short-lived relationship, he knew a thing or two about her. And the dimple deepening in the right side of her face was one of the red flags he'd come to recognize.

Something was up. Scheming Annie was at it again. Wiping down the already clean counter, he braced himself for the worst.

Finally, a gleeful Annie reached into her purse and withdrew a golden envelope. Elegant fingers tipped with pastel-blue polish moved the invitation across the table until it settled directly in front of him.

"I'm throwing an eighties-themed party at my house on Saturday to introduce some of my friends from L.A. to my new friends here in town and I want you there."

"It's a kind offer, but as I'm *sure* you remember—"

"You don't do parties. I know." Before he could protest, she scrunched her face up into a cartoonish caricature of a grumpy expression and spoke in her deepest, most masculine voice. "Wine tastings, industry events, pouring hours. Sure. But no parties."

"I don't sound like that."

"You do. You definitely do."

This time, Tom's smile was genuine. Most everyone else in town went out of their way to keep their interactions cordial, but decidedly short of friendly. Besides his own family, Annie was the only person in his life who ever had the guts to joke with him anymore.

His mind flitted to May, like it usually did when he thought about the past. Their lives had been nothing *but* jokes and laughter; he missed that. Which, of course, was why he couldn't go to Annie's party. Not Saturday night or any night.

"Thanks for inviting me, but I don't go anywhere I might embarrass myself."

"I've never seen you embarrass yourself. Ever."

Yeah, and I'd like to keep it that way, thank you very much. This entire town already hates me. I'm not going to get anywhere with them if they think I'm a joke, too.

"And I think this party could actually be good for you. We could publicly bury the hatchet. Everyone loves their whispers and rumors in this town, but once we're seen together laughing and having a good time, we'll put it all to rest." Her eyes flickered to the empty shop around them, and the implication was clear. *Maybe if we make nice publicly, the customers will start coming back.* But what Annie didn't know was that the rift between him and the people of Hillsboro went back long before her. "Besides, I have someone I want you to meet."

Tom's heart stopped. "Who?"

But his ex-fiancée was already halfway to the door before he got the word out. He had to admit: she had a way of persuading people, even if persuasion meant leaving the room before you could tell her no. She called over her shoulder. "You'll see her if you come to the party on Saturday. Eight o'clock. Don't be late or you'll miss the cake shaped like the *Ghostbusters* logo!"

"But, Annie—"

Ding! No use. The bell above his door clanged, announcing her departure. The sound reverberated in his ears, knocking around in his skull until it was the only thing he could hear or think about.

An eighties throwback party. He wasn't sure what other people saw in revisiting the past. Especially when the past never really seemed to leave him in the first place.

Chapter Three

May

May couldn't remember the last time she'd been to a house party. Barn dances and town festivals, sure. But a real house party with Jell-O shots and unofficial make-out corners and music so loud she could barely hear herself think? She probably hadn't been to one of those since high school.

Sitting in front of Annie's vanity mirror, May inspected her (admittedly, phoned-in) Claire Standish costume, her red hair a perfect fit for the Molly Ringwald costume. She'd found the perfect thrift-store outfit to mirror *The Breakfast Club* character and her height already mirrored Molly Ringwald's taller-than-average form, but still... something felt off. Wrong.

It took May a moment to realize that *she* was the broken element. She was all wrong.

In some ways, May could see the appeal of a night like this. Sure, she didn't get to parties much these days, but if she managed to avoid Annie's matchmaking schemes, maybe a night of thought-numbing music and pointless conversations would be a good escape.

But escaping any of Annie's plans was a very big if. The

longer she thought about the night of unknowns before her, the less sure she was that it was a good idea at all. A swirling vortex of nerves took hold of her stomach, which she tried to numb with another sip of wine.

Well, the sip was actually more like a glass-finishing gulp, but whatever. She would need a little liquid courage if she was going to make it through the night. Obviously, she didn't want to be drunk—drunkenness, in her experience, usually led to her making a fool of herself—but a little bit of a buzz to loosen the knots in her neck was necessary.

Turning her attention to her slightly chipped nails, she pulled a vial of red polish from Annie's extensive collection and tried to fix it. Anything to take her mind off things.

Only problem was, her hands were shaking so badly she could barely hold the brush.

"How are you doing there, kiddo?"

May didn't need to so much as glance in the mirror of Annie's vanity to see that it was her eldest sister, Rose, standing in the doorway. She'd recognize that soft, light voice anywhere. But when she did brave a glance, she found her sister wandering across the expansive bedroom toward her, freshly dressed in a soft pink dress she'd sewn herself for this party, perfectly channeling Baby from *Dirty Dancing*. May tried to put on a brave face.

"Fine."

"Really?" Rose asked in that gentle way of hers, all measured and concerned. Even when she was teasing, even when what she said might have sounded rude coming from anyone else, she always spoke with such love that it was impossible to be hurt by her. Her lips curled into a kind, knowing smile of her own. "Because you are the one who taught *me* how to do my nails and right about now you're starting to look like a Jackson Pollock."

"Sorry," May replied, shaking her head clear and reaching for the polish remover as her sister took the seat beside her at the vanity. "I've just got a lot on my mind."

"Like what?"

Oh, nothing much. Just the fact that I've spent the last few years trying to be invisible in this town because I'm afraid of what they'll see when they look too closely at me. I've spent the last eight years of my life trying to hide who I am and what I've done because I'm terrified of losing the people of this town. If I lose them, if I do something to embarrass myself or step out of line, then I won't have anyone.

I gave up my dreams of traveling the world because I was afraid that I would lose this community and be all alone. I gave up Tom and have regretted it every single day since because I was afraid that if he dumped me, the town would never forgive me for leaving in the first place. That, if I came back after leaving, I would be a pariah and an outcast just like he had been.

I've been hiding behind myself for so long. What if I go out there tonight, put myself out there, and I mess up all of that hard work?

May couldn't say any of that, obviously. Instead of talking about her existential problems, she decided to talk about her literal ones.

"My bees and the shop and what the hell I'm going to sell at the Food and Wine Festival and—"

"Come on. You know you can't fool me. We're Anderson women. When it comes to our businesses, there's nothing we can't handle." Rose paused and tilted her head as their eyes locked in the vanity mirror. Even though they weren't looking directly at one another, May still felt as though her sister were rifling through her heart. That was the thing about being an Anderson. There was no hiding. Well, there wasn't *much* hiding. "You're worried about something else, aren't you?"

Guilt knotted in May's stomach. The truth was complicated, too complicated to ever confess to her sister. The last time she'd tried to be with someone in the way that Annie wanted her to be with this guy friend of hers, May had thoroughly ruined everything. She hadn't been brave enough back then to go out on a big, brave adventure with Tom. She hadn't been brave enough to tell the truth afterward and save his reputation.

The truth was, she was afraid of trying again. Afraid that, after years of a small life, she didn't have the courage to put herself out there anymore. But even more than that, she was afraid of history repeating itself. What if she *did* meet this guy of Annie's, fall hard for him, and hurt him just like she hurt Tom? Yes, she did know that she was a chronic overthinker. And yes, she did know that she was getting too far ahead of herself, but still, she couldn't live with that. No, it was easier just to hide. Just to let life and love pass her by. She didn't want to hurt anyone else. She couldn't bear it.

"I just don't know if I can do this," she said carefully. "I haven't been to a party like this since I was eighteen and had a boyfriend and thought everything was going to be all right for the rest of my life."

"Well, isn't it? Aren't you fine?"

Rose had a terrible habit of always asking both the exact right and the exact wrong questions. May squirmed under the scrutiny.

"Yeah, but... going out there and trying again? What if I screw it all up? What if I mess up so badly that I'm *not* fine again? I mean, she wants to set me up—"

"I thought she promised she wouldn't," Rose countered.

"Have you met Annie? Of course she's going to."

"Good point."

With her nails no longer looking like an abstract painting, May laid her hands out flat to dry. Anything to keep her mind off of the growing weight of guilt balling at the base of her throat. This was why she avoided talking about Tom and the past with her family. Every discussion led to another evasion.

"So if I like this guy, then I could be starting over again, you know? *Trying* again. And I just don't want to fail. Not like last time."

Rose seemed to consider that. "Is that why you've been this way? You haven't talked about it at all over the last few years; I just thought...I thought that maybe this was what you wanted."

May shrugged. This, at least, she could be completely honest about. "I like my quiet life. I like my bees and making candy and letting the calendar pages slip by. But...there are benefits to not searching for anything more, you know? Infamy wasn't really a good color on me. Invisibility is much better." May's throat tightened, and she realized that her sister's gaze was very intense...maybe a little bit too intense. She nudged her with her elbow, trying to lighten the mood with as sweet and easy a joke as she could manage. "Besides, you never even date at all. I don't see why I'm getting a lecture from you about this."

"Well, would you rather I pull Harper in to lecture you about it?"

"No."

"Good. Now, do you want to know what I think?"

"You're my sister. I always want to know what you think."

All traces of humor dissolved from Rose's eyes when she spoke. "I think you need to make a promise to yourself that you're at least going to try again. Try to live a full and big life again. It's who you are, May. It's always been who you are."

"But—"

"And if you fail, then you'll still have your family and the people who love you. And we'll always be there to help you pick yourself up, dust yourself off, and try again. A ray of sunshine like you can't spend her entire life in the shadows."

Each syllable felt like hydrogen peroxide on an open wound. It burned at first, but then it made everything clearer and better. She swallowed hard, knowing her sister was right. It *was* time to try again. Falling in love again was out of the question, but living her life didn't have to be.

"Why do you always have to be so wise? When will I be like that?" She smiled ruefully at Rose.

"It comes with the oldest sister territory, I'm afraid. You can never hope to be as great as me." She waved her empty champagne flute with a wink. "And I think I've already had one too many glasses of Prosecco."

"You've had a single glass of Prosecco."

"What can I say? I'm a lightweight."

"Well," May teased, nudging her sister with her shoulder, glad they were out of the wilderness of their heart-to-heart. "Don't drink three glasses or you'll hit mean-drunk territory."

"One little fistfight in the parking lot of the Bronze Boot and your kid sister never lets you live it down!"

Grateful laughter welled up in May's chest, and she relished the sound as it left her lips. No matter what happened tonight or in any of the nights that came after, she'd always have her sisters. And knowing that could get her through anything.

Just at that moment, the door to Annie's bedroom swung open, revealing the woman of the hour, dressed in her Madonna finest.

"What are you two still doing in here? The party's started, ladies, and you don't want to miss one minute of the nostalgia fest!"

Reigning queen of the dramatic exit, Annie left them both behind with a flourish of braided ponytails and a huff of excitement. No arguing with that. Rising from the vanity, May barely suppressed a groan.

"Nostalgia. Just what I need right about now."

"A blast from the past can be good for the soul, you know," Rose gently reminded her, raising her voice slightly as they neared the wall of sound emanating from the first floor of the house. She reached down and gave May's hand a confidence-building squeeze that, in reality, did nothing to dull her fears. Perhaps her older-sister vibes were all used up. "The decorations tonight might be old, but it feels like a good time for some fresh starts."

May could feel her smile getting wistful. "I hope you're right."

Arm in arm, they tripped down the rest of the steps, until they finally reached the living room, where the party was already raging on without them. Annie, of course, couldn't resist a grand declaration.

"All right, ladies. Welcome to eighties night."

Upon their arrival this afternoon, Annie had hustled them up the back staircase to "preserve the mystery," which meant that when May stepped off the staircase and into the open-concept first floor, she was seeing the grand spectacle for the first time. And what a spectacle it was. It was only too bad that the party wasn't nineties themed, because that first step into the party was almost like what May imagined it was like for the scientists in *Jurassic Park* the first time they saw those dinosaurs: complete awe and terror. What had been a maze of boxes and bags and carts just a few days ago was now a magazine-ready bash, complete with a collection of the most beautiful people May had ever seen. Annie's Angelino friends had made the trip to the country in droves, and they were as much decoration as the neon lights dancing overhead and the so-tacky-it's-cute tower of Cheerwine in the corner. Cyndi Lauper blared over the house's sound system, her lyrics about falling and time drowning out any reasonable attempts at conversation, while every television—and she counted at least three—played a different eighties rom-com or music video mutely in the background. And, true to her word, right in the center of everything, was a replica of the couch from *The Golden Girls*.

One thing was certain. Hillsboro had never seen a party like this.

Rose let out a low whistle of approval, barely audible over the music, and May couldn't help but mutter to herself, too.

"Wow."

Annie's bright eyes danced as she reached toward one of the small high-top tables littering the floor. She retrieved two small boxes and handed them over, dumping them in Rose's and May's hands before they could protest.

"I even got disposable cameras. I have no idea where we'll go to get the film developed, but grab one and make sure to take plenty of pictures. And speaking of photographers...May, why don't you come with me? I want to introduce you to someone."

In that moment, with that request somehow managing to strike her ears louder than the blaring music all around them, a stone of dread settled into May's stomach. Now? So soon? Couldn't she at least stuff her face with canapés first? Even condemned women were given the dignity of a last meal.

"But—"

Her protests, unfortunately, fell on deaf ears. Even Rose—the traitor—wasn't having any of it.

"Remember your promise," she scolded, her voice getting smaller and smaller to May's ears as she was pulled by her one free hand through the moving sea of bodies populating the living room. For a brief moment, she caught sight of Harper and Luke—May's middle sister and her fiancé, locked in an adorable embrace as Westley and Buttercup from *The Princess Bride*—and wanted to call out to them. Maybe *they* could rescue her from the romance-happy Annie and her plot to make her fall in love. But before she could even open her mouth to call out to them, her captor dragged her out of the house entirely, onto the house's sprawling front porch—a terrace of reclaimed wood and stone overlooking the valley below. Annie and her decorators had dressed it up to look like an exterior shot from any high school dance scene in an eighties sitcom. Oversized, brightly colored Christmas bulbs flooded the pergola overhead, dousing them in artificial light that was occasionally interrupted by the natural starlight of the night sky.

The relief from the pounding noise and heat of the party inside was instant, but her discomfort returned when she saw a lone figure standing against the terrace railing, holding a camera to his face and letting quiet *clicks* ruffle the air as he snapped shots of the landscape all around them. *This* must be the one.

Well, not The One, obviously. But the one that Annie wanted to introduce her to.

"William!" Annie called, her voice too loud and still not adjusted from the party inside. But if this William guy was surprised by the sudden disturbance, he didn't give it away as he coolly lowered his camera and turned around, smooth and easy, as if the movement had been choreographed.

"Annie, it's so good to see you," he said, his voice so rich and deep May wondered momentarily if he was faking it. "Thanks for inviting me."

"Throw a legendary Annie party without my favorite photographer in attendance? Not for the entire world!"

That was when this William person noticed *her*, standing behind Annie and trying to disappear into her shadow. And when he turned the weight of his eyes on her, it was like falling into a deep, dark chasm she didn't know she'd be able to escape from. He was...Well, suffice to say that Annie had excellent taste in men. Maybe he carried a camera, she thought, but it would make just as much sense for him to be in front of it. Tall and all lean, packed muscle, he showed off his impressive form in a get-up that she could only assume was supposed to be Tom Cruise in *Risky Business*. The look was disturbed by his shock of perfectly styled blond hair, very un-Cruise-like, but she could forgive that if he kept smiling at her as he was doing.

"Hello, back there," he said, raising up one hand in a wave.

"Oh, William," Annie said, acting as if it were a complete coincidence May happened to be standing right next to her. "This is my very dear, very lovely, very single friend, May Anderson. She lives here in town. May, this is my very dear, very lovely, *terminally* single friend, William. And if you'll both excuse me now, I have just seen an old friend."

In a flash of skirts and pigtails, once again, Annie pulled her trademark no-arguments disappearing act, leaving May very much alone with a stranger she didn't know the first thing about. Except that he was beautiful. And everything inside of her told her that he was *very, very* dangerous.

But maybe that was just her doubt talking. Or the part of her brain that was now in real danger of losing the argument for heading home to watch episode seven of her latest murder mystery drama. Maybe he was actually a great guy and it was her fear—and not her instincts—telling her to run in the opposite direction from this handsome guy. In any case, she'd promised Rose that she would try.

A groan escaped her lips before she could hold it back. "She's not very subtle, is she?"

"Subtle as a sledgehammer," William agreed, that deep voice rumbling and resonant, like a nearing thunderstorm. He quirked a smile at her.

"I'm so sorry. She promised me she wouldn't do anything like this."

"Like what?"

May tried not to speak without thinking, but this time, it was unavoidable. She had too many competing emotions fighting for dominance inside her; her mental energy was too thoroughly depleted to control her mouth. "Like try to set me up with any of her oh-so handsome and eligible bachelor friends. I think she's aiming to have the whole town married off by the end of the night."

Just at that moment, a handful of refugees from the party inside—including her two sisters, mercifully—emerged onto the terrace. Instead of trying to join her and William's conversation, however, they gathered around the swing bench at the other end of the porch.

William took one step forward and glanced up at May from under long eyelashes. She suddenly had the overwhelming urge to step back, but she held her ground. She didn't want everyone who'd just slipped outside to think she was running away. "Well, at least she's got one thing right."

"What's that?"

"She paired the most beautiful woman at the party with the *oh-so* handsome guy."

May's words lodged in her throat. This was exactly why she didn't go out, especially not around guys like this. She couldn't be trusted with her own voice. She somehow managed to screw even the most simple of encounters up. "I didn't...I wasn't trying to—"

But before she could even get the words out to wipe that infuriatingly handsome smirk off of his face, she heard Rose's familiar voice cut across the din of noise from the party, sharper and harsher than she could ever remember hearing her before.

"What is *he* doing here?"

That's when May turned. And saw Tom Riley standing at the foot of the front steps, his gaze resting squarely upon her.

Chapter Four

Tom

When Tom had mentioned—only mentioned, in passing—that he was considering going to a party tonight, his grandmother laughed as if he'd just told the funniest joke she'd ever heard. When he expressed to her that he was mildly insulted that she was cackling at the idea of him being sociable, she'd continued to giggle while saying, "Oh, Tom. You spend your Saturday nights watching British murder mysteries and trying to pretend the rest of the world doesn't exist. You won't be going to that party, especially if there's a chance that May Anderson might be there. And if you do go, I bet you'll drive there, sit in your car for half an hour, and then drive home before anyone is the wiser."

Defiantly, stupidly, Tom told his grandmother that she didn't know what she was talking about. He would go to the party and May Anderson wouldn't be there, and even if she was, it would be totally and completely fine. *He* would be totally and completely fine.

Except, he did sit in his car for half an hour and consider not going inside. May Anderson was there. And he was absolutely, under no circumstances, *fine*.

For the last two years, since he'd returned to town, seeing May in passing was inevitable. But every time he saw even a suggestion of her fiery red hair, he ducked away and out of sight. Seeing her here though, under the full light of a million strands of fairy lights and her face warmed by laughter and moonlight, was suddenly unavoidable.

Especially when she felt him looking, turned, and faced him so that her eyes blazed against his dark ones.

Suddenly, the oh-so clever John Bender costume burned against his skin. Things only got worse when he realized she was dressed as Claire Standish. He'd thought it would be funny, showing up to the party as the ultimate eighties bad boy, but now it felt too on the nose, like he was making fun of their tragic, doomed, beautiful romance. He felt as much like a villain as everyone else at this party seemed to think him. He could only imagine how much worse he looked in their eyes now, with his dark hair covering his equally dark eyes, his big, hulking figure casting a long shadow across their perfect party.

His chest tightened when those green eyes of May's met his and melted slightly. For the briefest of moments, it was as if he could fool himself, convince himself that she was relieved or happy to see him. But as soon as the thought crossed his mind, the green hardened to jade, blocking him out once again, and he remembered the truth.

She'd let everyone silently judge him for years. She and her rumors were the reason his family business was failing. His stomach turned at the sight of her, no matter how beautiful she looked now, all grown up and more striking than ever.

She wasn't the only one staring at him. The rest of the terrace, too, gave him the thousand-yard-stare treatment, the same kind of look you'd give to a plague victim who'd just swanned into a party full of healthy folks. Tightness constricted his chest, making the simple act of breathing normally suddenly one of the most difficult tasks he'd ever faced.

The moment—unbearably awkward—could have stretched on for a second, or maybe a lifetime. Tom wasn't sure. All he knew was that when it ended, it ended with Annie's piercingly happy voice and the clacking of her high heels against the terrace flooring. Moving gracefully across the slats, she crossed the space between them and launched into a friendly hug, speaking maybe a little bit too loudly, apparently for the purpose of diffusing the tension. Even as he welcomed the hug and the help, Tom wasn't sure it was working.

"Tom! You came! It's so good to see you!"

"Thanks," he said, echoing her volume before ducking into a whisper only she could hear. "You know, I don't know if this is such a good idea—"

"It's going to be an amazing night. The best."

She smiled up at him in all of her short, cutesy glory, and he remembered why he'd fancied himself in love with her once. Sure, their relationship never would have worked out and it was for the best that they were just friends, but there was something so easy to love about her unending optimism. And he, a man who found it hard to be optimistic about anything, couldn't help but admire that.

Optimism in this moment wasn't something he could share, though. But still, he admired her ability to see the good in everything, like one might imagine the glimmer of a distant star in a completely dark night.

"Come on," she said, when she finally released her hold on him. "Let me introduce you around."

A small hand tugged at his, but he stayed rooted to the top step leading to the terrace. Her guests had slowly returned to the business of party-making, but their eyes still followed his every move. "I really think I should go—"

It was exactly the wrong thing to say, and he'd said it a little too loud. Loud enough that Harper Anderson, May's older sister and Annie's soon to be sister-in-law, turned on her heel and cast a face full of fire squarely in his direction. Of all the things he missed about his relationship with May, he hadn't missed her two warrior-queen older sisters, who were always poised at the ready to defend their family.

"What?" Harper barked, completely ignoring the pained, torn look of her fiancé, who kept a tight hold on her hand, as if he was afraid she'd lunge at Tom any second now. "You can't bear to be around my sister? She's not good enough for you to grace us with your presence?"

"I didn't say that—"

Annie beamed, tapping Tom's shoulder conspiratorially. "Of *course* he didn't! And I'm sure Harper didn't mean that."

Rose, May's eldest sister and generally considered the nicest, softest of the three, didn't look so convinced. She also looked about ready to spit glass if Tom dared to get too close. "No, I think she did."

"C'mon," Annie said, her voice wavering slightly as she spoke. "It's a party. Time to bury old hatchets, right? Right?"

It was then, with her false eyelashes fluttering and her eyes wide and wet, that Tom realized. She hadn't done this purposefully. She hadn't wanted to orchestrate some grand conflict or to manufacture drama to entertain herself. She hadn't even thought that it would be a problem.

Annie Martin truly believed the best in people. She invited them all here because she genuinely didn't understand the way that this town worked. The way that old scars kept opening and bleeding again and again and again.

He must not have been the only one whose heart bled for

her, for the soft and breezy way she saw the world. Because May stepped away from the safe corner of the terrace and out into the center of the action, the very place he knew she never wanted to be.

It didn't surprise him. Even if she hadn't shown it to him these last few years, when it came to most of the world, May had always been—or at least tried to be—an enduringly compassionate person. She wanted to save Annie from herself, from the humiliation of being the only one here who didn't realize how messed up and tangled their lives all were. The cynical part of him chalked this up to May trying to publicly save face, to cast herself as the hero in this little drama of theirs.

But he was surprised when she stepped in front of him and held out her hand, raising her defiant—and quivering—chin to meet his eyes.

"Do you want to dance?"

Their eyes locked once again, but this time, there wasn't any of the hardness or coldness he'd sensed in her earlier. Now, she wore a mask of strength, one that he might have believed had the hand she extended in his direction not been shaking like a leaf.

Their moment of connection didn't even break when Rose's voice cut through the quiet stillness. "May—"

"It's okay, Rose," May said, before extending her hand again. From inside the house they could hear the music of the party turning slow and deliberate, the kind of sappy song that reminded him of high school dances and kissing May like he would never kiss anyone else. Except this time, *she* was asking *him* to dance, and kissing was definitely off of the table. "Do you want to dance?" she asked again.

"Sure."

He answered the question out loud before he'd answered

it in his heart. Did he actually want to dance with her? She'd let the entire town believe the worst of him, closed herself off from the world and from him, and now she wanted to *dance*? If he were a different kind of man, he would have turned her down there and then.

But he wasn't that kind of man. He wasn't the kind of man who would publicly reject any woman, not even one he resented every single day.

He couldn't hurt her. Better yet, he *wouldn't* hurt her, not like she'd hurt him.

And besides, it would only make things worse. If he rejected her now, the rumor mills would be turning double-time tomorrow, and she would be the poor, innocent victim to his mustache-twirling villain.

Slowly, fully aware that the terrace part of the party was carefully filing away their every move for further inspection and dissection, Tom slipped his hand into hers and opened his arms to her. Her smooth, soft body pressed perfectly against his, familiar and warm.

It felt like home. Even after everything, holding her this close was like coming home. And how he hated that. Hated feeling like he belonged with her, like what happened to them was the kind of cosmic accident that sent planets out of alignment. He really needed to get a grip.

Getting a grip proved difficult, though, when his mind began calculating not all the ways that it was awkward to be here, in this moment with her, but instead turned its attention to all the ways she'd changed and grown over the years. She wasn't still the eighteen-year-old girl from his memories. She was a woman, soft and curvy and alluring enough to send his pulse racing.

All around them, the party feeling resumed at Annie's rushed insistence. But as far as Tom was concerned, there was nothing but the two of them. The rest of the world—the party, the town, the rumors and the reputations—faded into a jagged, distant focus, until he could see and think of nothing but her and the awkward sway of their bodies, out of time with the music.

They danced upon a very thin line here. That line between hate and love.

"So, what?" he asked after a moment of silent dancing, his annoyance at having let May save him from an awkward situation making his voice a little too tight. "Are we just going to shuffle in silence?"

"Sorry if I thought it was better than seeing you excommunicated from the party," May answered, deliberately refusing to look at him.

It took a surprising amount of effort for him to do the same, for him to tear his eyes away from her cheek. At this proximity, he couldn't escape the physical manifestations of all the ways she'd changed over the years. The way his hands yearned to drift to the generous curve of her waist, which had grown more dramatic since he'd last touched her. The way her chest pressed against his. The way her soft breaths now came higher up on his collarbone than they used to.

But, as best he could, he pushed that awareness away. All he had to do was survive this dance with May, and then he would be free once again. Free to go on pretending she didn't exist.

"Strange that you would be so worried about my excommunication," he said, his voice a flat, disinterested line. "You haven't worried about that before. You've seemed pretty happy to leave me to the wolves."

A million times, he'd imagined this conversation, where he screamed and begged her to understand his pain and what she'd done to him. But now that he was here, he couldn't muster up anything more than cold indifference.

He'd gone out into the world and made something of himself—he'd studied languages and wine and seen a world outside the county limits. May had stayed here, trapped in the very life she'd always told him she didn't want.

Part of him still hated her. Part of him pitied her. But in this moment, he just wanted to be done with her.

"It's been difficult, being here—"

"You had a chance to leave," he reminded her. Her breathing against him became more erratic, more desperate.

"I know—"

"But you didn't want to leave with someone you clearly hate so much," he filled in. "Don't worry. I understand."

"But that's not true," May protested, her voice sharp and fast, as if the reply was more reflex than a carefully considered response.

"Then what *is* the truth? There's not a lot of that going around these days."

"The truth..." He could feel her heart pounding against her chest, could feel the way her body betrayed what she apparently couldn't say out loud. "The truth is that I have to go."

"May."

"Thanks for the dance, Tom. I'll see you around."

It was as good as a promise that she'd never see him again. On a breeze of honey-scented soap and a flash of Titian curls, she disappeared, taking her sisters and their scathing stares with her.

Tom remained, left behind by the rescinding tide of the party, motionless as a pebble buried deep in the sand. His mind and his heart raced.

As he stared at the spot where she stood only a moment ago, trying to sort out his thoughts, a small, broken voice muttered over his shoulder. Annie.

"That . . . That didn't go how I wanted it to."

"Yeah. Me either." Turning to leave, he raised his lips in something like a smile at his host. He knew firsthand the damage that little white lies could do, but he couldn't force himself to tell Annie the truth: her party was less than ideal. As was the company. "Thanks for inviting me, Annie. It was a really nice party."

Annie's eyes widened, distress writing itself into every line of her face. "But you can't go now! You haven't met Joanna yet."

"Really, Annie, no one is going to want to get set up with me after that little display."

After all, that's why he was here, wasn't it? So she could set him up with some great girl she had in mind? He couldn't imagine that anyone would ever want to date him after what had just happened. Word would spread through the party like a tray of canapés.

"Tom, anyone who wouldn't have you isn't worth knowing. Come on. Let me introduce you."

She offered her hand, small and steady as a life raft, and he allowed her to lead him into the party. He wanted to remind her that, actually, she *did* know plenty of people who wouldn't have him. In fact, she was best friends with three of them.

The bitter taste of that knowledge burned more than anything. Even in this, he was alone.

Chapter Five

May

May was aware that most women her age didn't want to spend their Sunday mornings swathed in a dense cotton beekeeper's duster, checking on flying insects with tiny poisoned knives attached to their rear ends, but she was also aware that everyone needed a way of decompressing. May, Rose, and Harper all had their side ventures, of course. May had the sundries shop, Rose ran a flower arranging business, and Harper managed the farm. But it was their hobbies that really gave them breathing room in this life. Her oldest sister crushed flowers into homemade perfumes, the other one liked testing the brakes on their family car by driving through muddy hills after rainstorms, and May liked to coax and calm her hives of bees until they gave her the sweetest honey this side of the Mississippi. Which she could then sell for twenty-two bucks a pop at her store in town.

She loved the ordered chaos of the beehive, the way these brilliant creatures worked together to create something beautiful. Whenever she felt her life spiraling out of control, she found herself wandering to this back part of the property, where they could remind her that everything would *bee* okay. No matter how disorganized the hive may have looked on the outside, everything was working together for a greater plan and purpose. She could only hope the same could be said of her life.

All night she'd been up, tossing and turning. Thinking about Tom. About that first glance across the terrace. About everything he said. About everything she couldn't say. About how *right* it felt to have him hold her in his arms again.

And about how wrong it was for her to be there.

He'd changed so much in the years since he'd last held her. His body had gotten harder, leaner, more touchable. His dark eyes were darkened by experience; his dark, almost black hair had grown out, giving her the urge to run her fingers through it. He'd grown into his face, his perfect jaw becoming more perfect than it had been when they were young. Even the scent of him had changed; last night she'd struggled not to be intoxicated by the woodsy, earthy, fire and tannic scent of him.

He was a man. Not the memory, not the ghost, who lurked in the corners of her mind. And that almost made things worse.

He hadn't wanted to take her hand and dance last night, that much had been certain. She could almost feel his distrust humming beneath his touch. He hadn't been rough or violent or anything like that, but she knew how loving, how kind his arms could be. All she'd felt from them last night was disgust.

She'd earned it. And seeing him last night, so close, yet so distant that they might as well have been dancing in different counties, only reminded her of that shame. Yet she couldn't help but still feel his arms around her and be aware of a small yearning that they could be like that again.

Because that was the dirty little secret, wasn't it? She missed him. She'd missed him every day for the last eight years, from the first moment she had to wake up and face her small town alone, aware that he was on the road, in that ancient truck, driving away from her. For years now she'd been able to tamp down that loneliness and that want, but he'd been too close last night for her to ignore it now.

She regretted it. Not going with him. Being with him last night, with all of that worldly wisdom he'd found after his adventures and travels, with all of the knowledge lurking behind his long, dark eyelashes, the regret grew thicker, heavier, harder to carry.

All of these thoughts hummed in her skull, buzzing in time with the bees she was handling. *Order can come in even the most profound chaos*, she reminded herself, remembering the phrase from the beekeeping guide she'd been reading last night in an attempt to lull herself to sleep. But just as chaos came to her mind, it also came into her field of vision as Annie—impractically dressed as ever in a leather skirt and flowing top straight off of a runway somewhere in Europe—made her presence known.

"So . . . last night was intense."

No greeting. No friendly formalities. May lifted her face from her current hive work and blinked through the netting obscuring her vision. "I beg your *unbelievable* pardon?"

"Last night. You and Tom. That was intense."

This couldn't be real. This had to be a nightmare, right? Surely Annie wasn't going to try and talk about Tom now, not after last night. May had a hard enough time forcing her own heart and mind and wants to cooperate with her decision to completely excise Tom from her life. There was no way she could keep Annie in line, too.

"Annie, is this a lecture? Because I'm sorry if I ruined

your party, but I'm really not up for discussing Tom Riley right now."

"Don't be silly! You don't need to apologize. It all turned out fine in the end, actually. Well, better than fine, actually. I introduced Tom to my friend Joanna last night, and I think they really hit it off nicely."

"Oh ... You tried to set Tom up, too?"

"You're both such fantastic people. Just because the two of you didn't work out in high school doesn't mean you have to cloister yourselves in these loveless prisons forever. I thought setting up you and William, along with Joanna and Tom, might smooth things out nicely, don't you?"

May didn't know how to answer that. "I'm not in a loveless prison."

"Breeding those bees is the most action you've seen in the entire time I've known you."

"This conversation isn't happening. And if you get any closer, you're going to get stung."

Cautiously, Annie's heels carried her a few steps away from the hive. "Well, take that thing off and talk to me."

For a moment, May considered sticking as close to her bees as possible, seeing as they were her only real defense. But when Annie had something on her mind, not even a swarm of angry bees could deter her. Slowly, May started for her friend, slipping out of her face cover.

"I'll walk you back to your car as long as you stop talking nonsense."

"Fine." Annie's mouth disappeared into a long, thin line. Such an easy surrender raised the hairs up on the back of May's neck. "But you should come into town with me. There's the big emergency council meeting about the Food and Wine Festival."

The council meeting. In all of last night's drama, May

had completely forgotten. She checked the aging watch on her wrist—an old gift from Tom's grandmother that she'd never had the heart to part with—and groaned.

"Is that the time? I'm supposed to be down there now."

All thoughts of Tom and the past momentarily forgotten, May wriggled out of her beekeeping uniform and dropped it on a nearby tree stump. She'd just have to pick it up when she got back. The Northwest Food and Wine Festival was one of the biggest things ever to happen to Hillsboro, and with her business one of the first signed up to participate, she needed to be at every meeting and in every conversation. Every year, the National Association of Food Entrepreneurs and Business Owners (a fancy name for a bunch of rich guys from New York who wanted to throw themselves a party every year) selected a different part of the country to highlight, hosting a weeklong celebration of the local food-related businesses in the area. Last year, the Gulf South Food and Wine Festival brought over fifteen million dollars in new business to the small town of Crawfish Creek, Louisiana, and now that they'd chosen her small town to feature, May needed a chunk of that change.

If she made a splash at this event—which would be awash with foodie influencers and critics, restaurateurs, chefs and grocery buyers—then it could be the event that propelled Anderson's Sweets and Sundries to the next level. Contracts for supplying honey and sweetmeats to big retailers would give her financial security that diversified from relying on small purchases from locals and tourists and finally allow her to contribute in a meaningful way back to her family and the farm. So, she needed to have a say in the process. Over a year and a half of planning, she hadn't missed a meeting yet; and she wasn't going to start now.

Annie seemed to be on the same page, throwing herself

in the driver's seat of her sleek, black sports car and waving
at May to follow suit.

"I'll give you a ride. Hop in."

The car was one of those high-tech automobiles that,
upon entering it, immediately made May feel as though she
would break it just by breathing wrong. As Annie revved
the engine and started down the hill, May carefully flipped
down the mirror and inspected her appearance. Not exactly
super professional to show up to a meeting looking like she'd
been wrangling bees all morning, even if it was true.

"I look like a puddle of sweat made sentient by an evil
witch."

"And a very cute sentient pile of sweat, if I do say so
myself," Annie said, a bright, beaming smile crossing her
face as she reached to press open the glove compartment.
The small door opened with a soft *click*, revealing a silver
case that shone in the morning light like some kind of holy
relic. "Look in there. I've got a whole beauty kit tucked away
for emergencies. Instagram doesn't care if it's a million
degrees outside. Help yourself."

Gratefully, May set to work rifling through the kit. Blot-
ting paper. Concealer. Lipstick. Enough to make her look
presentable in front of the committee. Presentable would
just have to be good enough. As Annie drove them from
the Anderson farm down into Hillsboro, May artfully set
to work. A lifetime of taking this old town road meant she
knew and could anticipate every bump and jolt, meaning she
could avoid smeared mascara and liner. A small miracle.

But even as she did so, she couldn't escape the sinking
feeling that this whole thing had been part of Annie's plan.
Now, she was trapped in this car with no bees and no distance to protect her. If Annie wanted to talk about Tom, May
would have nowhere to run.

"So…" Annie said after a few minutes of soft music, proving May's suspicions right. "To return to the subject—"

"We're not having this conversation. I had a good time last night, even with everything that happened. I don't need to be saved from some *loveless prison*, even by you. Your friend William is…" May considered the William guy. He was…not *really* for her, but fine enough. A little intense. A little too handsome. May had always found herself more drawn to relaxed men, the ones who didn't need to perform themselves, but rather *were* themselves. William didn't seem like the type. "Well, William is interesting."

Annie giggled and gave a slight roll of her eyes. At least she understood that he wasn't exactly May's type. May had been worried about knocking her friend's matchmaking self-esteem. "Look, I know he's a lot, but I thought maybe you could use someone like him. A little shock to the system to wake you up."

Oh, a rebound. Great. Just what May needed.

"I don't need to be woken up. I need…"

"What?"

I don't need to be woken up. If anything, I need the past to go to sleep. She wanted to live a life where she could finally step away from the girl she'd been back then and the stupid mistakes she'd made. Her entire being ached for a fresh beginning.

Saying that out loud, of course, wasn't really an option, though. And even if she did say it out loud, she wasn't going to follow through on it. She was too safe where she was now, coasting by in her own life. She settled for another truth. Tom had been right about one thing last night. There wasn't enough truth going around these days; May would take all of it that she could.

"I *need* to get to this meeting."

"Can I ask you a question?"

"You can ask. I don't promise I'll answer."

"What really happened between the two of you? You and Tom? Harper told me he did some pretty bad things to you," Annie said after a moment of silence. May shrugged. Tom had been honest with her last night; she wasn't going to make the same mistake by being honest with Annie now.

"You've heard the rumors, I'm sure."

"Rumors aren't the truth. No matter how many people might want them to be."

Guilt twisted, deep within May's heart. She changed the subject. "What really happened between the two of *you*?"

Annie shrugged. The truth didn't seem to bother her. She repeated it as easily as a weather report. "I wanted someone to keep my brother from worrying about me the rest of his life and he wanted someone to help him pretend he wasn't still broken up about something that happened when he was eighteen. Harper helped me see that as nice as that was, it was hardly a strong foundation for marriage."

Here she was again. Despite the fact that Annie's car was ambling down a long, uninterrupted stretch of back country street, May found herself at a crossroads. To tell the truth, to lie, or to avoid speaking altogether? Telling the truth felt impossible. Lying felt just as incomprehensible. So, May did what she always did in times like these. She defaulted. Fell back into familiar, easy patterns and habits. Dancing around the truth like a pre-programmed animatronic, sweeping and diving in circles around a rusty, well-trodden path.

"I don't really talk about it anymore."

"Have you considered that might be part of your problem? That you don't talk about it anymore?"

Annie was hitting *way* too close to home, way too close to everything May feared about her own life. Maybe it was impossible to break free of this life she was trapped in *because* she didn't want to. Because comfort was safer than bravery. As they turned into town, May tried to keep her voice as light and airy as she could.

"What are you getting at?"

"I don't know." Annie shrugged. "You're my friend. I just want to see you happy; that's all. You could use some closure. You seem…"

"What?"

"Stuck."

Stuck. The word landed like a blow straight to the center of May's chest. Annie was right. She was, absolutely, totally and completely stuck. When May didn't respond, Annie gently followed up.

"Do you think you're stuck, May?"

Yes. Of course she thought that. She'd never thought about it in such explicit terms herself and no one had ever called her on it so bluntly before, but… yes. It was true.

Not that she was going to tell Annie that. She couldn't tell anyone that she was anything less than overwhelmingly satisfied with her life. That was how you survive in this town—treading water until you can't anymore. And ignoring any doubts that you should have left for a taste of something else when you had the chance.

May considered about a dozen responses and even more ways to subtly change the subject. *Hey, let's talk about William's abs* was the first and most obvious. But she swallowed them all away in favor of three deep, cleansing breaths. *Thank you, sunrise yoga.*

Okay, so maybe she was stuck. But stuck was safe. It was the safest thing for everyone, including Tom. Especially Tom. Last night had just proven to her what she'd known all along. He was better off without her.

The car pulled up to City Hall, a small, ornate building

across the town square from May's shop and dating back to California's incorporation in the Union. Annie made no move to kill the engine.

"You didn't answer my question, you know."

"Yeah." May swallowed and released her seat belt. "I know. Come on. I want to get a good seat."

Moments later, they situated themselves in the front of the council chambers. Dating back to the days of the old west, the council chambers looked slightly more like a saloon or a hunting lodge than the traditional marble-and-white columns of most town halls. Wood paneling surrounded the lower half of the walls, while the higher half reaching toward the ceiling stretched with fading, California-poppy-painted wallpaper. Benches, like those in a courtroom, lined up in tidy rows facing the high bench, where the council currently waited to bring the room to order.

All around them, folks spoke in hushed whispers, no doubt trading gossip about last night's party. May's battle to tune them out was won when she caught sight of her sister, engagement ring flashing even here under the low-watt lighting, sauntering up the center aisle. May waved her over.

"Harper!"

"May," she replied, sinking into the seat beside her with a *thump*. Her eyebrows knitted with concern May didn't know how to carry. "How are you holding up?"

"Oh, everything is great," May lied. Her smile actually hurt from how fake it was. "What do you think they called the meeting for?"

"No idea." Harper shrugged. "It has to be something big or they wouldn't have called an out-of-schedule meeting."

"Maybe my contact from L.A. came through and got Beyoncé to agree to perform," Annie whispered, her eyes wide with possibility.

Before May could gently inform her that there was no way in hell Beyoncé would ever agree to be seen in a back-water like Hillsboro, Mayor Andrews and the rest of the council slipped into their assigned seats. The room settled into silence, and the aging, balding man pressed the speech button on the microphone in front of him, calling the room to order.

"Good morning, everyone. This emergency meeting will now come to order. Miz Greyson, will you begin taking the minutes?"

"I've done so," the secretary, a wizened old lady who had been one hundred for all of May's life, said in outrage, waving a little pen carved to look like a quill.

The town council may have been made up of busybodies with more time on their hands than sense, but May had to admit that at least they had a sense of humor about things.

"Thank you. Now, as I'm sure you're all aware, our lovely Caroline Perez is the current head of the Northwest Food and Wine Festival planning committee."

Mumbles of agreement and confusion rippled through the room. May frowned. Mayor Andrews pressed on.

"Unfortunately, due to an illness in her family, Caroline has been forced to go to Boston for the foreseeable future. Which, of course, means that we will be requiring a new coordinator. Just someone to get our big festival across the finish line."

The dull mumbles of conversation sparked into full-on discussions, ones that May was too shocked to engage with. They didn't have a coordinator anymore? This couldn't be happening. Not now, not when so many people here were depending on this event.

"Now," Mayor Andrews said, raising his voice to quiet the crowd. "I know that this is a lot of last-minute responsibility.

But considering that this is the biggest thing to happen to this town since, well, the 101 was built, we need someone smart and capable who will do their best to make this event and our community shine—"

"I'll do it."

May was out of her seat, on her feet, and speaking before she could register what she'd just done. The rest of the council, apparently, was similarly shocked. Jaws hung low all around.

"Uh," Mayor Andrews stammered. "The chair recognizes Miss May Anderson, of Anderson's Sweets and Sundries."

Pointing to a microphone and podium facing the council, he invited her to speak. Four long steps carried her from her chair to that microphone, meaning she had exactly four steps to decide *why* the hell she had just done this.

Unselfishly, it was because she knew that someone needed to step up and lead. The town was counting on this festival. It might as well be her, the one who'd been lurking over Caroline's shoulder and taking note of every vendor and phone call and email chain.

Selfishly, though…She needed a distraction. There wouldn't be any time for Annie's meddling if she was busy planning the biggest event this town had ever seen.

"Well, I've been a member of this community for as long as I can remember. I'd already offered Caroline my help once the festival got closer. I think I could do this."

Not much of a rallying argument for her leadership, but it was all she could manage at the moment. She couldn't stand the sensation of people staring at her, the weight of their gazes upon her. Their judgment. Mayor Andrews exchanged a few glances with his fellow council members before leaning back to address the crowd.

"Any objections or other offers?"

For a moment, no one spoke. May didn't even breathe. But then, the resolute sound of two high heels tapping against the hardwood floor of the chamber broke the silence of the room, alerting May without even looking that Annie had just stood up.

"I have an objection."

What?

"The chair recognizes Annie Martin, local citizen."

Annie didn't step up to the podium. Instead, she raised her voice, letting the sound of her sickly sweet tone bounce against the walls of the chamber. "My objection is that this is a very big and incredibly important job to do on one's own. I move that May Anderson be given a partner to help shoulder the load."

May opened her mouth to object, but Mayor Andrews spoke first. "That seems reasonable, given the time frame. Do you have anyone in mind? You, perhaps?"

"Oh, that's incredibly flattering, Mr. Mayor, but I was thinking that a local would be better suited to the position. Someone like Tom Riley."

The room, which had been seemingly in Annie's corner, suddenly revolted. Conversations broke out like wildfires through the assembled crowd. But she was not deterred. Instead, she just raised her voice even louder and spoke again, even firmer and more deliberate than before. Meanwhile, May's knees had begun to shake so hard, she had to grip the podium for support.

"Tom Riley would be a great choice. He's proven himself as an upstanding member of this community, a fine business-man, and he has a proven track record of doing events like this with the wine tasting events he does around the county now and used to host when he was traveling around the world. I nominate Tom Riley as co-chair for the festival."

Panic rushed through May's veins. Her and *Tom*? Working together? There was no way. No way she was going to do it, and no way anyone in town was going to agree to it, least of all the man in question.

"What do you think you're doing, Annie?" she hissed, turning away from the microphone.

Annie didn't even glance in her direction. She confidently tossed a long lock of hair over her shoulder. "I'm unsticking you."

The council shifted in their seats, clearly torn between a compelling argument and their belief that this interloper, this out-of-towner, clearly didn't understand what she was proposing. Had she not heard the rumors? Politeness won out. Mayor Andrews stumbled over himself to be diplomatic about the whole mess, while May stared at the fake wood grains in her podium and begged whatever invisible forces might be out there to help her dissolve into the floorboards.

"I'm sure Mr. Riley is very busy, and—"

"No, I'll do it."

That voice. That familiar, sweet, deep, rich voice she couldn't escape or forget. It came from the back of the council chamber but still shook her to her core as if he'd come up behind her and whispered it in her ear.

The man who, it seemed, would now be her partner.

Mayor Andrews seemed as shocked as anyone else. "You will?"

"Sure." She felt Tom's stare shift to her shoulders, and she turned, finally, to face him. His eyes were unreadable at the surface, unmappable in their depths. "Yeah, I mean...if May doesn't object."

The room was silent as a tomb. Miz Greyson's quill stopped its scratching. Everyone stared at her. Waited for her decision. She knew as well as Tom did that there wasn't any turning down this deal. To do so would be to leave them both suddenly plunged back into high school drama, to smear them both with the black brush of controversy and gossip. She couldn't do that. At least, she couldn't when he was looking at her like that.

"I don't object," she said, her quiet voice picking up and blaring through the nearby microphone.

"Well, then..." It took Mayor Andrews a moment before he properly composed himself enough to make a coherent thought pass through his lips. May knew how he felt. "Are...Are there any other nominations? Anything else we should discuss before adjourning?" The moment of hesitation stretched out too long, as if the old man was mentally pleading for someone, anyone to put a stop to this. But when no one answered, he raised his gavel. "Going once. Going twice. This meeting is adjourned. Miss Anderson, Mr. Riley, if you'll come to my office now, I'll hand Caroline's binders over."

The banging of the heavy wood against the desk ended the meeting. Just like it sealed May's fate.

Chapter Six

Tom

He couldn't believe he'd said it. Even as he sat in the back of the auditorium, staring at his hands and trying to ignore the steady stream of passing, judgmental eyes as they filed past him and out of the building, Tom couldn't believe that what had just happened had, well, just happened.

How could he have been so stupid? So impulsive? Sure, he needed this festival to secure his family's business and his own future, but that didn't mean he had to shackle himself—very publicly!—to May Anderson while also carrying the town's incredibly important festival on his shoulders. For so long he'd been so careful to do nothing that would set the town's rumor mill into motion with gossip and tall tales about him. He'd done everything in his power to make sure they could have nothing to even speculate about.

And then he had to go and do the one thing that would ensure months upon months of gossip to come. He'd probably be hearing about this particular stunt until the day he died.

No, worse. They'd probably inscribe it on his tombstone. *Here lies Thomas Keats Riley, the man who disturbed an entire city council meeting by agreeing to team up with his ex-girlfriend so they could plan a festival. May he rest in whatever the opposite of peace is.*

Knowing that it wasn't entirely his fault—Annie loved to meddle more than she loved just about anything on this planet, apparently—didn't make any difference to him, just like it wouldn't make any difference to anyone who picked up the story around town.

But it was important. Necessary. This festival was a big deal. And if being part of it meant facing May Anderson, then he had to do it.

No, he wouldn't just be facing her. He would be joining her, teaming up to create this event that the entire town was depending on. His mind raced as he considered all of the implications of what he'd just done. He hadn't just agreed to meet May on equal terms on a one-off basis. He'd just agreed to bear the weight of Hillsboro and its dreams—*his dreams*—with her.

He tried to keep his mind on his own investment in this matter. Maybe focusing his thoughts there would temper the war in his heart. He needed the festival to go well if he was ever going to save his family business from drowning. The thing about business in a small town like this was that if you didn't have great word-of-mouth—if the people at the grocery store and the hotel check-in desk and the gas station weren't talking you up to the tourists—then you might as well not even exist. Everyone who ever drove into Hillsboro from San Francisco or Los Angeles or the big cities up north came here for the *authentic, small-town experience*; if the locals didn't recommend you, then the tourists would walk right on by to the truly "authentic" place next door.

His business was going under because of small-town gossip and grudges. No one would recommend the vineyard run by the man who had left the town sweetheart for dust—not because they were still angry with him or because they hated him, but because they were indifferent to him. They'd written him off long ago. And now, as a consequence, he was barely grasping on to his family legacy by a thread.

If this festival was a hit, though? If he could manage to make a big splash and impress people from all across the country? If they grew to like him without the whispering of the small-town biddies constantly surrounding them?

Well…that might just save them. Volunteering for this assignment wasn't about May Anderson or their past together; it was about—it *had* to be about—saving Barn Door Winery. Saving his family's legacy. And he was going to do his damnedest to see it through. No matter how much the thought of spending time with her made his heart want to leap out of his chest and run into the center of a busy four-way intersection as the less painful option.

The sound of someone clearing their throat shook him from his thoughts. When he glanced up, he saw Mayor Andrews standing there, his dark face filled with deep lines of thinly veiled concern. Ah, so it seemed that the last few years of his being a fine, upstanding citizen of Hillsboro hadn't erased the man's memory of that time when a nine-year-old Tom sent a baseball straight through his window.

"Thomas," he said, hands in his pockets and voice low and deep, the patter of a disappointed school principal. "Could I see you in my office, please?"

"Yeah. Of course."

That's it, Tom. Just be smiley and compliant. Give them no reason to think they're right about you. That had always been his strategy, and it was one he kept to now. By the time they reached the mayor's office in the back of the town hall, Tom wondered if he still had the strength to keep up all of this fake smiling. Mayor Andrews hesitated in front of the door, his hand halting on the brass handle.

"Son, I don't know what you think you're doing, but—"

"I just want what's best for this town, Mayor Andrews." When the man didn't look convinced, he reiterated his point. "Honestly. I want what's best for everyone."

Tom wasn't entirely sure his happy-go-lucky-don't-let-them-see-your-real-feelings gambit worked, but, in any case, Mayor Andrews pressed open the door to his office.

The plain wood paneling and cheaply decorated interior looked like any other municipal office Tom had ever visited. He'd seen dozens of desks just like the one in the center, with its laminate finish and Arial typeface nameplate. The mayor had a few personal effects scattered around the room—diplomas framed up on the taupe-painted walls, a few horseback riding ribbons he'd won back when he did that professionally, framed pictures of his family and memorable cut-outs of newspaper articles on his desk—but none of them drew his attention quite like the redhead waiting there.

Tom had known she would be here, but being so close to her sent a jolt of electricity through his body. Not the romantic kind, obviously. The kind they used to feed prisoners who sat in Old Sparky.

May focused on the wall in front of her, not deigning to give any attention to the men who'd just arrived. She was cold. Removed. Polite. Indifferent. Just like he had been before he'd agreed to this. She seemed as remote and unknowable as a statue in the Greek wing of some great museum.

Without any ado, the mayor got down to brass tacks, moving to take the chair behind his desk and the only comfortable looking one in the room. Tom followed suit, taking the last chair. The one directly beside May.

"Well, there's not much to say here," Mayor Andrews said, pulling a cardboard office organizer from beside him and slamming it up on the desk for their inspection. With every jerky, mechanical movement he made, it became overwhelmingly clear to Tom that he didn't want to be here, stuck in the middle of Hillsboro's most infamous breakup. "Caroline gave me this box with all of her festival paperwork and—"

"Thanks," May cut him off, reaching for the box and dragging it onto her lap. The feeling of discomfort with this current situation was, apparently, shared all round. Tom couldn't decide if that was a good thing or a bad thing. He watched as her fingers clenched white around the edges of the box. "I'll take it. Anything else?"

Mayor Andrews blinked at her abruptness. Sure, she laid the smiles and courtesy on thick, but everyone could tell she was trying to make good a quick getaway. Tom's heart thundered. She couldn't just *leave*. He needed to talk to her. And so did the mayor, who tried his best to rush out a reply before she could leave them both in the dust. "We'll need to get you both signed up for city email accounts so everything can be documented, but for the moment—"

"Great." May rose to her feet and nodded at them both. "I'll keep you posted on our progress."

And with that, May Anderson was gone in a flash of fiery red curls and the faint scent of honey. Tom didn't wait for the mayor to dismiss him. Instead, he shoved himself to his feet and followed her. He'd just invited even more unwanted gossip and scrutiny from the whole town in order to get his hands on this festival. He couldn't let her get away. For better or for worse, they were now in this together, and he needed to speak to her if he was going to make that torture worthwhile.

Letting his feet carry him past the handful of onlookers waiting outside of the mayor's office and the administrators who lingered in the hallway to watch the encounter, he followed May's retreating form, holding his tongue from calling out to her—carefully obeying the *No talking in the hallways! Meetings in progress!* signs hanging all throughout the Town Hall—until he finally broke free of the building and followed her down the rustic staircase leading to the street.

His eyes darted back and forth, assessing the situation on the town square. A handful of tourists dotted the sidewalk, gaping at the precious storefronts, but he didn't recognize anyone who would trade on the sight of him chasing May down. Still, he kept his voice low as he called after her, trying to remain as calm and cool looking as possible. Even if someone happened to look out of their store window and spot them, he wanted to give them no more excuse than he already had to magnify this interaction to the level of scandal.

"May!" he half called, half stage whispered. When she made no indication that she heard him, he tried again. "May, I need to talk to you."

If you had told him a few days ago that he would have *willingly* been going after May Anderson, asking her to talk, Tom would have called you crazy. He didn't want to speak to her. Better yet, he didn't have anything to say. Her lies had put him in a chokehold that his own honor wouldn't let him slip out of, and the steady loss of air was slowly crushing him. Why would he ever want to speak to her again?

But still, there he was, calling out her name like the foolish, wide-eyed kid he'd been at eighteen, when he'd called after her as she left him, his truck, and their dreams behind.

The solid beating of her booted feet against the aging

concrete didn't slow at the sound of his voice, but she didn't pick up the pace either. Instead, she called over her shoulder as she single-mindedly walked onward. "What?"

Oh. Right. Now that he had her attention, he actually had to say something, didn't he? One thing the town gossips and reputation-cementers had gotten right about him as a boy was his impulsivity. Sometimes, a thought or an idea captured him, and he was already halfway to getting it before he realized he didn't actually, you know, have a plan. Swallowing hard, he choked out the first thing that came to mind.

"Don't *you* want to talk about this?"

It wasn't like he wanted to talk about it. But it was necessary. Very, very necessary. If they were going to put on a decent festival, then they needed to at least come to some kind of agreement about what that would look like. And how best they could avoid each other. That did seem to be what she wanted, after all.

"What is there to say?" May asked, stopping in front of one of Hillsboro town square's many quaint storefronts. He recognized the familiar painted window and the lace-wood awning immediately. Anderson's Sweets and Sundries. No, he'd never had the guts to actually go inside, but on evenings when the place was closed and he was certain May wouldn't be in, he'd sometimes wander by and peek in through the window. Not for any sentimental reasons. Just out of curiosity. Just to see what life she preferred to one with him.

Now, though, as May fumbled with the box and her keys, she looked about as far from delighted as someone could possibly be. She wasn't outwardly hostile or anything, but the politeness and indifference in her voice strained and stretched, a dead giveaway that she was uncomfortable.

Some things had changed since they were kids. But one

thing May Anderson apparently hadn't been able to shake was her biggest tell. Her neck flushed red whenever she was nervous. And right now, her neck was as red as the carnations the Andersons grew on their farm.

"I don't know…" he said, lowering his voice. Towering over her, he tried a little bit of old-fashioned brooding. "Maybe that you could use my help to make this festival a success. Maybe that we should come up with a plan."

As May finally located her key and opened the door, her gaze flickered between the lock and his reflection in the glass doorway. Slowly but surely, the red began to recede from her neck. "I don't need your help to make sure everything goes smoothly. I can handle this on my own."

"Right." He breathed a laugh. Sardonic. Bitter. "Now I remember why we don't talk anymore. You never tell the truth."

"Ex*cuse* me?"

Anger of his own started to rise up inside of him, which he quickly tried to tamp down. His grandmother would remind him about flies and honey and vinegar and all that. No matter how deep-seated his feelings about the woman in front of him, he needed her. He needed her to let him make this festival a success. He hated the idea of being vulnerable in front of her, but there was no other option.

"Look, I need this, May. I need this festival to go well and I need Barn Door to have a *really* great quarter, and forgive me if I don't exactly trust you to make those things happen."

"And why shouldn't you?"

Because you're the reason we're failing in the first place.

"Everyone in Hillsboro is loyal to you. They aren't doing me or my family's business any kind of favors. They aren't helping us get any footing. If I'm going to make any kind of progress here, then I'm going to need to do it myself."

"Ah, I see, so you want to babysit me. Want to make sure I don't do anything to sabotage your chances," May muttered, bitterly.

Tom choked out a scoff. There was nothing he wanted less than spending time with her, than having to be forced back into her orbit. "Want to? No. I definitely don't *want to*. But let's think of it as a tactical alliance. I'll help you, and you'll help me, and in the end, we'll both be heroes."

A bitter, sad note entered May's tone. "Just like old times, huh?"

Tom blinked. His chest constricted. "No. I don't think so."

For a long moment, neither of them said anything. He stared at the intricate glass sea-jars holding delicate candles and wondered vaguely what they would smell like. Was she still partial to vanilla and brown sugar like she had been? Or was she using her sisters' cast-off flowers for scents now?

If May was anything like him, she was also thinking about those old times, and about every agonizing, stretching day that had happened since. Folding his arms over his chest, he cleared his throat and tried to move on.

"Listen. Let's . . . let's divide up the work and make it happen, okay? It's probably for the best that we don't, you know, hang out together very much."

"I'm sorry your business is struggling. I know what that is like. Maybe, we could try to be friends," May muttered into Caroline's box of festival documents, so quietly he almost didn't hear her.

What? "Friends."

"You know. Like Annie said. Publicly bury the hatchet, even if we can't in private. Get away from where we've been. Try to give everyone a reason to forgive us."

We. Us. He didn't miss the way she'd lumped them both

together instead of pointing out the obvious—that everyone clearly hated him more than they hated her. It was more charitable than she deserved, but he managed to swallow most of his protests. This, crazy as it sounded to him now, could have its theoretical advantages.

She was the reason his business was failing. If everyone thought that they were okay again, if everyone thought the tide of their relationship had turned, if people thought she'd forgiven him…

Then maybe they would, too.

"So, what? You want us to play-act like we're friends?" Tom asked.

"It might help with your business. Give you a little boost even before the festival."

He hated to admit it, but she was right. And he wasn't exactly in a position to turn down good ideas. Even if it meant spending more time with her.

"This business has been Gran's entire life. I can't give up on it now."

"Truce, then?"

No, a truce sounded too much like forgiveness. A truce wasn't possible.

"How about partners in crime? Each of us just in it for ourselves."

A flicker of a small, almost imperceptible smile danced across May's lips. She nodded. That was good enough for her. "Deal."

And when Tom walked away a few minutes later, after the terms of their agreement had been set, he couldn't help but think he'd just made either the best or the worst decision of his life.

That's usually how things with May went. The best…or the worst.

Chapter Seven

May

Ever since the moment May had heard Tom's voice volunteer to be her partner for the planning of the festival, she'd been dreading family dinner. Usually, at the end of a long day, she wanted nothing more than to take her place at the table with her sisters and her parents, drinking in everything Harper and Rose had to say while trying with all of her might to ignore her mother's input. The woman loved nothing more than trying to micromanage her daughters' lives, but they did their best to skirt around her as best they could. With flowing glasses of wine and plates piled high with home cooking, dinner with her loved ones was usually the shining beacon at the end of even the most difficult, grating of days.

Usually was the operative word in that sentence. And tonight, she knew she wasn't going to get the peace and quiet she was used to. Tonight, she prepared for dinner like she was going to war.

But, much to her surprise, the interrogation didn't come. They talked about the weather and the new crop of sweet pea flowers—May's favorite—and a funny interaction Rose had today at her shop, and preparations for Luke and Harper's wedding. For the most part, things seemed calm. Normal.

Except, of course, that they weren't. May could tell. The dead giveaway that everyone had been firmly instructed *not* to speak about the whole encounter with Tom was that her mother, sitting beside her father at the far end of the table, practically twitched with pent-up anxiety every time the conversation lulled or steered anywhere near the direction of the Northwest Food and Wine Festival.

By the time the meal ended and the girls had been dismissed outside to eat their cobbler beneath the summer sky while their parents took care of the dishes, May's nerve endings hummed in anticipation. They'd been playing her this whole meal, waiting for their opportunity to strike. Her sisters found it now, as they sat in a familiar row of garden chairs—still painted with the handprint decorations they'd given the wooden monstrosities when they were in grade school—beneath an overhead curtain of stars.

For a moment, they sat in silence, their spoons scraping against the bowls and the sound of their chewing and their speechlessness so deafening May was convinced it would drive her to the brink. She might as well be the first one to say something. Not only because she couldn't stand the tension for another second, but also because, well, she needed someone to talk to. She needed her sisters. After everything that had happened today, she craved the kind warmth and clarity that could only come from a long, cathartic talk with the two people she loved most in this world.

"All right," she said, pulling her knees into her chest, partly for comfort and partly as a defense mechanism. "What's on your minds?"

"Hm?"

"Us?"

Rose and Harper shot her a matching pair of *oh-so inno-cent* masks of surprise. A dead giveaway that they were up to something. Her sisters were so different that for them both to have the exact same reaction to something was practically a signed confession that they'd been scheming together.

"You two have been dancing around it all night and somehow you looped Mom and Dad into the mix. Just say what you're going to say."

"Oh, thank God," Harper said, her body going slack and a large, guilty smile breaking across her face.

"Harper!" Rose replied, scandalized that their perfectly laid plan had been thwarted by such a blatant confession.

"What? I was going to explode not talking about it."

Rose shook her head, tutting at the two women sitting beside her. She even threw in a slight eyeball for good measure, which, by Rose's standards, was a positively flashy display of emotion. "How I ended up with the world's most dramatic sisters, I'll never know."

"Mom and Dad wasted all of the good genes on you, obviously." May shrugged. "We're just whatever's left over."

"You're changing the subject," Harper warned, spooning a glob of halfway melted ice cream and cobbler into her mouth.

"You caught me," May confessed. As much as she'd wanted to talk all of this through with her sisters, there was something so concrete about discussing it. If she spoke about it out loud, then that meant it actually happened. And if it actually happened, then that meant she'd have to do something about it. That meant she was actually going through with this whole "fake friends to save the festival and the town and our reputations and our butts from Annie" plan.

It meant that, for the next few weeks, her life would be consumed by Tom Riley.

Harper wasted no time. "What are you going to do? What

happened to the two of you during that dance? Didn't you just want to haul back and punch him in his stupid face?"

His stupid, handsome face. And no. No, she hadn't. If anyone in this scenario deserved a good punch, it was probably her. Not that her sisters knew that.

"Honestly, Harper," Rose said, waving her spoon like a disappointed math teacher who just discovered no one did their homework. "You're not going to get anywhere asking questions like that."

"But aren't you curious?"

For a moment, Rose hesitated. The truth was written clearly across her pretty, moonstruck face, and it was easy for May to track the line of her thinking from *yes, of course I want to know* to *but it's not kind to treat someone else's life like an episode of reality television.* Rose was too nice to ever call Harper out directly for cheering on Tom and May's feud like a blood sport, but May knew that her sister was torn on that particular front.

When Rose did finally speak, she did so with the quiet diplomacy that only a measured, calm elder sister could have. "Can you just tell us what happened?"

"Nothing," May said, shrugging. "We're going to run the festival together. Bury the hatchet, just like Annie said. Rose and I need good returns for our shops. He needs help with his family's place. The whole town could use a boost. We're all just going to have to get along and make this work."

Rose and Harper shared a look, sending May's stomach plummeting. She knew that look. The Older Sister Stare of Very Serious Concern™ was one that her sisters had perfected over the years. Any time they shared it, she knew she was in for a deep and meaningful talk.

"You..." Rose began, wincing slightly as her voice cracked. "You do know that when I said you should get out there and try again, I didn't mean you had to try to bring him back into your life, right? You don't have to relive high school to prove to me that you're trying to live at all."

May's heart caught on a thicket of brambles in the center of her chest. They were completely misunderstanding the situation. She wasn't trying to go backward at all. She was trying—and Annie was basically forcing her—to move forward. Confronting the past wasn't the same as trying to go back there. No, she wasn't trying to recapture her old life and her old love. She'd had Tom in her rearview mirror for years now. Any hope she might have had for them died a long time ago.

"That's not what's happening here," she said, staring into her cobbler, watching the galaxies of cream and blueberry swirling in the bottom of the bowl. Even she could tell she was more trying to convince herself than either of her sisters.

"Then what *is* happening?" Harper asked.

"Apparently my sisters don't trust me, that's what's happening!" May said, a laugh punctuating her slight accusation.

"Of course I trust you," Rose rushed to say. "We both trust you. It's just that…"

"It's just that we don't trust *him*," Harper supplied.

That wasn't fair, and May knew it. But seeing as she couldn't defend Tom without explaining an eight-year-old secret to her sisters, she settled on defending herself.

"I'm not the same teenage girl I was last time he was in my life. Things are going to be different this time." Now she was just repeating things she'd been telling herself all afternoon. Reassurances that everything was going to be fine. "We're just working together, for one thing. No romantic attachment involved."

Harper raised a curious eyebrow. A questioning one. "Not even on your part?"

"Definitely not."

If she'd been hooked up to a lie detector, the needle surely would have been unsure which way to move, because she wasn't really sure herself. Even now, when she thought about the way his amber eyes had flashed, the way his lips tugged in that familiar way that brought back memories of pulling him down and kissing him with reckless abandon...she couldn't deny that she did still have some feelings for him. Her heart had raced when he'd stood above her, when his lips wrapped around her name. But she'd convinced herself those feelings were for the Tom she had been with eight years ago; he had changed while he was away as much as she had, and she wasn't sure she knew the new, angrier man he was now.

And having ancient feelings didn't mean she was going to act on them. It didn't mean she was going to lose herself to the new Tom. She knew that she couldn't. It was better for everyone that way. She'd caused too much damage to ever hope that he could feel anything for her.

"We just don't want to see you get hurt again," Rose muttered.

"Don't worry. There's no risk of that," May replied, returning to the last remnants of her cobbler.

"And how can you be so sure?"

"Because Annie has set me up with her *very eligible, terribly handsome* photographer friend, and I intend to see that through."

"Will you be serious for even one second, sister?"

"Harper, give me some credit. You just said that you trusted me."

"I'm just worried about you. You've never been the same since your breakup with him. I don't want to see you go through that again. I feel like he shattered you, like he ruined your life, and I'm just concerned. That's all."

There were so many problems with what May had allowed to happen in the wake of the breakup with Tom. She'd ruined his reputation. Caused an entire town to basically pretend he didn't exist. Proven herself to be a coward for not going with him in the first place. Proven herself a double coward for not setting everyone straight when they spread lies and rumors about him. But one of the other unintended consequences of her cowardice was that everyone now thought of her as some wilting flower, a pathetic little thing that had been trampled and never bothered to blossom again. They thought she was weak. Broken. That her life had been ruined.

Maybe she could endure that from the folks in town, but she wasn't going to sit here and listen to it from her own sister.

"My life is pretty damn good, thank you very much," she protested. Her mind suddenly filled with thoughts of Harper and Luke, their perfect little love story. Jealousy curdled in the pit of her stomach, threatening to spew out of her. Her sister had a kind of happiness with Luke that most people could only dream about, the kind of happiness she might have had if she hadn't thrown it all away. "And no one is going to tell me that it's not, especially not my sister looking down from her perfect setup."

Harper reeled back as if she'd been slapped. Her jaw hung loose and limp. For a rare moment, she was actually speechless. "My life isn't perfect."

The urge to roll her eyes was too strong. May gave in and scoffed. "Yeah, I'm sure your impending marriage to a billionaire who looks at you like you threaded the stars is a real trial."

Even as she snapped out the retort, May knew she was speaking in anger. She knew she wasn't being fair. But the pain currently clawing at her heart made giving her sister a fair shake too difficult an ask.

For her part, Harper dropped her bowl to the small end table beside her chair with another deafening clatter that disturbed a nearby cluster of birds in the high magnolia trees. Her nostrils flared. A cold, flippant smile tugged at her lips.

"Fine. You know what? Forget I said anything. I just hope you know what you're doing. That's all."

With that, Harper turned on her heel and left, questions and doubts hanging in her wake. May's mind only traveled in one direction though. Pity. Overwhelming pity that her sister still thought she had a heart to break when, in reality, she'd locked it away the same day she let Tom Riley drive out of town without her all those years ago.

It had been for the best. Letting him go without her. She was sure of that. She *had* to be sure of that. Just like she had to be sure that what she was doing now was for the best. No matter how her sisters felt about it, she couldn't turn back now. Because she meant it when she said that she liked her life. She had done a lot in the last eight years, which she could never have accomplished traveling around the world with Tom, and she had to believe that it was worth it.

After a long moment of silence, Rose's voice piped up from her chair.

"She just wants what's best for you," she said, idly swirling the remnants of her dessert in her bowl, not looking up.

"And you think I don't want what's best for me?"

More words said in anger. May regretted them almost instantly, but she didn't take them back. Not even when Rose stood from her place and gave her a small, sad pat on the shoulder.

"I know tonight wasn't a good example of it, but if you need anything, you know we're always here to talk. Always."

"Yeah. Thanks."

But that was the problem, wasn't it? Wanting to talk would mean wanting to tell the truth. And May had always been too big of a coward for that.

She'd have to bear this like she'd had to bear everything over the last eight years. Alone.

Chapter Eight

Tom

As far as Tom could tell, there were two main problems with agreeing to run a festival with the ex–love of his life and the woman who kept him the object of rumor. One, he now had to spend all of his time either with that woman or thinking about that woman. And two...he had to, you know, actually help plan an entire festival, something he didn't have the first clue how to do.

On the morning of his first meeting with May, Tom found himself out in the vineyard for one of his early-morning walks. He'd always been a restless kid by nature, ready to break out and become something bigger than the infamous small-town nothing he'd been growing up, but even back then, he hadn't been able to deny the natural beauty of the land. Mountains gave way to rolling hills, green and lush in the morning sun. The dew caught all of the natural light, filling the vineyard with the golden haze of morning. In an hour, all of it would be gone, sacrificed to the day, but for now, Tom was totally content to wander the paths between the vines and soak in all of that morning excess, drinking in the natural luxury of this place.

Tom rolled a grape between his fingertips, checking the strength of the fresh skin. They were too young and too new to be anywhere close to the level they would be come fall and harvest time, but he checked anyway. At this point, he'd take literally anything to avoid having to think about working with May.

Why *had* he accepted? Turning her down would have been disastrous for both of them, another blight on his permanent record where she was concerned. There, in front of the whole town, he couldn't possibly have turned her down without incurring all of their collective wrath. And he did *really* need this festival to work. He needed the business; the way everyone in town treated him…it was like Barn Door didn't even exist. And this was their only hope of really getting their name out there again, connecting with bigger markets outside of Hillsboro.

Outside of Hillsboro. His heart tugged at the thought. Unlike May, who'd turned tail and run before they could even put the keys in the ignition on that fateful graduation night, he'd gone out into that greater, bigger world for a while.

Sometimes, he still missed it. Sometimes, he missed train stations where none of the signs were in English. He longed to get lost in the backstreets of a small French village because they'd last printed their maps in 1951. He daydreamed about Hungarian ruin bars. But even when he'd been out there, he hadn't been satisfied. There was always a piece missing, a piece that made him wonder if he should go back to Hillsboro. Or maybe he just didn't belong anywhere.

He let the grapevine fall from between his fingers and was about to move toward the next row when the sound of familiar, slightly off-time boots crunched behind him.

"Good morning, Grandson."

Tom fought back a groan. Great. Gran must have heard the news. His grandmother—his mother's mother and his only living grandparent—was a sharp-eyed, silver-haired woman with a permanent mischievous smile dotting her weathered face. There wasn't a problem in the world she couldn't solve or a difficulty she couldn't stare down with a laugh.

She was also, without question, the world's best, as she called it, "bull dinky" detector. If he so much as told her a half-truth about this situation, he would never hear the end of it.

"Morning, Gran."

Tom stooped to inspect a slightly twisted sprinkler system near his feet; Gran wasn't deterred or content to stand a few feet away or polite enough to give him some space, though. Her short body cast a long shadow over him as she stood so close he could smell the pillowy scent of her fabric softener.

"So," she began, tapping one of her booted feet on the ground, kicking up a bit of mud as she found her rhythm. "Why did I have to hear about this May Anderson mess from Camilla at the Barnett's deli counter?"

Word traveled fast here. He'd been afraid of that. Tom fought back a wince. He knew better than to lie to Gran, but he couldn't help it. He didn't want her to worry.

"It's not a big deal," he said indifferently.

"Not a big deal? You're about to take on planning assignments and make schedules and manage budgets and Hendrix knows what else with *that girl*. It sounds like a pretty big deal to me."

Two quirks of Gran's language. She never attributed anything to God in the traditional sense. Jimi Hendrix always stood in his place. And May Anderson was almost always *that girl* where she was concerned.

There weren't many people in Hillsboro who questioned the party line when it came to his and May's breakup all those years ago. His own parents even seemed to believe it, never asking any questions too personal that might accidentally confirm that their son had broken the spirit of Hillsboro's Sweetheart. Gran, on the other hand, had never bought what any of the whisperers around town were selling. She'd made it very clear on multiple occasions that when he was ready to tell the truth about the end of his first love, she'd be there to listen. That moment of readiness had never come for Tom. He wasn't sure it ever would. It definitely wasn't going to be here and now, when he was ankle-deep in mud and filled to the brim with anxiety about what lay ahead of him.

Satisfied that the sprinklers were finally untangled, Tom rose to his full height and tried to think of anything he could say to possibly dissuade his grandmother from this line of questioning. He came up with nothing.

"Yeah." He shrugged. "I guess it is a pretty big deal."

"You agreed to this?"

"Yeah."

Another moment of silence as Gran surveyed him. Tom did his best to look out at the distant fields sprawling around them with some semblance of dignity, but he already knew Gran would find any weakness in his armor. She always did.

"All right. Spill. I want to hear everything."

"Well…"

Waving her hand for him to pause, Gran fished in her pocket for a moment before presenting him with a tiny bottle of whiskey, one of those shooters you'd normally find in an airplane.

"Do you need a little liquid courage?"

His grandmother was many things, but subtle wasn't one of them. Usually, that was an endearing quality, but right now he couldn't help but blink in slightly horrified shock. *Batty old woman.* Why couldn't he have the kind of grandmother who always carried cookies? He definitely would have taken a cookie. Or muffins. Like the kind May used to make with her honey. Did she still do that? "Gran, it's seven in the morning."

"It's never too early for the truth," she said, waving the bottle at him encouragingly. Its glass caught the light, sending shards of glare in every direction. He blinked the light out and shooed her.

If the choice was between speaking and downing a shot of whiskey at 7 a.m. and *then* speaking, he'd take the former any day. Picking his way through the rows and rows of vines, letting the soft scent of earth beneath his boots ground him, he filled her in as carefully and delicately as he could. There was still so much hurt in him, so much resentment and betrayal at what had happened between him and May. He never wanted Gran to see that side of him.

"I saw May earlier this week. At the party."

"And?"

"And I'm over her." His voice tightened. He strained to speak softly, measuredly. Their encounter turned over and over again in the back of his mind, hinting at uncapturable truths he couldn't even begin to reach for. "I guess I still want to hate her. But...it feels like things are different. She feels different. But she can't be different, you know? Like... she can't be different because she hasn't done anything different. I'm...I'm talking myself in circles, aren't I?"

"You should have taken the whiskey. Come on. Tell this old woman everything."

A lie would have been so easy. *We didn't work out in high school and now it's awkward. I just don't like her like I did back then.* Lies would have been easy; that didn't make them any less wrong. Tom swallowed, hard. Sure, protecting May's reputation meant never running through town with leaflets explaining the truth or doing a local TV PSA correcting the record. But if he really wanted closure or to move on or whatever, then that started with telling the truth whenever he could. Confessing to Gran seemed like as good a place as any to start. This was it. Now or never.

"It's all a lie, what they say," he choked. Honesty flowed from his lips, rushing after years of being kept behind a dam in his heart. "I didn't break up with her. I didn't leave her. I think...I think she got spooked before we left town on graduation night—she decided I was going to break up with her and leave her out there, alone—and she dumped me. But the entire town believes it was me. She let them believe a lie."

"So, *she* left you?" Gran asked, seemingly more for confirmation than out of some sense of shock.

The memories of that night—long ago as it might have been—still burned fresh in his mind. *Look, Tom, you know what everyone says about you. You're unreliable. A reckless loner who can't be trusted. Why would I leave to drive across the country—why would I travel the world with you—if I can't trust you?* He'd shoved them in a locked drawer in the bottom of his mind, from where he only dragged them when he wanted to particularly torture himself. Refusing to mentally revisit that night very often meant that every time he *did* throw himself back to the worst night of his life, the wounds ached, tender and raw. He hadn't offered them any time to heal, hadn't tended to them in the way he should have.

Patterns in the clouds above them swirled into images of a stoic-faced May standing beside the aging pickup truck that was supposed to carry them to see the world. He could still see the unshed tears pooling in her eyes, clear and unmovable as crystal, still recall exactly the way the wind rushed out of his lungs when she said, *I'm not going with you.*

It wasn't, as he first thought, just in his mental memory banks. It was also in his muscle memory as well. His body ached now the same way it had back then, like she'd delivered a swift blow straight to the center of his solar plexus.

He swallowed hard, trying to banish the sensation. Maybe he wasn't as indifferent as he'd thought. Gran wouldn't care that he'd shown emotion—in fact, she'd probably encourage it—but he wanted to prove to himself that he could move past it. If he couldn't prove it to himself, he had no chance in hell of proving it to May or anyone else in town, for that matter.

Then, a small, slightly wrinkled and sun-spotted hand reached out through the smooth morning air and wrapped its ringed fingers around his. Gran had always been something of a hardworking hippie type—she'd been among the Tribe who'd tried to levitate the White House in the sixties—and she'd always been generous with physical affection.

The softness of her hands almost made him want to cry. When was the last time he'd touched someone like this? He'd been running away from people and letting them run away from him for so long that he'd forgotten the simple pleasure of accepting when someone else offered to reach out. He gripped her hand back, letting her strength bolster his courage.

"She sent me away. She told me she couldn't trust me because of the way everyone in town talked about me. She was convinced that we'd get halfway to freedom and I'd leave her at a truck stop somewhere. She just stopped believing that I loved her because a few people got in her head."

That's what she'd said. That *everyone in town* was *concerned* about the way he tended to be, about his reputation. She was afraid, despite years of across-the-tracks friendship and dating that he was suddenly going to realize he didn't want to be with her and abandon her somewhere.

She'd let the small-minded gossip of people they didn't even particularly like—gossip they'd spent most of their lives laughing at and ignoring—completely alter the trajectory of their lives. Thrown away the future they'd planned together because someone persuaded her that he didn't love her enough.

In the end, he had a sneaking suspicion that she'd been terrified of becoming just like him. An outcast in her own home. Among her own people.

"Oh, Tom," Gran said, squeezing his hand sympathetically. Her voice had none of its usual strength and humor. If she'd been, as he thought, expecting that something had happened between him and May that the town didn't know about, she clearly didn't think it was *this* bad.

He pressed onward, trying to articulate the private war he'd been waging ever since he came back home to Hillsboro.

"Now our vineyard is suffering because of this rumor that I broke her heart. Everyone in town is pretending we don't exist, and it's hurting the business. *She* let this happen and now . . . now I have to go back and try to pretend like nothing is wrong? How can I . . .?"

How can I forgive her?

The question died on his lips. Even speaking the possibility out loud shook him to his core. Did he even *want* to forgive her? Was he strong enough to try?

Worse yet, what if he wanted to forgive her but she turned out to be the kind of person not worth forgiving? What if he'd spent all of these years protecting the reputation of someone who wouldn't even apologize or thank him if she was given the chance?

It was fear holding him back. He knew that. Fear of discovering that all of these years, he'd been controlled by a long-buried love for someone who wasn't worthy of it.

Tom stared at the flowering leaves of the grapevine, examining the filament and the green pigment. It wasn't ready yet. Just like he wasn't.

His gran seemed to be on a similar track. Tilting her head slightly up to catch the full glow of morning, she let out a small sigh and spoke in her usual, frank, unsentimental way.

"Grandson, at the risk of the obvious metaphor, you work with these grapes every day. You watch them grow, you care for them, and because of that, you know that if you took them off of the vine and crushed them this very morning, they'd be useless, wouldn't they?"

"Yes."

He could see where this was going, and every fractured piece of his pride desperately didn't want her to go there.

"You were a pair of stupid eighteen-year-old kids. *You* drove off and proved her point, that you were the kind of guy who left. *She* let her fear rule her life and hurt your future. Maybe—just maybe—you should see what time has done to the two of you. How have you aged? How have you grown? The answers may surprise you. May surprise you both."

Tom didn't want to. He didn't want to let go of his pain, didn't want to get too close to it. But the honest parts of him knew that Gran was right; he couldn't go on living like this forever.

"So, what do you think I should do?"

Gran shrugged. "Kiss her. Slash her tires. Go on a bender. Run away together to Reno. I don't know. Just do *something*. You can't keep living in the past. You don't belong there anymore."

"I'm not living in the past." When Gran's face made it clear that she didn't buy that load of garbage, he added, "I mean, I went to that party and I let Annie introduce me to this really nice girl from Los Angeles."

Her name was Joanna Avery. She designed jewelry and loved wine and laughed at his jokes like she really meant it.

He was sure that the longer she stayed in town and the more she heard about the man everyone thought he was, that would change. Everyone eventually left. May. Annie. And Joanna would be next. Better to just cut off the seedling of a relationship before it could really take root.

"And you've seen her again since then?" Gran asked, inspecting a nearby butterfly that had made a temporary stop on one of the vines before her. Its wings fluttered in the light breeze as it settled; the colors were so bright and piercing it felt like they were almost taunting him.

"No."

"But you've called her."

"No."

"But you've texted her."

"No."

Gran's eyes danced with humor as she raised one distinguished, thinning eyebrow. "Ah, but you sent her a singing telegram."

Tom sighed. Deep and long and low and only halfway annoyed. She was right, after all. He hadn't done a damn thing. "No, Gran."

"And when was the last time you went on a date? Or looked at a real, human woman?"

"All right," Tom said, a laugh escaping him. He held up his hands in mock surrender. "I get the picture."

"Good. Now, go send this Joanna a text, and then go plan your little festival with the Anderson girl. I've been dying for a half-decent fireworks show."

The whole thing was a bit of a joke, but Tom knew that there was some truth to it. For so long, he'd been dark and hidden and silent as a still, summer night. Maybe now... maybe now it was time for some Fourth of July style shake-ups.

Chapter Nine

May

Sometimes, when May got into one of her riskier moods, she'd allow herself to daydream about what it would be like to throw all of her stuff in the back of her truck and drive out of this town. She would wonder what the air tasted like outside of California, what kind of person she would become once she stretched her wings.

But she wasn't ever going to leave the safety of this place, not after all she did to secure her place in it. Dreams like that were foolish. And May Anderson was no fool.

Well, she wasn't *usually* a fool. Today, however, was quite the exception.

"All right, Stella. Monster. Let's make a pact, all right?"

As May glanced into the rearview mirror of her beat-up, hand-me-down Jeep, she addressed the two animals waiting there. Her sister and Annie were on their way out of town for the weekend on a wedding-planning trip, leaving no one to watch Stella—the Andersons' oversized Maremma Sheepdog—and Monster, the adorable, squish-faced, pocket-sized mutt Annie had picked up at the local shelter last year.

One of the problems with having a reputation as the reliable sister who never went out and never saw anyone was that May was always the first person anyone asked when they needed a favor. Paired with the fact that she always felt too guilty and was too afraid of the damage to her reputation if she told people *no*, she always found herself doing the chores no one else wanted to do. Today, that meant keeping a close eye on the two most trouble-making dogs to ever run wild over the fields of Hillsboro.

The pups, at the sound of their names, perked up, huffing with excitement as the green of the town square called to them. With festival prep and a full house of tourists getting ready for the weekend, May had a full day ahead of her, but she couldn't leave the animals to their own devices, so that meant clicking them into their harnesses and turning this into Take-Your-Dog-To-Work day.

"You're both going to behave today. And in return, I get to keep my sanity and you both get lots of T-R-E-A-T-S, all right?"

Of course, the pups didn't respond, so May climbed out of the truck and slowly moved them out into the world beyond her car. This was a process that usually had to be done delicately, as Stella was the ultimate escape artist, and with every movement May made, she felt more like she was trying to defuse a bomb than get a dog out of her car.

All around her, the square was beginning the warm, summer morning with a buzz of activity. People bustled back and forth between coffee shops and the bookstore. Children and their matching adults threw pennies in the center fountain or picked at the weeds growing in the green grass. The familiar faces of shopkeepers and cooks passed in May's peripheral vision, distracting her even as she tried to dedicate her every last thought to the all-consuming process of keeping a rowdy puppy and an overprotective herd dog from tearing her arms off with their aggressive sniffing and exploring.

"Okay, girls, just a few minutes out here, and then we'll go ahead and open the store—"

But, May realized with a sinking feeling, she wasn't going to get the chance to finish that sentence. Across the square, a familiar, busted-up red pickup with a handful of empty wine cases in the back bed drove up, parked, and the door swung open to reveal the angular, sharp-jawed, heart-stopping face of Tom Riley.

That, in and of itself, wouldn't have been a massive problem. They were working together, after all, and she was determined that things were going to change between them.

The problem was that Tom Riley had been there the day the Anderson family had gotten Stella. Tom Riley had played with Stella as a puppy, run all across the property with her and let her teethe on his favorite pair of boots. Stella knew his face, his voice, even his scent. And like a reliable elephant, she never forgot. The second the wind blew and Stella sniffed the air, she recognized that long-lost friend.

May didn't stand a chance.

Stella bolted, using all of her strength to tear her lead out of May's hands. Her powerful legs carried her across the square, dodging small children and leaping over benches, defying anything that stood in her way. It happened so fast that May barely had time to register the rope burn before she was gone.

Of course, not to be outdone, Monster took off too, but the poor little thing's little legs barely had enough strength to strain the lead, especially when May took off after Stella, her entire body flushing red with embarrassment as she watched the giant hound of a dog approach Tom like an old friend.

Which, she guessed, with an ounce of melancholy, he was.

At the sight of Stella, Tom's face lit up, and he bent down

with such tenderness and affection—such love—that May almost fell backward from the shock of it. How easy it was to forget, in the haze of everything that had happened in the years since they broke up, that they'd once been better than family. He wasn't *just* a scar on her past. He was a part of it. A good part.

"Stella!" Tom crooned, welcoming the oversized pup into his arms and burying his face in her fur. "Hey, girl!"

The whole sight reminded May of those feel-good videos that sometimes popped up on YouTube of lion keepers who were reunited with their former beast-pets in the wild, where the animal would instantly recognize them and excitedly leap into their arms again like they would have when they were cubs. Stella, it seemed, still thought she was a puppy when it came to Tom, and the force of her knocked him flat on his rear.

Not that he seemed to mind. He took the dog kisses and sniffs with so much good-natured laughter that May's stomach turned. She wanted to move on from her past, not to be sucked back into it. Rushing forward, she snapped up Stella's lead and pulled the animal away. She didn't have the emotional energy to consider how this might have looked to everyone in the park currently watching this exchange.

"Stella, come."

Fighting against the command, Stella tried to keep close to Tom, but May marched firmly back toward the other side of the park.

"No, it's all right!" Tom protested. "She's just—"

"Stella. Come." But the dog still wavered between them, her legs carrying her back toward May and then tugging on her leash to strain toward Tom's outstretched, welcoming hands. "Heel, Stella. You're setting a bad example for Monster."

Tom, apparently, thought he was being helpful by trying to give the dog all the attention he hadn't been able to over the last few years.

"Really, May. It's okay if they—"

"No, Tom. She can't just run away like that." She turned her attention on Stella as she tried to lead the two dogs on their leashes toward the store. Distance was what she needed. Distance between her and Tom and all of the memories and guilt he brought with him. She'd thought she was strong enough for this, but one look at him and Stella and she knew she was lost. "It's very bad. Very bad!"

That's when the scuffle started. Tom reached for Stella's leash, while Stella wedged her way between Tom and May. Monster, ever the tag-along, emulated Stella, nipping at her heels all the way. May tried to handle all three of the creatures currently making demands on her attention and strength, an almost impossible task.

"Here, let me—"

"No, don't!"

"Stella, stop—"

It all happened as if in slow motion. Monster followed Stella. Stella followed Tom. Their leads wrapped around May's ankles. They tightened. And in a flash of both shock and acceptance of the inevitable, May fell backward into the fountain in the center of the town square with a *SPLASH!*

Water engulfed her, but she recovered as quickly as she could, trying to resurface and escape the cold, watery clutches of the fountain. She wasn't a germaphobe by any stretch of the imagination, but the thought of that water quality sent shivers down her spine.

Problem was, when she finally managed to get back on her feet, she couldn't find it in herself to move entirely out of the fountain. Because everyone, including Tom Riley, who now held the leashes of the two dogs heeled and at his side, was staring at her. She couldn't imagine what a sight she was, dripping wet with pond water and red-faced from the humiliation, but she could see, plain as day, what a sight Tom was.

He was laughing at her. Or, more precisely, he was covering up his mouth as if he could possibly begin to hide the fact that he was very clearly laughing at her. An exasperated half laugh escaped her lips before she had the chance to hold it back ... or before she could remember that there were plenty of people watching this exchange with keen interest.

"Oh, you think this is funny, do you?"

Tom's eyes widened. His jaw tensed behind his hand. But that didn't stop the laughter. "It *is* a little funny. I'm sorry, but—"

"But you think it's *funny*?" she repeated, gesticulating wildly in his direction. This was intended to be intimidating and devastating, but it only succeeded in spraying droplets of water from the ends of her sleeves and fingertips, highlighting her current predicament.

A smile-grimace pulled at Tom's lips, one she recognized from all of their years of pranks and inside jokes. That mischievous grin he had tried so hard to hide lately, the one that promised even more trouble to come. She'd fallen in love with that smile once. It was even more beautiful now, even more striking on a slightly aged and weathered face. "A little bit."

"A real gentleman. Come on," she said, rolling her eyes. She thought about leaving the fountain on her own, but then an idea struck her instead. Reaching out her hand, she played the role of the poor innocent victim. "Help me out of here."

Switching the dogs' leads into one hand, he reached to take hers ... but she wasn't going to let him get away so easily. For one electric breath, their fingers touched, and she dragged him into the fountain beside her, where he released the leads and landed with a *SPLASH* of his own!

Now it was her turn to laugh.

The towering and imposing figure that was Tom Riley now lay in a pile of wet clothes and discarded pennies at the bottom of the wrought-iron fountain, spluttering as he wiped his long locks away from his forehead.

"Hey!" he cried, much to the laughing delight of the nearby children.

May joined in their laughter as she reached for the dogs' leashes and took them back in hand. The last thing either of them needed was to have to chase the animals all over town while soaking wet.

Though, to be fair, she didn't mind seeing Tom soaking wet. She knew she should have looked away, turned from the sight of his wet T-shirt clinging to his rippling, muscular chest. All thoughts of what he would have looked like with that shirt *off* also should have been out of the question. But they weren't. She couldn't help it when her eyes slyly examined him and the body her fingers itched to touch again.

She tried to hide the longing with a joke. "Not so funny now, is it?"

"Actually," Tom said, splashing her, "I think it might be even funnier."

Oh, he wanted a fight? She'd give him a fight. Rearing her free hand back, she readied herself to disturb the flowing fountain behind him, showering him with water, but a voice cut over the din of the town square, shocking May straight to her core.

"Hey! You two!" Mrs. Elaine Bates, the town's foremost busybody apparently didn't realize who she'd just caught breaking about fifteen civil ordinances. "Get outta that fountain before I call Chief Ramirez on—"

"Sorry, Mrs. Elaine!" May said. She couldn't see the woman from her vantage point, but she didn't want to stick around to meet the face of the one-woman rumor mill who also happened to have her mother on speed-dial. "We're going now! Sorry!"

But fate had other plans. They both staggered out of the fountain as best they could, struggling to regain their footing and recover from their dip. Monster—following Stella's gentle example—and Stella had both sat beside the marble-and-metal monstrosity, tilting their furry heads up so that the nearby children could rub their ears or knot their fingers in their soft fur, and when May tugged the dogs leashes, urging them onward, she thought that maybe—just maybe—the arctic sheets between her and Tom were finally thawing.

It felt…well, it didn't feel like it had been when they were kids. For a moment, things had been *better* than when they were kids.

She couldn't remember the last time she felt this kind of warmth within her. The last time she'd had this good a time with someone who didn't share her last name.

"Tom, do you want to head into the shop so we can get—"

When she looked up, though, to finish that thought, she realized that Tom was no longer interested in her or their fountain adventure. His head had been thoroughly turned by a tall, slender woman walking across the park in their direction. She was incredibly beautiful, the kind of beautiful that could only come naturally. Tom raised one hand.

"Joanna!"

The woman lowered her red, heart-shaped sunglasses—which would have looked kitschy and ridiculous on May's face but looked perfect on her, May thought with a bitter pang—and blinked as she recognized him. A smile grew across her lips.

"Tom!" Long-legged strides carried her across the park, closing the gap between them. She looked like she was going to go in for a hug, but then peeled back when she clocked that he was dripping wet. "It's so good to see you again! Annie told me your phone was broken, or else I swear I would have been heartbroken when you never called—"

May bit back a snort. Of course Annie was behind all of this. And of course Annie would have made up some ridiculous excuse for why Tom hadn't called her.

Though...come to think of it...why *hadn't* Tom called this Joanna? And why was he trying so hard to pretend as if he wasn't swooning under her attention?

"Oh, yeah, I'm...getting it fixed right now." Tom swallowed hard, a little quirk of distress that he apparently hadn't grown out of since their high school days. Straightening, he remembered his manners and introduced the two of them. "Joanna, this is May Anderson. She owns the Sundries Store down the street and she keeps bees. May, this is Joanna. Annie introduced us at her party."

"A beekeeper? Really?" Now, as she spoke longer, May detected a soft, British accent. Figures. Annie *would* set him up with someone so perfect. "That's so impressive! I've always been so fascinated by beekeeping. They're so important today, with all of this climate grief. You must be so incredibly talented, to run your own business and take care of your creatures."

And she was *nice* too? The unfairness of it all. If she was going to come in and try to date Tom, the least she could do was have the decency to be a jerk. But no, when she spoke, nothing but enthusiasm and friendliness poured out of her. It was so intense that May felt herself blush. Her eyes went straight for a crack in the sidewalk beneath her feet.

"It's not a big deal, really. I raise the Queens and sell them or donate them to help expand the world's bee population. It's the largest operation of its kind in Northern California. And my family has a flower farm, so of course the bees are good for our system."

"Incredible. Absolutely fascinating. You know, I have a friend who does a *Thirty Under Thirty* for *California Mag* every year. Could I introduce you?"

Tom answered for her. "That's awesome, May—"

May's mind immediately went to Barn Door. She couldn't take this away from Tom, too, not after he'd cut his adventuring off early to come and help his grandmother run the place . . . or so the rumors said. "You know, Tom here has his own vineyard. Makes his own wine. He'd be a great candidate."

"I know," Joanna agreed. "I would have recommended him for the *Thirty Under Thirty*, but he hasn't invited me to the tasting room yet."

"Yeah," Tom said, his fake smile firmly in place. Stammering wasn't usually in his repertoire, but he couldn't stop it today. "You'll—you'll definitely have to come over some time. Everything's just so busy with the Food and Wine Festival—"

"Don't I know it! Busy worker bees over here. Get it, bees? Well, you two get to it. I'm sure I'll see you around. It was nice to meet you, May. Good to see you again, Tom. Call me."

She dismissed herself, walking away with a small wave over her shoulder that Tom answered despite the fact that she couldn't see it. May watched the entire interaction with acute interest . . . and something else she didn't quite have the vocabulary to name. When Tom watched Joanna go and made no move to reenter their conversation, May tried her hand at it.

"That was—"

"Don't say it."

She couldn't read Tom's expression, but his tone made her smile. A bittersweet smile, a conflicted smile, but a smile all the same.

"I wasn't going to say anything."

"Good. Don't."

"Good. I won't."

"Come on." He sighed and ran a hand through his hair. The universal sign for burying deep, deep emotions. "We have a lot to do. And we need showers."

Yes, they did have a lot of work to do. A lot of stressful, high-pressure, anxiety-inducing work to get through together. So... why couldn't she stop thinking about Joanna and Tom? And why did she get the distinct impression that the green acid growing in her stomach with every breath was the bitter, unfamiliar sensation of jealousy?

Chapter Ten

Tom

Even completely covered in ribbons and glitter, Tom couldn't stop thinking about that moment. In the handful of hours since it'd happened, he and May had cleaned gross fountain water off themselves, run a handful of errands, wrangled the dogs, made it all the way back to the vineyard, and begun constructing elaborate, over-decorated welcome baskets for the Food and Wine Festival's most esteemed patrons, and *still*, he hadn't been able to wrench that moment from his head.

Well, two moments, really.

There was the suggestion that he be interviewed for the magazine, when May had talked about his accomplishments as if she were really, truly proud to know him.

And there was another moment. More subtle and endlessly more confusing.

When they'd both landed in that pond, for a split, brief moment, their eyes had met. With the rich, coppering sun shining down above them and the splashing water dancing like falling diamonds overhead, she'd met his gaze and smiled at him.

It only lasted a second, but hell, it had been a *good* second, being there with her. No, not just good. Right.

Which was ridiculous, of course. He couldn't allow himself to feel right in May's presence.

They'd agreed to do the baskets together and separate out the rest of the festival chores soon. Here, in the quiet of the tasting room porch, which overlooked the entire Barn Door estate, they worked in almost complete silence, letting the rustling of the leaves in the gentle wind and the crinkling of plastic wrapping be their only music. In the distance, Stella and Monster chased butterflies. The moment was perfect.

He should have known that wouldn't last.

"So...Joanna was nice."

Tom's jaw tightened and he fumbled with a ribbon. "I thought we were supposed to be arranging these baskets. I need to concentrate if I'm going to make them look halfway decent."

"Sure. Sure." A moment of silence. Then May couldn't take it any longer. She kept her voice in the upper, nonchalant tonal register, immediately giving away how invested she was in this conversation. "It just seems to me that you'd want to talk about her. If I had some pretty woman traipsing after me, I'd never let anyone forget it."

"She wasn't traipsing."

"No, of course she wasn't. She was springing. Bounding. Frolicking."

"I wasn't aware you'd gone to thesaurus school."

To his surprise, May barked out a laugh. The familiar sound washed over him, sweeter than summer rain. He'd missed this. He'd missed her. And he hated himself for it. "Man, you have been away from me for a long time. You used to have better comebacks than that. You must be losing your touch."

"Yeah. Whose fault is that?"

The snap of a retort escaped from him before he could contain it. The silence that followed made his hands sting as though he'd slapped her.

Just because he was angry at her, just because she'd hurt him, didn't mean he had any right to hurt her back. Not even by accident. Swallowing his pride, he tried to clear the air.

"I'm sorry. That was...that was low."

Braving a glance up at her from beneath his eyelashes, he stole a peek at her as she struggled with what he'd just said—the insult and the apology both. At first she sunk slightly into a frown, but then she faked a smile as she returned to her work.

Tom could tell a fake May Anderson smile from a real one any day. Years without practice hadn't changed that.

"No, you're right. It is my fault. It's all my fault." Her voice trailed off before regaining steam. "But really, Joanna seemed nice. Why haven't you asked her out?"

"She wouldn't want to be with someone like me. No one would."

"She was practically begging you to ask her out. Come on. You had to see that. She did everything short of hopping in your lap and crying about it."

To his surprise, Tom was glad that May hadn't entirely lost her fighting spirit in the years since they'd last spoken. Somehow, she was even more abrupt, even sharper, than she'd been back then. He shrugged, still fumbling with the same ribbon he'd been trying to curl for ten minutes. It was better to struggle with that than to think about the way May's oversized shirt was slipping from her shoulder, giving him a perfect view of her kissable neck...and the swell of her chest just beneath her collarbone.

"I've just been...I haven't been socializing, really. It wouldn't be right."

"Why not?"

Tom shot her a look. "You know why not. Anyone I dated would become the newest target of the Hillsboro Gossip Market."

"Maybe she doesn't mind that. Maybe Annie has told her and she doesn't care."

"Yeah. Right. Sure. I haven't…asked anyone out in a long time."

Apparently, May thought that this was the time for commiserating. Focusing on her basket—the third she'd completed in the time it had taken Tom to curl one half of one single bow—she explained.

"I haven't been dating either. Haven't been doing much of anything, to be honest."

"Yeah. I'd heard that."

A sigh and a smile. At least, in some things, they were equal. Equally broken. Equally at the mercy of others. "Hillsboro Gossip Market strikes again."

This was something that Tom had struggled with for a really long time. Ever since he'd come back to town, in fact. May Anderson had everything. She still had her good name. She still had the affections and the defense of everyone in town. She could do anything she wanted, while he was relegated to the shadows, forced to smile and placate and beg for crumbs from people who were determined to punish him for something he didn't even do.

With all of that privilege, with everything she had at her fingertips, why was she…this? A woman who purposefully made herself insignificant so no one would see her or look at her too closely?

"Why is that?" he asked gently, not wanting to spook her. "Why haven't you been, you know, doing anything?"

"I'm doing this right now. With you," she teased, picking

up another empty basket. Tom shook his head and bit back a laugh of his own.

"Come on. Tell me."

"I'm...I feel..." He watched carefully as her breathing grew labored. As she furrowed her brow and her hand gripped blindly at the air, as if she were trying to pluck the right words from herself. It wasn't dramatic or anything, though; she was calm, deliberate, and very, very sad. Mostly because she wasn't trying to be. Tom always found that people who pretended everything was all right were usually the ones who broke his heart the deepest. "You know that thing when you park your car in a safe, dry place, but then you go inside for a few hours and it rains? And then your car has totally sunk in the mud and you turn the key in the ignition and the wheels are spinning, you're burning gas and your battery, but you're getting nowhere?"

"Yeah. Yeah, I've been there."

He was there right now, in fact. He'd been there since the day he got back into town. May ran a hand through her hair, a dismissive gesture meant to make the very big, very real thing she was feeling seem small and forgettable.

"I guess that's how I feel. That's why I haven't been doing anything."

Tom didn't know what to say. He'd spent all of this time and energy building her up into some big monster in his mind, this creature worthy of his hatred and his grudges, but really? She was just as broken by this system as he was, wasn't she?

It didn't make everything okay. But at least...at least he now knew she wasn't a monster.

"You're stuck."

"Yeah. I'm stuck."

Tom met her gaze. And for the first time, when he looked

at her, he didn't see the eighteen-year-old girl who'd broken his heart and cracked his future in half. He saw May Anderson, the lost, stuck woman before him. "So am I."

"But we don't have to be," May said, coughing to clear her throat as she went back to her basket. Tom narrowed his gaze.

"What do you mean?"

"Annie may be a bit of a wild card, but maybe she's right. Maybe we should go out and try to get out of our comfort zones. You should ask your girlfriend out."

Joanna. He'd totally forgotten about her. He'd been too lost in the woman in front of him.

"She's not my girlfriend."

"Not yet, no. Look." May jumped to her feet, the baskets totally forgotten, and tried a new tactic, one Tom couldn't help but laugh at as soon as he realized what she was going for. "We'll practice. I'll be Joanna. You be—"

"Harrison Ford."

"I was thinking you'd be you, but if you think you could get Harrison Ford to play the role of Tom Riley when you ask her out, then, by all means."

May-as-Joanna adopted the slouched, affected posture and pout of a model as Tom considered this proposition. Could he use the help? Yes. Was he a little rusty when it came to asking out beautiful women? Also, yes. But was it safe to test out his skills on May Anderson?

He wasn't sure about that. Especially not when she was looking so adorable, with her slightly damp curls and her flushed cheeks. He wondered if her hair was as soft as it looked, how it would feel beneath his fingers. A muscle in his stomach twitched.

"This is stupid."

"Yeah, probably." May shrugged. "But we've both spent

a lot of time being safe. Maybe we have to try something different."

Tom straightened and tried his best to play the game. "Okay. Um...Joanna, look, I was thinking—"

May turned over her shoulder, and the sun caught her at just the right spot so that she glowed. She was radiant. It knocked the wind right out of him, especially when she smiled. Joanna couldn't be farther from his mind. "About me?"

"Yes. And stop looking at me like that."

"Like what? I'm just a humble socialite-slash-bee-slash-wine enthusiast who—"

The words died between them. Tom should have let it be, but he couldn't help it. He had to know why she'd stopped herself.

"Who what?"

"Who can't take her eyes off of you."

His stomach twisted with want. Unfamiliar and conflicting. He shouldn't want May Anderson again. But here she was, standing in front of him, looking so beautiful and feeling so real. He tried to keep up the pretense of their little game, but the closer he drew in to her, the less and less he was thinking about Joanna.

"Well, I could say the same thing about you. I was actually wondering if we could go out sometime."

"Really?" May asked, breathless.

"Yeah." He had an urge to laugh. "Just the two of us. Candles. Wine. Music."

"I'd like that. I'd like that very much."

With every word, her lips breathed against his. When had they gotten so close? Why did he want to lean in and close the space between them? Why did he want nothing more than to throw the past away and start over with the one person who'd made that very thing so impossible?

Did he...? Did he still feel something for her?

Tom dropped the act, blinking to try and clear the stardust from his eyes. "You know, I think I can handle it. I can...I can handle her, I mean."

"Right," May breathed, her warm air settling upon his lips. "Absolutely. Of course."

But neither of them stepped back. Tom wasn't sure he had the strength to even try. But then—

"And what is all this?"

He didn't think he'd ever moved as quickly in his entire life as he did then, when his gran walked up to the porch and interrupted their moment. In less time than it took to breathe, he was across the porch and breathing heavily, trying not to look suspicious as she stood with her hands on her hips, staring at them both as though she knew something they didn't.

"Gran!" Tom cried, trying to catch his racing heartbeat.

The woman's secret, know-it-all smile did little to assuage his discomfort. Her eyes flickered between him and May, who stared down at her feet and, apparently, tried to melt into the floor. "That's what they call me."

"Gran, you remember May Anderson."

"I think I remember that name. How are you, dear?"

With her attempts to turn invisible thwarted, May's neck snapped up, and she looked up at Gran with her jaw slightly open. Panic whitened her face, and she immediately set about collecting some of the stray baskets still left unwrapped around the porch.

"Good. I'm good. Uh, you know, Tom, I might just finish some of these back at my place, if that's okay."

"Sure, if you think that's best."

"See you tomorrow."

And with that, a terrified May Anderson practically

sprinted out toward her truck, where she called the dogs back to her, loaded them up in the truck, and drove off past the fields of grapes in a cloud of dust before Tom could really process what was happening. The whole interaction took maybe a minute and a half, from Gran's appearance to May's hurried departure, but that was all Tom needed to see her discomfort.

The sudden appearance of Gran in their secret, private moment had ruined everything. It had reminded her of everything she still had to lose if she allowed herself to feel anything for him.

Well, he told himself, that was mutual.

Gran, of course, wasn't inclined to agree. "That looked pretty cozy."

"It wasn't. She was just helping me get ready to ask that girl out. Annie's friend, Joanna."

"And I'm sure you hated it." Gran tutted, milking the situation for all the humor she found in it. "Every second of being close to her. Must be hard to have a woman like that in your life. Terrible."

"She's not . . . She's not *terrible*."

Gran's eyes danced with unspoken hope. "Who knows? She might even be good."

Chapter Eleven

May

The next day, May's lips still burned from the kiss she'd missed out on. The kiss she'd wanted. The kiss she now hated herself for even considering. She'd done her best to push Tom Riley away, done her best to try and protect him from her, to shove him squarely in the lovely Joanna's direction and now...now, she felt not her old feelings for him coming back, but new ones rising in their place.

She didn't love her eighteen-year-old's memory of him. She was starting to fall for the man she was spending more and more time with. Tom Riley, the slightly bitter, closed-off, hurt mystery of a man who couldn't want less to do with her. The man who was still, despite everything, funny and clever and gentle and kind.

A man she could never be worthy of, even if she tried for the rest of her life.

It was in this state that she went to the backyard of the family house, where she could fill crates upon crates with new candles and not be disturbed.

At least, she thought she wouldn't be disturbed until her father showed up.

"Candles, dear?"

"Hm?"

May looked up from the palette of candles—their fresh, sweet pea scents floating up on the breeze—to find her father standing there, looking down at her over his cup of coffee with a concerned, slightly amused expression on his face. She tried to respond with calm detachment, as if she hadn't spent the entire night stress-making candles and listening to ABBA and mainlining lemon-lime soda, which was the only sugary drink she could find in the entire house.

Her father made a small *hm* noise, though she couldn't tell if it was a humorous *hm* or a worried *hm*. "This seems like...an awful lot of beeswax candles."

"Yeah, I couldn't sleep last night."

"Any particular reason why?"

"Nope. Just...just couldn't sleep. One of those nights."

May and her father had never had a *bad* relationship, but like with her mother, it was always clear that she hadn't been the favorite child. Her other siblings were closer to their parents; May only felt, well, parented by them.

"And are you lying to me?"

"Dad, come on," May said, rubbing leftover beeswax from her hands onto her jeans. Guess she'd be having a special on candles at the shop today. "Throw me a bone here. I don't really want to talk about it."

"Sometimes the things we don't want to talk about are the ones we need to get out there the most."

"Did you get that out of a parenting 101 book?"

Her father didn't rise to the bait. Instead, he waited for a moment as she collected herself, then said in the calmest, flattest voice possible, "Is this about the Riley boy?"

"You know, not every problem in the entire world goes back to Tom Riley. I wish I could go one day without someone looking at me with sad, pitying eyes while they say, *Is this about Tom Riley?*"

He raised one bushy eyebrow in her direction. "So, it *is* about Tom Riley?"

"Obviously! You don't make a hundred beeswax candles in the middle of the summer because you're perfectly happy about teaming up with your old boyfriend."

May slammed the top back onto the crate, where it completely missed its mark and fell into the pine needle–strewn grass at her feet. She stared at it for too long.

It was so pathetic, wasn't it? Mooning over some boy. But this wasn't about a boy, and she knew that every time she thought about it too deeply.

It was about her guilt. And it was about her complete and total inability to do anything about it. If she told the truth now, if she cleared the air of all these rumors she'd allowed to permeate for all this time, then she could—and no doubt, *would*—lose everything.

But being around Tom Riley was a constant reminder of that guilt. She'd thought she could get through it, that maybe exposure therapy and a little bit of friendship would fix everything, but the opposite was true.

She hated herself now more than ever.

"You miss him, don't you?" her father asked.

"I don't miss him."

"*May.*"

"I don't!"

The old man had the audacity to smile that quiet, secret, fatherly *I know more than you, kid* smile. He nodded his head. "Except for all the times you do."

"Yeah. Except for all the times I do miss him, I don't

miss him." She laughed, but the guilt weighed down the sound. "Dad?"

"Yes, dear?"

She stared at the wood grains of the box top at her feet. Their patterns swirled and dizzied her, until she was certain she would pass out if she stared for another moment too long. But when she blinked, she realized that it wasn't the patterns that were making the world blurry. It was water pooling up in her eyes, unbidden and unwanted. "If you did a bad thing, but doing the good thing might ruin your life, change the way everyone sees you... What would you—I mean, how would you fix it?"

"Am I allowed to know the specifics of this hypothetical?"

"Hypotheticals don't have specifics."

"You know how to do the right thing, May. No one needs to explain it to you. You just need the courage to get your feet moving in that direction."

"Right. Yeah."

"It takes great courage to be good. But I think you're a lot braver than you've been letting on these last few years. Wouldn't you agree?"

"I don't know."

"Well, I look forward to finding out."

Without anything else to say, May started back for the house. She was already looking forward to a soak in the world's deepest bathtub, a snack of endless white cheddar popcorn, bottomless spiked seltzer, and a long, dreamless, thoughtless sleep.

But she'd barely gotten two steps toward home when her mother's shrill voice disturbed the birds in the nearby trees.

"May Anderson! You get up here right this minute!"

May paused. Maybe if she stood very, very still and tried very, very hard to disappear into the foliage, she'd manage it.

"May! May, did you hear me?"

For a split second, May considered ignoring her, faking ignorance and driving into town for the night, maybe crashing in a sleeping bag she had tucked into the back of the store for emergencies. If her mother was in one of these demanding, highly excitable moods, there was a better-than-average chance that it was about something she'd done wrong.

But, just as she was about to drag herself into the truck and speed away like the apocalypse was chasing her, May noticed something strange. A modest, simple car with a rental's license plate sitting up at the top of the hill, near the family house. May could recognize the cars of almost everyone who ever came to visit this place. This car? She didn't have the faintest idea whose it could be.

Curiosity won out over her instinct to bolt.

"May!" her mother called again, her voice somehow managing to get even louder than it had been a moment ago, a feat May had previously thought impossible. "Are you out there?"

"Yes, ma'am! I'll be right up!"

"Well, hurry! And maybe put on a fresh coat of lipstick!"

Lipstick? May paused with her bag halfway slung over her shoulder. What in the world would she need lipstick for? She kept her tinted ChapStick—the closest thing to lipstick she regularly kept on her person—in her bag and decided not to tell her mother that *a fresh coat* of lipstick would imply that she'd been wearing any at all today... which she definitely hadn't been.

She didn't want to give the woman another reason to start crying about the unmarried state of two-thirds of her daughters and how that was probably due to the fact that none of them cared what men thought of their appearances.

May stopped short as she walked up the hill, tripping over her own thoughts and her boots. That wasn't entirely true. She *had* cared what Tom Riley thought about her today.

She'd been self-conscious in that oversized T-shirt he'd leant her; she'd secretly wanted to look cute in front of him and not, like she was sure she did, like a drowned rat. She'd spent the better part of the morning comparing herself to the image of Joanna, using that woman's beautiful body as a template against which May knew she could never measure. Literally. She was at least a foot shorter.

At the foot of the stone-laid steps to the house, her mother ambushed her in a flurry of hushed, whispered commands and tugs at her less-than-perfect outfit. Tom's shirt hung over her like a dress, one she'd belted with a sweatshirt from the shop wrapped around her waist.

"Oh, my dear! It's so good to see you! Did you go to work like that? You know you're never going to make sales like… Never mind! Do you have a brush? And what about that lipstick? I thought we'd talked about lipstick—"

May held her hand out, suspicion pulling the hairs on the back of her neck until they stood upright. She'd been expecting anger, some kind of talk-down about what happened with the town council or whatever Mrs. Elaine Bates had told her mother about what happened in the fountain. She hadn't expected something approaching Christmas morning giddiness. "Mom, what's going on?"

"Your friendship with Annie is really paying off in spades. I knew it was going to. Don't you remember? Didn't I say on that first day that the Martins were going to be very important in our lives?"

"You did, but—"

"Apparently, one of Annie's very single, very eligible friends from Los Angeles was quite taken with you at her little party, but you didn't leave so much as a glass slipper or a phone number for him to track you down with! But don't worry. The poor boy's waiting inside with a nice cup of coffee and—"

A record scratched in May's mind as the pieces fell into place. Her mother was trying to doll her up for William, the photographer Annie tried to set her up with before the whole Tom thing got in the way. Great. Exactly what she needed today. "You let him in the house?"

Her mother reeled back, affronted. "Of course I did. What else was I supposed to do? Leave the poor boy to wait out here in the cold? Don't be ridiculous."

It was about 70 degrees outside. No, what was ridiculous was assuming that May wanted some strange guy she didn't know showing up randomly at her house.

May lowered her voice, trying to force the woman who birthed her to see reason. "Mom, I really don't think—"

"Don't think! Don't think at all. You girls always over-think relationships when you should just be diving in! Now, go around the back to the terrace. I've put out some wine and a cheeseboard, and I'll send him out back to meet you. Pinch those cheeks a little bit and get some life into them before he gets there, please!"

Before May could protest again, her mother disappeared into the house, leaving her no choice but to run away or to comply. Running away was an attractive option, but she knew that when it came to getting her daughters coupled off, the Anderson matriarch would probably call out the National Guard to find her if she went missing for even a minute.

She just wants what's best for you, May's internal voice of reason—who sounded surprisingly like Rose—reminded her. *She's just pushing you into this guy because she wants you to find love and she thinks this is the best way to go about it. Besides…if Tom has Joanna—which he should, considering everything that happened between the two of you—then maybe you should find someone, too.*

Maybe you should get unstuck, too.

So, while May didn't pinch her cheeks like her mother suggested, she *did* trudge around to the terrace and plop herself down in one of the aging metal chairs to await her unexpected date.

Just remember…you promised Rose that you would try to move forward. You promised Annie you would get unstuck. This William guy seems as good a place as any to start. Sure, he'd come on a little bit strong at Annie's party, but anyone can make a bad impression. She just had to keep an open mind. Just had to hope for—

But the second the back door swung open and he opened his perfectly crooked jaw—his one feature that kept him from looking like a villain in a made-for-TV movie about the evil, hot husband of some tormented suburban housewife— she knew she'd made a big mistake.

"May! May Anderson!" He paused in the doorway, the lights overhead casting him almost entirely in silhouette as he stared down at her. Ducking down, he took the seat next to her and helped himself to a heavy-handed pour of wine. "I'm sorry to barge in like this," he said, voice dripping with insincerity that told her he wasn't sorry at all. "I had been hoping to talk more with you at Annie's party, but you ran off like your carriage was about to turn into a pumpkin. Annie said I could drop by though."

"Sorry about that," May said, trying to sound more sincere than he'd been in his apology. "I didn't mean to blow you off or anything. I'm just not—"

"*Wow.*"

Before she could finish her thought, he leaned over toward her and breathed out that word like a soft, tender prayer. But one made by a devout believer or a liar fishing for miracles, she wasn't sure. Leaning back in surprise, she blinked at him.

"What?"

"You know," he said, his index finger lazily dancing along the rim of his wine tumbler, "your voice is very beautiful when it's not being drowned out by loud music."

"Um...thank you."

That *was* a compliment, right? She couldn't be entirely sure.

When was the last time a man had complimented her? A man other than her father, of course. She scraped her memory to think of a time, and when she came up empty, she chalked up her indecision about this...comment to her romantic rustiness.

In a surprising three gulps, William polished off his glass of wine before refilling it. May didn't drink red wine anymore—not that her mother, who laid out this spread, ever noticed or cared—but the fact that he didn't even offer to fill her glass nettled her. She stuffed a mouthful of cheese and quince paste into her mouth to keep her from saying something snarky and regrettable.

"Well," William said, relaxing back against the chair with his wineglass cupped delicately in his right hand. "I guess I should get right down to it, shouldn't I?"

"Only if you want your visit to make any kind of sense to me," May teased, singsonging the words to hide how deadly serious she was about them.

"I want to photograph you."

Just when she thought the world could hold no more surprises.

"*Me?*" she choked.

"Yes," he said, dark eyes dancing. "I've been low on inspiration lately, so when Annie invited me here, I thought I would get away from the high-flying life of an artist to drink in some small-town culture. Thought I'd drink some good wine and eat a few pies and have a little fun before going back to my real life. But then..." He turned those dark and dangerous eyes on her. It took everything in her power not to get lost in them. She may not have been immediately taken with him, but even she wasn't strong enough to resist a pair of handsome, entrancing eyes when they looked at her like she was the most precious piece of artwork to ever roam the planet. "I saw you. And I knew that I'd been brought here for a higher purpose. I knew I'd found my spark once again."

"With me?"

"Yes. You! A larger-than-life figure of a woman who rules her hometown like a queen from some high fantasy film."

Usually, when someone spoke, it helped her understand *more* of what they were talking about. When William spoke, though, she only grew more and more confused. And slightly uncomfortable. But was she uncomfortable with him specifically or the idea of being liked at all? She couldn't be certain.

"Are you at the right house? I think you must be thinking about someone else."

"I know it's a strange request," he said, holding out his free hand in a mock surrender. "But if you'd just sit for some pictures for me, I'd like for you to see just how beautiful you could be."

Her heart stutter-stepped. *That*, at least, she knew wasn't quite a compliment, or at least, it wasn't the kind of compliment her heart really wanted.

May's mind retreated back to this afternoon, when every look from Tom had been enough to warm her from the inside out. Even after everything she'd done to him, he still cared about her, still went out of his way to show her true, genuine kindness. Next to a guy like that, this William guy felt hollow as a cleaned-out honeycomb.

But her mind traveled back to the smile Joanna had given Tom. Joanna had noticed Tom's goodness as well, and May could tell that he felt something for her in response.

Get unstuck, May. "You know what? Sure."

William's eyes widened and his thousand-watt smile lit up the terrace; she could practically see the wheels turning in his head. "Really?"

"Yeah. Why not? It sounds like fun."

Go and pose for the sappy romantic photographer, she'd said. *It'll be fun*, she'd said. Famous last words. That hypothesis, Tom's gran would have said, was bull dinky. Because the next day, when the cool evening breeze wrapped around the mountains of Northern California like a comforting blanket to break up the summer heat of the day, she found herself perched precariously on a boulder, holding Stella by a leather lead in one hand and raising a golden scepter aloft in the other.

When he'd called her a queen from a high fantasy film, that (apparently) hadn't been an exaggeration for poetic effect. That had been his artistic vision. The ridiculous gown he'd clipped her into—using fabric stretchers to make the flouncy fabric cover her modesty when the stupid thing stubbornly refused to zip—covered very little of her shoulders and every time the wind picked up, it created a wind tunnel within the voluminous skirts swathed around her legs.

If she actually made it out of this alive, she was both (a) going to regret it and (b) spend the next few years recovering from hypothermia or pneumonia or whatever it was survivors of exposure came down with. Northern California summer nights were not the warm, temperate experiences everyone assumed they were.

"Hey, William?"

"Yes, my muse?" he muttered, still fiddling with some of the settings on the body of the camera, which he'd perched upon a tripod unsteadily leveled upon a few boulders. She wasn't actually sure he remembered her name. All around him, white tent lights and reflectors shone in her direction, and a few monitors faced him, meaning she could barely see in front of her, much less what she looked like to the outside eye.

Still, she had a pretty good idea of how ridiculous she looked.

"Do you think maybe we could take a break? Go inside for a hot chocolate or a glass of wine or something?"

Summer nights in Sonoma County often dipped into the forties and low thirties. May could feel every single dropped degree as the wind danced along her bare skin. Why had she agreed to this again?

Right. Because her sister thought she needed to get out more. Well, if this was what happened when she tried to do just that, then she considered getting out to be highly overrated. She tried not to think about the fact that Tom was probably on a nice, normal *indoor* date with Joanna this second.

"And lose all of this beautiful light? I wouldn't dream of it!"

"But it's getting pretty cold..."

"Oh, don't you worry about me," he said with a beaming smile, completely ignoring the fact that she might, you know, be the one freezing parts of her anatomy off. "I have a pair of hand warmers in my pockets if things get too dire."

She thought of the warm flannel shirt Tom had let her borrow the day they'd fallen into the fountain. He'd gone out of his way to make her feel safe and comfortable, so unlike this moment with this stranger. A sour sickness descended into the pit of her stomach as the contrast between the two men—the one she'd tried to keep at arm's length and the one she was now stuck in the middle of the woods with—grew wider and wider with every comparison she made between them. Shifting uncomfortably in the too-small sandals William had given her to wear, she searched for any more topics of conversation that could keep her mind off of the dropping temperatures. A bright flash filled her eyes with spots.

"Oh!" She blinked, rapidly. "Should I be doing anything? With my face or anything?"

"I'm just testing the light out for the minute. If you want to do something, you can tell me a little bit more about yourself. Everything I know about you I know from rumors and gossip. I got talking to a fascinating woman in town earlier. Mrs. Bates?"

"Then I'm afraid you've gotten a pretty bad picture of me."

"No such thing as a bad picture of you, Amelia Anderson. Not when I'm taking it."

There it was again. That smile he'd given her at the house, the one that told her she was the most precious piece of artwork he'd ever seen. But she didn't *want* to be a painting or a piece of art. She didn't want to be a thing.

She didn't want to be stuck on someone's wall, frozen in time forever. That's just…that's just the way her life had turned out. That's the way she'd *let it* turn out.

Heat pooled beneath her collar. What was she doing here? Why was she posing for this guy and settling for him, settling for lying to everyone, settling for doing all the wrong things?

Right. Because it was easy. Safe.

"You know, I was really thinking that, if we worked together, you might consider hiring me to do the promo and press work for the Food and Wine Festival. I think you and I could have quite the mutually beneficial partnership."

"Yeah," May said, not believing a single word of it. "Maybe."

Chapter Twelve

Tom

May Anderson had come down with a cold, and as was usually the case any time anyone so much as breathed wrong in
May's direction, the entire town was talking about it. Tom had
heard about her cold at the grocery store, at the bank, from his
bottle delivery guy, from three of his vineyard workers, from
Annie (both via text and in person), from the woman who
made him coffee this morning, *and* from the little girl sitting
next to her mom at the printing store—who had even asked
pointedly whether he had given it to her—and her symptoms
had been getting progressively worse with each telling.

In other words, as the end of her first cold-ridden week
drew to a close and they limited their communication to text
messages and brief, sniffly phone calls, Tom convinced himself that May Anderson was on the brink of death.

Not that he should care. Not that he *did* care, really. Caring about May was pointless; she had plenty of people to
worry about her. The rumor mill proved that.

And he himself proved that. He cared about her. At least
a little bit.

His pride whispered in his ear that it didn't matter.
That with May Anderson out of the picture, he could push
Barn Door Winery to the forefront of the festival, make all
of the changes he wanted to the program, and by the time
she eventually returned to planning with him, it would be
too late to change anything back. It would even help him
avoid the inconvenient feelings that had been plaguing him
since that day in the fountain. Out of sight, out of mind,
right?

Wrong. Because here he was, standing at her front door,
holding a fresh box of Gran's famous grilled cheese and
tomato soup he'd made from scratch.

He hadn't *meant* to make tomato soup from scratch.
He just couldn't sleep and then, next thing he knew, he had
reduced a garden's worth of tomatoes and seasoned them
just right, and added just a dash of cream until he had a bubbling pan of fresh soup. Fresh herbs from his gran's garden
completed the aromatic, warming scent, one that awakened
his senses and reminded him just how long he'd been working on this soup. It could have happened to anyone.

And it definitely didn't mean anything. No, it was just
because he needed his festival partner back. Nothing else.
Nothing deeper than that.

He wasn't worried about her or anything.

Going to the Anderson Family Farm had been an incredibly harmless decision. It was the middle of the day, when
he expected Harper and her father to be out working with
the blooms that filled the wide fields cocooning their hillside
home, and the rest of the family to be at their jobs. His plan
was just to drop off the grilled cheese and the soup at the
front door and ring the bell, and run away like a teenage boy
doing "Ding Dong Ditch" before May would even realize
he'd been there at all.

He hadn't counted on Mrs. Anderson, May's mother, sitting on her front porch when he walked up.

"Tom Riley?"

The second she called his name, in that bracing tone of hers, the muscles in Tom's shoulders tightened in embarrassment. *Busted.* Wincing, he gave a wave as he made his way toward the house anyway. No use in turning back down. That would only make things worse.

"Hi, Mrs. Anderson. Is May home?"

Face flushed with excitement, the woman beelined for the front door and threw it open. "I don't know how I got so lucky. Two in one week. May! May, come down here!"

Two in one week? Tom couldn't even begin to guess what she meant by that, but he did try to bow out as gracefully as possible, offering her the bag he'd carried here.

"She doesn't need to. I was just going to bring her—"

"May! May Anderson I'm not going to ask you again! I'm so sorry, Thomas. This is just the absolute *rudest*—"

With every word the woman spoke, Tom remembered how May had struggled in high school with her parents. Everyone outside of this house thought the Andersons were this practically perfect family, but he knew better. May had always felt like the black sheep, the one left out. It seemed that nothing had changed; her mother was still as biting as ever. Sure, he knew that Mr. and Mrs. Anderson loved May, but he also knew that if May was sick, her mother wasn't going to be the one to look after her properly.

Glancing up at the roof, Tom caught sight of a familiar streak of red hair dancing on the wind.

"It's okay. I think I know where to find her."

A few minutes later, an overly obliging Mrs. Anderson had led Tom upstairs to the door to May's room. Every step through the house was like crossing through a long-remembered dream space. The smell of the flowers. The creaking of the stairs. The chipped paint in one of the upstairs door frames. Tom remembered it all so well.

Yet, when he found himself outside May's door, he hesitated to open it. He could just leave—leave the soup and the grilled cheese, and run off without having to see her. That would probably be best. Safest. After all, what did he care if she was sick?

He reached out and turned the door handle anyway, letting himself into the bedroom. As he'd expected, the space was empty and the window was open—a sure sign that May was in her favorite hiding spot. Everything else, though, shocked him. Gone was her wall-sized map, marked with tiny gold stars for all the places she wanted to visit. Gone was her small but well-kept library of language guides and travel booklets. The collage of photographs of them? Missing. Even the bedspread she'd dyed by hand during eleventh grade—using the discarded purple flowers her family couldn't sell—was gone and replaced with a plain, white down comforter.

A chill gripped at the center of Tom's chest. *What happened to her? Where are the concert tickets from shows she snuck out with me to see? Where are the posters for all the planets she wanted to visit once space travel became possible? Where is the terrible painting she did of the Eiffel Tower in tenth grade, the one she loved too much to ever take down? What the hell happened to May Anderson?*

No. No, he didn't care. Refused to care. He was just here to deliver the provisions and get out as soon as possible. His concern began and ended not at the woman May Anderson had become, but at the Food and Wine Festival and what it could do for his business.

That was it.

Going straight for the open window, he stuck his head out

and inclined his face toward the roof, where, sure enough, May was sitting, wrapped up in a pair of mismatched pj's and a blanket that would have looked more at home on an ice-fishing expedition than a rooftop in California during the summertime.

"Don't you know you'll catch your death up here?"

May started, then blinked down at him in surprise. "What are you doing here?"

He waved the brown paper bag in his hand. "I heard from just about everyone in town that you were dying. Thought I might bring you some provisions."

With a wave, she invited him up, and he put the handle of the brown paper bag in his mouth so he could swing himself up onto the roof like he used to. Strange how long muscle memory lasts, how his hands knew exactly where to grip so he could easily pull himself up into place.

The roof of the Anderson house overlooked the entire valley, where an endless sea of flowers painted a portrait of sun-drowned beauty before them. Instead of looking at him, May stared out at those colorful blooms, quiet and contemplative even as she thanked him for the grilled cheese and the soup.

"It's good to know you haven't forgotten my hiding spot," she said, the smallest of smiles teasing her lips. "Even if Mom has."

"Everyone needs their place in the world. This one was always yours."

"Yep. Nothing's changed since high school. Nothing."

That cold hand squeezed his heart again. She sounded so, so *bitter*. He hadn't expected that from her. After all, hadn't she stayed here in Hillsboro for just that reason, so that nothing would change?

Tom shifted uncomfortably. He tried to lighten the mood. Tried being the operative word.

"It's a pretty gnarly cold you've got. Should I be worried?"

"Doctor says I'm not contagious anymore. And I didn't catch it from anyone, I don't think. Annie set me up with one of her friends from Los Angeles, and he had me out in the cold for *hours* taking pictures."

That must have been what Mrs. Anderson meant by *two in one week*. It had never been a secret that Mrs. Anderson thought the key to a long and happy life was a long and happy marriage; she hadn't changed her tune, it seemed.

Tom felt his throat tighten slightly at the thought of someone else swooping in and knocking May off her feet. Annie wasn't what anyone would call the world's best matchmaker, but still, he couldn't help but imagine moony-eyed May looking up with admiration at some handsome, worthy guy. He tried to swallow back the feeling.

"He...he sounds nice."

"I thought he was, too. Or, at least, Annie seemed to think so. But turns out he was just using me to try and get a gig with the festival. He didn't even call me after Annie's party. And he wasn't going to until he heard that I had hiring power. Apparently, it's always been his dream to get a paycheck for drinking and palling around picturesque NorCal vineyards and town squares."

He shouldn't have felt relief at that. He also probably shouldn't have felt the urge to find the guy and throat-punch him. He shouldn't have felt the urge to laugh at her adoption of his ridiculous accent. Her cheeks were pink now, but not from the fever and not from the wind up here on the roof. From embarrassment. Tom shook his head dismissively. "What a loser. He doesn't deserve you."

"I know," she said, without a hint of self-pitying woe. She spoke as though every word were an undeniable, irrefutable fact that everyone just had to live with. "No one does. Not after what I've done."

Tom balked at her sudden honesty. "Is this the cold medicine talking?"

"No, this is just a girl trying to talk to her best friend."

"You're not my best friend anymore."

He regretted the words as soon as he'd said them. Not because it wasn't the truth—it was; she'd given up her place as his best friend the day she let him drive away from this town alone—but because of the way she flinched when he delivered them.

"I know." She bit her bottom lip. Her fingers toyed with the handle of the brown paper bag he'd given her. "But I think you're still mine. You've always been mine."

His heart stopped. Then raced. He searched her face for understanding. *She'd* been the one to give *him* up. "Even after everything?"

"Yeah. Even after everything." The wind brushed between them, a quiet intruder into their private moment. "You know, for weeks before graduation, I'd been thinking about lasts. Last time I'd go down to the creek for a swim. Last time I'd eat Dad's blueberry muffins. Last time I'd ride up to False Mountain. And at first it was exciting. *Think of all the cool firsts you'll have.* But then...then I started to think that the only person I really felt myself with, the only person who really saw me and knew me...was you."

"And what was so wrong with that?"

"I was lonely, Tom. I *am* lonely. Rose and Harper have always had each other. They've always been my parents' favorites. I was alone in this house until you showed up. What...what would happen if I left town, left everything I'd known, my support—flimsy as it was—only for you to leave me once we were out there? I'd gone through my entire life only being good enough to make one real friend. Why did

I think anything would change once I left town? I started to believe that once I was out there, you'd leave me, too. And it was better to stay here and to stay safe than to risk everything."

This was the first time she'd ever laid out her reasoning so clearly. On the night she'd pushed him away all those years ago, she'd said things like *I can't trust you* and *this is for the best*, but she'd never told him the entire truth. Now...now, he knew. And the knowing was all the more heartbreaking and terrible.

"I wasn't going to leave you."

"I didn't know that."

"You let other people convince you—"

Finally, she tore her eyes away from the horizon and focused on nothing but him. After wishing she would just give him her attention, now he wished she hadn't. Seeing the pain, the conflict, the cavernous emptiness in her eyes threatened to tear him apart.

She wasn't a monster. She was a broken woman who'd made a bad choice out of fear.

"I know. I know. And I'm sorry. I was just...so afraid. The kind of fear you can't even put into words. It made me act like a stranger." Her head dropped. Then, she mumbled, mostly to herself, "I still am acting like a stranger."

"Because you don't want to be alone?" he asked.

"Yeah."

A dozen retorts floated to the forefront of his mind. *Yeah, now you know what it feels like. I've been alone all of these years and it was your fault. If you didn't want to be alone, you could have just come with me back then.*

The cruelty tasted sweet, like victory, like finally getting one over on someone who'd hurt him. But when he looked at her again, he didn't see someone he actually wanted victory over.

He didn't want to be her enemy anymore.

They'd both been marooned on these islands of isolation for so long. Too stubborn, too proud, too hurt, and too afraid to reach out.

Not anymore.

"You're not alone," he said, clear and quiet.

May shook her head miserably. "I should be. I thought you hated me."

"I stayed up all night and made you soup," Tom said, nudging her shoulder. "Can I ask you something, though?" he asked, thinking back to her bedroom, thinking of this person beside him who lived in such a sad, lifeless place.

She nodded. "Anything."

"Do you still dream of getting out of this place?"

"Every damn day, Tom."

For a moment, both of them were still and silent, their only entertainment being the bright and somehow soothing colors of the sunset in the distance. Then, eventually, May's small voice piped up.

"What was it like out there?" she asked, distant and wistful. "I mean, you made it out. You saw the world. Was it everything we'd ever hoped it would be?"

He considered that question for longer than he should have, thinking about all of the times he'd been sitting at a table in Paris or at a bar in Andalusia and looking at the empty seat beside him, only to wonder what it would be like if she was there to fill it.

"It was beautiful," he said, meaning every word. "You would have loved it."

"Will you tell me about it sometime?"

Tom smiled and raised an eyebrow at her. "Are you busy now?"

"Not unless this fever drops sometime soon."

Readjusting himself to sit more comfortably, he edged closer to her. There wasn't anything particularly sexy about a sick woman in her pajamas, but he couldn't ignore the thrill he felt at her closeness.

"You know, I hear stories are pretty good medicine."

"Then go on. Tell me."

And over the next few hours, as the bronze haze of sunset gave way to the first twinkling stars of evening, May's head slowly descended to Tom's shoulder, where it rested as he traced his journey. There was the car that took him all the way to the East Coast, where he studied under an apple and peach farmer with farms from Maine all the way down to Georgia. From there, he'd gone to France. To Spain. To Hungary. To Argentina. To Japan.

He told her stories of bull riding and uncooperative donkey transportation, of the best glass of wine he'd ever had, of the days he'd spent learning about soil and sunshine and how important it was to pour love into every glass of wine he ever bottled. He told her of waterfalls the height of skyscrapers. Of salt flats so smooth they doubled the sky. Of caves and cities and valleys and deserts.

The longer he talked, the more deeply he thought about those places and the memories of them, the more he wished things were different. When he'd left eight years ago, he'd shoved all thoughts of her into a tiny little box, which he only opened every once in a while. He hadn't let himself miss her. Hadn't let himself want her there.

But now he regretted ever leaving without her. He loved those memories... but they weren't the same without her in them.

And somewhere between all of the stories and the longing, May fell asleep on his shoulder. And he didn't have the heart to wake her.

Chapter Thirteen

May

She wasn't alone. He'd said she wasn't alone. It was more than she deserved, but still, the thought swam in her head like champagne, even until the next morning.

May had hoped—hoped, and not thought or believed, being the keyword here—that her mother would keep everything about her glut of male visitors this week a secret. She should have known better. As usual, her hope in her mother had been wildly misplaced. By the time she finally descended the staircase to take on her first full day of festival prep since getting sick, she was almost immediately set upon by a pack of rabid friends and family, all equally excited about squeezing information out of her.

Rose and Annie sat at the kitchen counter, drinking coffee and pretending not to be waiting for her arrival. Annie spoke first. "May Anderson! You didn't tell me you had a date! Two dates!"

May went straight for her travel mug and the coffee pot. If this was any indication of how the day was going to go, then she would need a lot of caffeinated courage to face it. "I don't know what you're talking about."

Annie tapped Rose with her newspaper, like a properly scandalized gossiping coquette in a Regency romance novel. "Don't know what we're—Rose, have you *ever*?"

"I *never*!"

May rolled her eyes. She couldn't help it. Everything was already overwhelming enough as it was. She was juggling a festival, a career, and this…thing she had going on with Tom. Dealing with two excitable women wasn't exactly high on her list of priorities, even if she loved them both to death. "You two are impossible."

Rose spoke softly, her eyes cautious. May could tell almost immediately that Harper had encouraged this, wanting to know the details but not wanting to take the hit to her pride that would be required to actually ask any questions herself. "We just want to make sure that you're all right. Juggling two men, an old flame reappearing—"

Annie interjected. "I'm just glad that you're not stuck anymore."

"I wouldn't say that," May answered after a moment of consideration. "Just that I'm trying not to be. And I'm not juggling two men. One is pretty much out of the picture and the other one is just a work colleague. That's all."

"Is that so? Then…" Annie gave her one long, lingering look from head to toe, then waggled her eyebrows suggestively. "What are you doing right now?"

May was wearing a soft, old-fashioned dress in a red-checked pattern that she knew brought out the green in her eyes; she'd braided her hair into a simple twist at the back of her neck and even donned a little makeup.

But so what? It wasn't for Tom. It was in celebration. A joyful acknowledgment that she'd finally been able to get out of the house after dealing with that cold for a week.

"I'll have you know that Tom and I are going to a square

dancing class to see if we might want to add it to the free events for the festival. That's all."

"Kind of last-minute. Was this your idea or his, this date?"

Now Rose was in on it, too, adding to the fanciful delusions of her and Tom's relationship.

"They reached out to us, actually. Sorry to burst your bubble, but Tom and I are..." She weighed how to finish that sentence. They weren't allies or co-workers anymore. But everything else seemed to be more than she deserved. "Friends. We're friends. And that's all that I think we'll be."

"He *is* going out on a date with my friend Joanna," Annie agreed, nodding.

Against her will and her better judgment, May's heart skipped two beats. He was going out with Joanna? Her mind flashed back to their game of make-believe, to the craving she'd had to press her lips against him and forget everything that had ever happened between them.

It seemed he'd taken her advice and their practice more seriously than she'd thought.

Well.

Fine.

Yeah. Good. Good for him. May was happy for him. Or...May would be happy for him. She swallowed, hard, and tried to get her breathing under control.

"He is?"

"Yeah, he called her yesterday and asked her out." Annie shot her a pointed look. "When I heard your mum's story, I was worried that he was going out with two girls at once, but I should have known better. He's not that kind of guy."

"Right," she replied, her throat closing slightly. "No, Tom's decent."

The half-smile May offered as she rushed to the cab of

her truck did nothing to convince Rose, who immediately dropped into sister-therapist mode.

"May, are you all right?"

May settled into the front seat and slipped the key into the ignition. She could feel Annie's and Rose's hot stares on her cheeks, but she kept her eyes set firmly on the windshield in front of her. "Mm-hm. I just hope I'm still a good dancer. I haven't done square dancing since I was in middle school."

Apparently, there was a good reason for that. When May and Tom met in the Hillsboro Pavilion, just a block away from the town's square, they walked in only to be greeted by Gertrude Rohan. Also known to the middle schoolers of Hillsboro Middle School as *Ruthless Rohan*.

She'd been their P.E. teacher in school and, apparently, in her retirement, had decided to follow her life's true calling by starting her own traveling square dancing school. Though her base was here in the county, she'd been traveling all across the country with her bandana-tied microphone and her collection of fiddle music, teaching children and adults alike the finer points of square dancing. No, *American Folk Dancing*. That's what her website had said. *The popular dances of American culture*. May wondered if, as part of her curricula, she taught the Cupid Shuffle and the Twerk alongside the square dance, but somehow, she doubted it.

The main room of the Garcetti Dance Academy—the small, extracurricular dancing school that May had basically flunked out of when she was nine and refused to dance to any music that wasn't ABBA—was a popular site for everything from children's ballet classes to wedding dance rehearsals, and the golden, varnished floor smelled like paint and memories. The soft lighting and the mirrored walls left everything in the present out in the open though.

May and Tom waited, side by side, for Mrs. Rohan to arrive, like two naughty children who'd been told to wait for the teacher after class. May wanted to ask about his date with Joanna, what had finally made him go for it, what they were planning, but she couldn't make the words form. Instead, they chatted idly, coolly, about the prospect of square dancing at the festival, about programs, about phone calls they needed to make and dates they needed to remember.

If he'd wanted to mention the date to her, he never made any indication.

At first, even without the inclusion of *actual* popular dances of American culture, May considered the possibility that this might be a fun, interactive element for the kids who visited the festival. But then Ruthless Rohan had to go and open her mouth.

"Well, well, well. Look what we have here. The Hillsboro High Prom King and Queen. Or did they strip you of that title when you skipped town?"

The muscles in May's jaws tightened; the hair on the back of her neck raised on end. "Mrs. Rohan—"

"I'm just messing with y'all," Mrs. Rohan lied, slapping a big, bright sticker of a smile onto her face as she tapped May on the shoulder. "How are you doing, kid? Are you all right?"

"Um, I'm not bad. Just trying to get this whole festival off of the ground."

"Of course. Too right. Let's get to work. I hear Mr. Riley is pretty light on his feet. Always jumping from place to place."

Oh. Right. *This* was why Tom Riley didn't show his face around town. This was what she had done to him.

"It's good to see you too, Mrs. Rohan," Tom said, smiling and offering his hand as though he hadn't just been insulted to his face, his usual defense mechanism. She'd seen it in his too-cheerful interactions with everyone they'd met and seen over the last few days of festival prep.

"Yes. I'm sure it is," Mrs. Rohan replied with a sniff, tossing her head and returning to her small CD player in the corner rather than taking his hand. "Now, are we ready to start? I want to give you a taster class of what we'd be doing with your festival guests. It *was* going to be an increased fee because of the last-minute nature of the event—"

As the woman droned on and on, beginning her preparations with bags of bandanas and stacks of CDs, May resisted the urge to roll her eyes. Apparently, Mrs. Rohan had forgotten that *she* was the one who'd contacted *them* about joining the festival and wasn't in any position to be making demands. But that was Ruthless Rohan for you. She got them in the room with false promises of "contributing to the town's cultural outreach" during the festival, only to show her true colors now that they were trapped in here with her.

Soon May and Tom found themselves standing at the ready, side by side, and equally trying to hide their amusement at the whole scenario. The mirrors proved that they weren't doing a very good job at hiding how hilarious they found the square dancing lesson; May could only hope Mrs. Rohan didn't notice.

"Okay. Take your girl by the hand. Or, not your girl, but—"

"Done," May said, grabbing Tom's hand up in hers to avoid any more snide remarks. She was surprised to discover just how much she liked holding Tom's hand again, how easy his touch was. "What's next?"

"So, we have a selection of music; and I will reserve the right to pick what we dance to."

May felt silent chuckles shaking Tom's shoulders as the small sound system in the corner of the room started blaring "Achy Breaky Heart" at top volume.

"Are all the songs going to be this...?" May scraped her admittedly limited vocabulary for something that wouldn't get her in deep, deep trouble with the woman who could easily use her walking stick as a baton with which to beat her over the head for any perceived slight. *Abrasive? Awful?* "Are all of the songs going to be this catchy?"

"It's square dancing. It's about finding songs that match with the rhythm of the human heartbeat!" By now Mrs. Rohan was beaming, and with every passing second, May wished more and more deeply that she was doing something else. Anything else. Brushing Stella's teeth. Having her eyebrows waxed. Getting caught at every red light in town. "Right. Well, should we get started, then?"

"This'll be good," Tom muttered under his breath.

"You and I have very different definitions of the word *good*."

"Then let's leave. We don't have to stay here."

"If we leave she'll freak out and tell the whole town. And then where would we be?"

May tried to swallow the guilt welling up within her as those words crossed her lips. She knew they were true. Every move in a place like Hillsboro had to be calculated, and lashing out at Mrs. Rohan would land them both in serious trouble. It was difficult, though, when her every instinct told her to throw down the stupid bandana she'd been given, stomp—sorry, heel dig—on it a few times for good measure, and storm out of the room before the woman even knew what hit her.

Tom didn't deserve the hatred he got. But the thought of risking everything—her security, her reputation, her family's businesses, even—proved a tight wire sewing her jaw shut and a heavy stone keeping her firmly in place here in this hall.

Her own cowardice made her want to curl in a ball and hide forever. But her cowardice was the only thing keeping her afloat.

He must have noticed something shift within her, because

when they started the dance all over again at Mrs. Rohan's behest—apparently, she couldn't have them basing their judgments on a flawed dance—he gripped her hand all the tighter, immediately injecting her with a flowing, aching warmth.

Soon, they were side-stepping and twirling in time with the gratingly down-home country tunes, letting their boots scoot all over the polished dance floor. The whole thing was ridiculous, but May couldn't help but feel exhilarated, flushed, by all of the movement, by his closeness, by the feeling of her hand in his.

They were singularly ridiculous. And for a brief, blissful moment, she was able to forget about everything else. She was able to just be here, in this moment, with him.

When, eventually, they were given a water break, Mrs. Rohan excused herself to the kitchenette in the back of the building, leaving May and Tom panting and recovering in the front room.

"This is actually kind of fun," Tom said, his cheeks red and his eyes bright. May rolled her eyes, but couldn't hide her smile. He'd gotten so handsome over the years. Years working in the sun had given him a rugged, rough exterior, like a cowboy in a classic western, and looking at him now, May couldn't help the flood of butterflies that fluttered in her stomach at their closeness. At how easy and right it felt to be here with him, doing this ridiculous square dance.

"Yeah, if you can manage to tune the old windbag out."

They both laughed at that, and the butterflies in May's stomach became too much to tune out. She couldn't feel anything for him, couldn't allow herself to. Maybe she'd been trying to convince herself that something could happen, that they could leave their pasts behind them, but now that she knew he would be going out with Joanna, the knowledge of how much she'd messed up hit her square in the throat.

Daydreaming about dancing close to him once again, of feeling his solid figure against hers, was definitely out of the question.

"So, I heard you're going on a date—"

"Yeah," Tom cut her off, glancing down awkwardly at his water bottle. "I mean...do you think it's a good idea?"

He spoke a little too fast. A little too expectantly. May's heart clenched. This was her chance, this was her moment to tell him that no, it wasn't a good idea. He should cancel their date immediately, throw her down on this floor and kiss her like she'd always dreamed of being kissed.

But, in this, she couldn't afford to be a coward, couldn't afford to give in. Tom deserved someone better than her. Joanna *was* that someone better. She would be cruel to stand in the way of something so perfect.

"She seems really, really nice," May said, surprised to find that it was the truth. "I like her."

"Good. Me too. I just hope she can see past, you know." He gestured to himself. "All of this."

"You just pointed to your entire body."

Tom fiddled with the water bottle in his hands, crunching at the plastic like one might crunch a math problem— anxiously and frustratingly. "You know what I mean. If she starts going out with me, someone's going to tell her the rumors. That I'm a good-for-nothing. They're going to try to push her away. I just hope she doesn't let them."

"I'm sure she won't," May said, unable to keep the quiet, wistful tone from affecting her words.

Moments later, they were dancing again, and this time, Mrs. Rohan seemed in a completely renewed spirit. If either of them had been hoping to get out of this "taster lesson" quickly and painlessly, they'd been seriously mistaken. The woman called dancing directions like bullets, sending them scrambling to follow her marching orders.

"And turn—"

They were halfway through the last skip-hop she'd commanded when this sudden interjection came. May scrambled to do what she'd been told, but not half so much as Tom, who threw his head back and laughed as he squeaked almost to the floor.

"Turn, boy!"

"I'm turning. I'm—"

It happened almost in slow motion. He reached out to take her hand, she looped his fingers securely in her own, then the squeaks of his boots got louder and before she knew it, they were both in a heaving pile of limbs and laughter on the floor, struggling to untangle themselves.

Not that May wanted to. This was the most fun she could remember having in…

Well, it was the most fun she could remember having. At least for a very, very long time.

Which, of course, meant that Mrs. Rohan had to come along and ruin it. Snapping the music off, she stormed over to them, casting her long shadow across them as she fumed.

"Tom Riley! I guess I shouldn't be surprised. You've ruined this just like you've ruined everything else."

The words were enough to silence May completely. Anger so intense and so hot welled up so quickly that she wondered if she'd ever be able to laugh again.

How could someone be so cruel? So downright mean?

Without thinking, May pushed herself to her feet. "Hey—"

But Tom shook his head and brushed her off before she could finish the thought. He shrugged. "It's okay. I'm used to it."

Used to it. She'd known that people around town were gossips and protective, yes, but she'd never imagined that *this* was the kind of thing he'd endured over the years since he'd been back home. That fire in May's chest burned even hotter now, but her voice went cold as ice.

"Mrs. Rohan. You know what? I think I've seen enough."

Tom's eyes widened. He shot to his feet, apparently to stop her. "May—"

"No. We are supposed to be representing our town, and if she's going to be talking like that to *anyone*, then she doesn't deserve the honor."

"How dare you say that to me, May Anderson! I'll have you know—"

Mrs. Rohan continued her protests, but May was already making her way toward the door, her mind thoroughly made up. It was instinctual, necessary, and she wasn't going to let anything talk her out of it.

"Oh, tell it to Billy Ray Cyrus," she scoffed. Her temperature was rising steadily now. The room almost spun with the frustration pumping through her veins. The injustice of it all. *She* was the one who deserved to be hated, but Tom was getting all of their ire. In this moment, May hated herself even more than Mrs. Rohan.

With a great heave of her arms, May threw the front door to the studio open and stormed out of it, trusting that Tom would follow close behind her. Rage clouded her, fogging the edges of her vision until she was finally sitting in the front seat of her car, staring at her hands and trying to catch her breath.

Then, when Tom took the passenger's seat, May finally realized what she'd just done.

Hillsboro was a town of rumors and reputations. And she'd just risked hers. She'd just risked both of theirs again.

What were they going to do to Tom and his family business now that he'd been party to her little temper tantrum? May stared at her still-shaking hands, not really seeing them at all.

"Oh my God," she muttered.

"May?" Tom's voice rumbled.

"Oh my God . . . Why did I do that?"

His jaw opened, then closed. She watched from the corner of her eyes as he made himself small, as he tried to avoid her eyes.

"I don't know."

"Now she's going to tell everyone and we're going to be . . ." May slammed her eyes shut, trying to keep welling tears at bay. She just couldn't help herself, could she? She did nothing but ruin things. She ruined *everything*. How could she even entertain the thought of ever being back with Tom? She couldn't condemn him to a life with someone like her. He didn't deserve that. "We're going to be in so much trouble."

"Maybe."

His tone was serious, but there was a slight quirk to Tom's mouth, and the corners of May's lips lifted in response. The funny side of it struck her, how ridiculous it was to be worried about getting into trouble like they were still sixteen. In the grand scheme of things, did it really matter?

But as she drove home that day, to the sound of her phone ringing off the hook with news and gossip and questions, she realized again that in this town, yes, it did matter.

Maybe keeping Tom Riley at arm's length was the best way to protect him from her, or maybe she could finally pluck up the courage to do something real to help him.

Chapter Fourteen

Tom

He was on a date with Joanna. He was on a date with intelligent, witty, kind, beautiful Joanna. He was on one of the handful of first dates he'd had since returning to Hillsboro with this fantastic person.

And he still couldn't stop thinking about May Anderson.

It was a problem. A big, overwhelming one that he tried—and failed—to shove from the forefront of his thoughts. For a few brief moments yesterday, when they were dancing in each other's arms, laughing together, he had forgotten how difficult she had made his life. But then reality had come crashing back down on him. Too hard and too fast and so overwhelming. He was buoyed by her defending him to someone who held a lot of power over them...and then disappointed in her almost immediate regret at having done so.

Which was it? Was she a changed person trying to be better, trying to recover from her past mistakes? Or was she comfortably content, just trying to float by on a calm sea even if it meant leaving him to drown in the rip tides?

Tom didn't know. All he knew was that he was out on a date with Joanna, he couldn't stop thinking about May, and he was frustrated with himself more and more with each passing second for not falling head-over-heels in love with the woman who might actually like him for real.

After he and Joanna had finished their perfectly pleasant meal—conversation and wine had flowed freely, she'd laughed at more than a handful of his jokes—they decided to go for a walk around the center of town. Saturday nights were sometimes called "Showcase Nights" around town, meaning that the shops stayed open later so that all the weekend tourists could have a peruse through what Joanna called the *adorably precious* shops on the square.

Tom had tried to steer Joanna away from this course of action at first, tried to tell her that it would be busy, that ice cream would be better, that they could even drive out to his place and have some wine under the stars if she wanted.

It had all been for nothing. Joanna was, after all, another tourist, escaping the hot Los Angeles sun and unrelenting traffic for an entire season instead of just a weekend like most of them, and she wanted to see the quaint little shops glowing under the street lamps just like the rest of them did.

Because Anderson's Sweets and Sundries was situated on the town square and because he was fully aware that everyone who lived in Hillsboro frequented the place, Tom usually did his best to avoid it altogether if he could manage it. If the town square was a place where people in this community went to see and be seen, then the best way to remain invisible was to, you know, not go to the most visible place around.

From the moment they started their trek toward the square, Tom kept the collar of his jacket up high, all the better to delay the inevitable. At some point, someone would recognize him out here—one of the busybodies who couldn't help themselves from making a mess of things—and they'd ask Joanna what a nice, sweet girl was doing with the boy who'd broken the mayor's window when he was nine, the boy who'd been accused of cheating on a test when he was thirteen, who'd lost the state championship baseball game with a bad pitch over home plate, who'd broken May Anderson's heart. He knew that something like that was coming, knew he'd eventually have to face the prospect of Joanna discovering that he was bad news, knew that she would eventually get smart and run off into the sunset, leaving him alone once again. He just wanted a few more precious moments of normal.

He'd missed normal. And if he could just get the memory of May out of his head, he would hold on to normal with Joanna as long as he could.

"It's just so *adorable*," Joanna said, clapping her hands together and staring up in awe at the light-lined trees above her. The sound of summer crickets underscored her words; the night wrapped its arms around them, drawing them closer together as they walked. "Don't you think it's just the cutest little town you've ever seen?"

"It's something, all right," Tom said noncommittally.

There were many wonderful things to love about this town. In its way, it *was* cute. All of those old buildings, lovingly kept up for hundreds of years, held small, independent shops like presents waiting to be opened. There wasn't a chain or a box store in sight; sometimes you could actually feel the love that the people of Hillsboro put into their town, into their businesses, into the lives they shared with one another. But Tom couldn't help but let the shadow of their small-minded gossiping and closed ranks cast a shadow over its good aesthetic and intangible qualities. They didn't hate him; he knew that. They were just trying to protect May.

Still, he couldn't help but wish the town held as much love for him as he did for all of them.

"I mean, you grew up here, so I'm sure you don't see how cute it is."

"Yeah, I guess distance can lend us some perspective."

"Yes! I mean, I bet you hardly notice. Like, for instance...uh..." As they window-shopped, Joanna let her fingers dance across the glass panes, her mind far off even as she stayed right at his side. "Here, everyone waves. Everyone says hello, asks how you're doing. It's so welcoming. So inviting. Where I come from, the people aren't half as friendly. Not in London where I grew up and certainly not in Los Angeles now. It's alienating. It feels like everyone is looking at you but no one really sees you. Like they're all talking about you but never talking to you."

She stopped herself short, a pink blush dancing across her face. "I'm talking too much, aren't I?"

Tom realized he'd been doing a lot of slack-jawed staring and not a whole lot of talking. The problem wasn't that he thought she was crazy or talking too much, but that in the few sentences she'd managed about her life, she might as well have been talking about his life here in Hillsboro. The isolation. The doubt. The nagging loneliness. It was just as real for him here, in this cute and friendly small town, as it was for her out there in the big city. He thought about his travels, too. About all the time he'd sat at empty tables wishing for someone to take the seat across from him.

Maybe their feelings weren't just about a place. Maybe their feelings sprung from somewhere deeper.

"No, not at all. It's nice. I was just wondering, how do you survive in a place like that?"

"Hm. I never thought about it like that before. I guess you just..." A small smile tugged at her lips as she looked in

the window of the Cooking Castle. Tom could not imagine it
had anything to do with the themed salt and pepper shakers
on display. "I guess you just find the person who makes you
feel seen. Who makes you feel heard. Who makes you feel
like you actually exist."

"And have you found that person?"

She spun on her heel and raised an eyebrow in his
direction; her smile turned cheeky. "A little forward, aren't
you, Thomas Riley?"

"I didn't mean—"

"No, I'm just teasing!" They started their walking again,
down toward the intersection where Tom most feared to
tread. "I mean, it's no secret why Annie was trying to set me
up. Actually...I'm totally hung up on this guy back in Los
Angeles. I'm crazy about him, but even though he makes me
feel all of that stuff—butterflies and champagne bubbles and
all of that—it's like I don't exist for him."

A wave of relief crashed over the top of Tom's head. So,
he wasn't the only one spending this date of theirs thinking
about someone else. Maybe Joanna's heart wasn't as available as Annie had initially suggested. Tom was all right with
that. He still needed time.

"That's a poetic way of putting it."

"I've had a lot of time to think about it."

Tom knew exactly how she felt. He'd spent the last eight
years since leaving May trying *not* to think about her, but
these last few weeks had given him plenty of unavoidable
opportunities to do so. He wasn't one for poetry, but he knew
what it was like to have one person so trapped in your mind
that they almost became part of you. He cleared his throat;
if she was going to be this honest with him, it was only fair
that he do the same.

"Well, I guess I should tell you that Annie is trying to

get me out of a similar entanglement, whether she knows it or not."

Joanna gasped; her eyes brightened. She, too, was clearly relieved at the revelation that neither of them was really available. "You're still in love with someone else, too?"

"I'm…" Realizing where they were, Tom skidded to a stop. His heart skidded, too. They were directly in front of Anderson's Sweets and Sundries, and inevitably, Joanna decided to turn her window-shopping into actual shopping. Here he was, faced with a question not just in the abstract but in real life. *Do you still love May Anderson?* He glanced through the window, where May was currently entertaining customers and offering treats from a wide cake stand base. She was so social, so caught in the center of everything. No wonder she'd been ashamed to defend him yesterday. "I wouldn't say that. Not exactly."

"Then what *would* you say?"

"I—"

Joanna pushed the door open. A bell overhead rang out, alerting the shop to their presence, but Tom hesitated.

A blond brow furrowed. "Are you coming?"

Tom couldn't very well say no now, not when everyone in the store was now staring at him through the front picture windows. "Yeah, right behind you."

From the moment he walked in, Tom was acutely aware of two conflicting pieces of knowledge. One: when Joanna had first opened the door, Anderson's Sweets and Sundries had sounded more like a party than a slightly crowded shop, filled with music and chatter and laughter and the clattering of coins as they were counted for change. And two: the moment Tom crossed the threshold, that atmosphere basically disintegrated. Except for the music, which still played from a small hook-up in the back of the store, everyone descended into shuffling silence.

Everyone, that was, except for May, who met his gaze across the room and did not flinch. Instead, her face lit up and she strutted through the small crowd toward them, not even trying to hide the fact that they had her pure, undivided attention.

"Tom! How good to see you! And Joanna! What a nice surprise." She swung her plate of treats in their direction, slices of some honey-soaked cake pierced by toothpicks. "Here, you've got to try some of these."

Joanna did not need telling twice. Immediately, she scooped up three and began making her rounds around the shop. Without even being told to do so—and without, apparently, worrying about what Tom would do without her at his side—she collected a basket and started dumping products and knickknacks into it, leaving Tom and May completely alone.

At least until Mrs. Elaine Bates swanned up, her sickly sweet smile promising lots of gossip about this later.

"Tom! I haven't seen you in here in some time."

"Well, get used to it," May interrupted, smiling just as insincerely as she looped her free arm through Tom's. "He's my partner-in-crime for the festival, so he'll be around quite a bit."

Tom's lips threatened to smile, but he held them back. Small-town decorum dictated that if you said something with enough polite charm, you could get away with pretty much anything. No matter how much Mrs. Elaine—May's mother's oldest friend and the town's supreme gossip—wanted to object to their pairing, if she did, she would be the one at fault in this exchange.

"Is something wrong, Mrs. Elaine?" May asked, cocking her head deftly to one side. "Are you sick?"

The old woman pursed her lips. "No, not at all, dear. I

was just leaving. My head, you know, it's been bothering me lately."

With one last withering glance in Tom's direction, she took her leave, and May started moving her way back through the store, taking Tom along with her. Tom's heart thrummed as though he'd just been in the middle of a brutal brawl. Braving a glance from the corner of his eye, he didn't see one trace of regret or hesitation in May's flushed, pink cheeks or her exhilarated eyes.

"What was that about? I thought you were . . . You seemed angry at yourself for what happened yesterday?"

"I was. But I was mostly upset because of how I thought they would treat you after what I'd done and said. I figured it was time for me to learn how to fight back better. How do you think I did?"

All around her, the party atmosphere once again rose up in tenor, with folks excitedly muttering as they clinked their wine-tasting glasses together.

Tom's stomach tightened. Wine tasting? The Andersons didn't make wine.

But that's when he saw it. Five cases of Barn Door wine, stacked high with labels out in the corner of the room, marked with the signature yellow sticker of their distributor. May had bought all of that for this event?

His heart soared. Hope was a hell of a pair of wings. He locked eyes with her.

"Thank you, May."

She smiled right back. More beautiful than he could ever remember seeing anyone smile before. "Anytime."

Half an hour later, after plenty of honey and floral snacks and after Joanna had filled her reusable tote bags with as much of May's product as she possibly could carry, they finally slipped out. In the cool summer night—the ones up here were always like that, and it was one of the things Tom had missed the most when he'd left—Tom suddenly felt light-headed. Dizzy. Like the sudden transition from the bright, warm shop to the cool night beyond had set him off balance.

Or perhaps something else entirely had set him off balance. He didn't know. He couldn't tell for sure.

"So…" Joanna said, eyeing him meaningfully. "Back to our earlier conversation."

"Which one was that?"

"You're still in love with someone else, aren't you?"

"I think it's…" *I think it's a definite possibility.* That's what he was going to say. But then, from the darkness of the sidewalk, he turned to face back into the golden glow of the window, where he could see May laughing and smiling with a small gaggle of customers. As if she sensed his attention, her gaze turned outward to him, where she held up one hand in a wave and smiled at him with her whole heart. The sight almost made him feel guilty. His whole heart wasn't quite ready yet. He wasn't sure he was ready to give it away again. "I think we should stop and get some ice cream before I walk you back to your place."

Chapter Fifteen

May

*First you take a deep breath. Then you pour the loose honey—
or honey crystals and a splash of water—into your stockpot.
Next you try not to think about Tom Riley and instead focus
on the ineffable beauty of a world that lets you take care of
small creatures and make candy out of the honey they create
from the nectar of flowers. Then you turn the boiler on and let
the aromatic scent of sugar and earth rise to your nose, wiping
away all thoughts of lost loves and undeserved second chances.
Breathe. Breathe. Breathe. Then you try not to think about how
happy Tom looked with Joanna last night, how practically perfect they looked in each other's company, how happy she could
make him when you couldn't…Breathe again. Then—*

May's internal directions tripped over themselves as the
loose floorboard at the far end of the kitchen alerted her to
the arrival of an intruder.

*Then…Then you catch the scent of Tom Riley's cologne
intermingling with the honey wafting through the air and
you try not to let him see that you've been thinking about
nothing but him for the last few hours…*

She kept her focus sternly on the silver pot before her, in which the honey she was tempering slowly crept toward a boil. "You really shouldn't sneak up on someone handling a pot of boiling honey in their hands. You know that, right?"

"Sorry," Tom said, and to her surprise, he sounded like he meant it. "I just didn't want to disturb you."

May couldn't help a laugh at that, even as she went digging in a nearby drawer for her candy thermometer. Creating candy from scratch was delicate work, yes, but she relished the complicated, intricate dance of this balancing act. Managing conversations and distractions and boiling hot sugar meant she didn't have much room for any of the other noise rattling around in her brain. And lately...there had been more chaos raging inside of her than outside, which was saying something considering the kind of life she led. "We've got a big, old farming operation, two renegade sisters, a guard dog who thinks she's our babysitter and a mother who doesn't know when to stop meddling. Combine that with running a store, making almost everything *for* the store, looking after several bee colonies, and planning a festival that has the future of our town resting on it..." She laughed again, the gallows humor letting off just a little bit of the pressure building up inside of her. "It's impossible for me to be any more disturbed than I am already."

"Point taken." Tom nodded and helped himself to one of the high barstools overlooking the kitchen burners and the connecting marble island. Many of the Andersons may have missed out on the baking gene, but May spent so much time at these stoves, slaving over hot sugar and aromatics, that she could have done the whole thing blindfolded, but with his practiced, warm stare suddenly on her, she felt her hands go sweaty and her stomach bubble as hot and delicate as the sweets before her. Tom didn't offer why he'd suddenly made this unannounced visit, and she didn't ask. She tried not to be aware of his broad presence, suddenly making the large farm-house kitchen feel cramped and hot. "What are you making?"

"Honey taffy with rosemary and vanilla," May said, nodding to the bundle of aromatics Rose had collected for her this morning. The plants didn't come from the family farming operation but from the eldest Anderson sister's personal garden; of all the strange quirks of sisterhood, May liked this one best. Her sisters coaxed life out of the ground, and she took that life and helped transfigure it into something else. Today it was candy, but it was also often soaps and lip balms and other useful, beautiful things that people really needed.

Oh, no. She was getting sentimental again, wasn't she? Shaking her head to clear it, May checked the thermometer again. Nope. Still not hot enough.

She couldn't say the same for herself. Every time she looked at Tom, her heart was filled with that same magnetic pull that seemed to follow her every time she was near him lately. Heat pooled beneath her collar, beneath the skin of her cheeks. Swallowing hard, she tried to focus on the sugar. *Yes. Honey. Boiling honey and candy making is a delicate thing, May. You know this. Don't let yourself get distracted. Don't let yourself think about last night, about how much you wanted him to leave Joanna behind and kiss you.*

"It smells amazing," Tom commented, peering over the stockpot and into its depths. The easy action drew him closer to her, and for a split second, she caught his scent mingling with the sugared steam.

Oh, no. She was feeling things for him. Things she couldn't rationalize or control or shove into a locked safe in the farthest, deepest corners of her heart. Jealousy. Want. Longing. Affection. Her body was reacting to him in a way that her mind couldn't—or wouldn't—shut down. *Pick a topic of conversation*, she told herself, *literally anything to stop thinking about his lips and the almost-kiss from the day you two practiced him asking Joanna out and how much you'd like to kiss him now.*

"Thanks," May said, hoping on hope that her smile was enough to hide the war raging inside of her. She grabbed the rubber spatula from the collection of utensils waiting on the counter and shifted some of the sugar crystals forming at the edges of the bowl, trying to distract herself from staring at his lips again. "Mrs. Chen's kids all came down with summer colds and these candies are really good for a sore throat."

"Can I have one?" Tom asked.

"They're not done yet, goof." She shot him a flat, conspiratorial gaze over the counter. For a brief moment, it was like old times again, like she was talking to her long-lost best friend once more. "I mean, I guess you can have one now if you like going to the hospital for internal third degree burns, but…"

"How do you make them?"

A shock seized her heart. That was something that no one thought of when they thought about breakups. Tom hadn't just been her boyfriend; he'd also been her best—and in some cases, her only—friend. Losing him wasn't just about losing someone to kiss and cuddle and call her own. It had been a devastating blow to her entire life. And it had been self-inflicted.

There had been a giant Tom-sized hole in her life and her heart. And over time, when she discovered she couldn't fill it, she'd just stopped remembering how good it felt to snark with someone. To joke and laugh without calculating how every word and snort would play against your public reputation.

She'd missed him. And having to miss him in the first place was entirely her fault. She'd been the one to screw her entire life up with her own fears and doubts and persuad-ability, in allowing someone to convince her that the man she loved didn't love her enough.

But what was frightening to realize was that more than all of that, more than missing him, she wanted him *now*. The man he'd become. This worldly, adventurous, dedicated man who'd given up his dreams of traveling to come home and save his family's business. A man who would put himself in the orbit of the person who'd hurt him just so he could try and do a good thing for his grandmother's legacy. She was falling for him, and she was already losing him again, this time not because of some mistake she'd made but because there was someone else who could make him so, so much happier than she ever could.

When she replied to his question, her voice was a little weaker but not unkind. More curious and distant. "Why do you care? Why are you even here?"

"Is it a crime for a festival partner to want to visit his other festival partner?"

"No, but I thought you'd be out with Joanna again."

She watched carefully from the corner of her eye as he prepared an answer.

"Joanna went back to Los Angeles. She'll be back to visit the festival, but she had some things she needed to take care of."

"What?"

"And besides, you and I have a festival coming up soon. This is more important than anything else. How *are* you feeling about the festival, by the way? Do you think we have everything under control?"

"Yes, of course."

That was mostly true. And besides, she didn't want to betray that she was cracking under any kind of pressure. She didn't want Tom thinking he needed to shoulder any more of her responsibilities. The festival was the main thing she used to distract herself from thoughts of him, so she needed all the extra work on it she could get.

But Tom wasn't convinced. Quickly, he ran through the list of things that they'd agreed would be her responsibility. *Banners printed?* No, they're being run on Tuesday. *Programs folded?* No, I thought I would do those on Thursday while I watched the two-hour premiere of a new season of that island romance show. *Lanyards strung? Welcome packets stuffed? Drink coupons for the welcome party printed? Name cards written?* No, no, no, and definitely not. Not with her handwriting, at least.

"You always did like to leave group projects until the last minute," Tom grumbled good-naturedly. Despite that fact, she always managed to get everything in on time.

"What can I say? I work best under pressure."

"I can see that." Tom peered over the pot of boiling sugars once again. May watched as the golden haze of hot honey bubbled in his eyes, bringing out the myriad subtle coloring in their depths. She could look at those eyes for hours. Which, of course, is why she tore her gaze away as quickly as she could. Best not to give in to temptation. Tom slid from his chair. "Hey... Do you think you could show me how to do that?"

May raised an eyebrow. She didn't really share these recipes with anyone. There wasn't a whole lot in this world that belonged to May exclusively. Even her reputation was partly owned by the gossips who propped it up. But these recipes were ones that she'd spent hours over hot stoves creating through trial and error. She guarded them with her life. "Are you going to try and steal my business?"

"No, I just thought... You know, you've been helping me with putting the Barn Door wines front and center at the festival, so I thought I would help you with a little bit of *your* work. It seems only fair."

"Okay. I mean, if that's what you want."

Gratified, he reached for one of the spoons near the cook-top. "All right, chef—"

"Oh, no you don't. Come here." She pulled one of her mother's frilliest aprons from the drawer and handed it to him.

"What is this?"

"Protective wear. Wouldn't want to get hot sugar crystals on that nice shirt of yours."

"You think it's nice?"

Uh, yeah. It was nice. Better than nice. With his pecs straining against that slightly too-tight shirt, the sleeves rolled up to expose the tanned skin of his lower arms, which she itched to reach out and touch, to see whether it was still as soft as she remembered, he looked sexy. She needed him to cover himself up just so she could focus. "Don't let it get to your head."

"You know, I always did think pastel blue was my color."

He'd said it teasingly, but May couldn't help but agree. He looked good in anything, but this brought out the gold in his eyes, the highlights in his dark hair. The soft red of his lips.

The rest of his clothes, too, caught her eye. Not only was his shirt the perfect cut and color, but his dark-wash jeans clung to him, making her heart beat a little faster. He'd always been the strong and sturdy type, but now she wanted to explore his muscles and see if they were as tight and powerful as they looked.

Okay, so covering his body in a frilly apron hadn't done anything for her concentration.

Returning her attention to the counter, she pressed one hand onto the cool faux marble, letting the chill rise up her arm and cool off her flushing skin. The other hand reached for the rosemary, and she grabbed two sprigs.

Distraction was the name of the game today. She handed him a knife, laid the rosemary on the cutting board, and began stripping the scented leaves, all while she tried not to think of how close he was, how soft his arm felt against her skin whenever their shoulders brushed against one another.

"So, it's really simple," she said, clearing her throat when it seemed that her voice was about to betray her and reveal all of the bubbly, excited energy fighting for her attention. "What we're going to do is—"

"Put tiny trees in these kids' candy?" Tom said, holding up a piece of the green stuff as May tried to make quick work of her piece.

"It's rosemary."

"I know what it is. I also know it's *not* what a kid would want in their candy."

"Well, kids also don't want your stupid wine," she teased, "so let's call it a draw, shall we?"

With the rosemary stripped, its green, musky scent filled the air and almost reminded May of Christmas. Those first few days of having a Christmas tree in the house were always marked by the musk of the fresh-cut tree, and this rosemary offered its new smell in much the same way.

At least it was covering up the intoxicating, singular smell of Tom Riley, the one that always drew her in whenever he was near. And the steady weight of the knife in her hand kept her firmly rooted to reality. No daydreaming with paring knives in hand—that's what her mother had always said.

"Weren't you going to teach me how to make the candy?" he asked, his voice still playful.

"Only if you stop sassing me."

"I promise," he said, crossing his hand over his heart in a solemn vow. "So, what do I do?"

For a moment, as she inspected the candy thermometer still sitting in the stockpot, she talked to him about the intricacies of candy making. Heat and sugar were both incredibly delicate; combine the two and you have a recipe for disaster. That was why they required complete attention.

And that was why she made candy when she was most desperate to banish him from her thoughts, though she didn't inform him of that little tidbit.

Once the temperature rose on the thermometer to the appropriate level, though, she cut the chitchat back to an absolute minimum, slipping her hands into burn-proof gloves and reaching for the pot.

"So," she said, grunting slightly as she lifted the heavy metal and gently—ever so gently—tipped its contents out onto the plastic pad currently laid out on the counter beside her. A golden river of bubbling liquid pooled forward, spreading like fresh lava. "You pour the candy out onto the Silpat."

"Good word. That could get you a win in Scrabble."

"What did we discuss about sassing?"

Tom tried to compose his face into a mask of seriousness but couldn't completely swallow his smirk. "Sorry, chef."

Without being invited, he reached out toward the sugar as May ripped the heat gloves from her hands. The impulse would have been unconscionably stupid had the sugar not looked so fun and had May not done the exact same thing the first time she tried to make these treats on her own.

"Don't touch that!" she shrieked, reaching out to stop him.

Their fingers brushed. Sparks followed in their wake. They locked eyes and stood, millimeters apart, staring at each other.

"Why not?"

"Because—" *Why wouldn't her brain work suddenly?*

"Because you have to do the actual flavoring. And also because it's about two hundred degrees and you'll burn your fingerprints off."

She considered making a joke about how that might be helpful to him, considering how many people around town still called him a criminal for that one time he stole a bag of Skittles from a local drugstore, but she decided against it.

Tom was still staring at her, his golden eyes unrelenting, asking her a question she couldn't answer right now. "What do we do now, then?"

She was going to take that literally. "We settle the aromatics, and we wait for it to cool down enough to mold."

As if sensing her sudden anxiety, Tom didn't push her, but instead let the moment pass and quietly followed her instructions. They made quick work of it, with May stripping the vanilla as Tom sprinkled the rosemary across the fast-hardening honey. He was *so* close. Every movement either of them made ensured that their skin touched in some way, shape or form. This candy-making scheme was supposed to get her mind off of him, *not* to let him completely consume every one of her thoughts and feelings and impulses. He struggled with the sugar in front of him, his fingers ghosting lightly over the surface of the strips but not quite touching them.

May reached for a knife again, which she used to score the candy into rollable pieces. The sweets were just soft enough now to mold, and they had to work fast or else they'd be ruined—too sharp and too rough to be eaten by anyone, much less sick children. She displayed her technique to him in a few simple words and gestures, but as she reached for her second piece, he piped up again.

Had he somehow gotten even closer in the last twenty seconds? Or was she just imagining things?

"Would you show me?"

"Show you?" she repeated, her voice strangled in surprise.

Hadn't she just done that? It wasn't particularly difficult. You just turn them into little candy rolls. But when he spoke again, she realized exactly what he meant. It wasn't difficult. And that was the point.

He was trying something. Trying to coax her out of the ultra-professional shell she'd been hiding in.

"Yeah, just…" Their eyes met. She lost her breath. "Take my hands and show me how it's done. I'm useless at this kind of thing."

An eternity passed in the moment they spent waiting on her decision. Like a magnet, her body and her heart were drawn to him; her mind, on the other hand, screamed about all of the reasons she couldn't, she shouldn't, she mustn't.

She listened to her body. She let herself be drawn in, once again, by the scent of him, by the warm, woodsy air swirling around him.

"Okay. So, what you want to do is take the piece between your fingers…" She laid her fingers atop his and gently rubbed the pads of her fingers along his knuckles, trying to mimic the action. She could barely hear her own thoughts over the sound of her own heartbeat, over the constant thrum of her own desire. With her head resting over his shoulder and her arms wrapped around him, she could feel his body respond to hers and couldn't help but notice the way his breath picked up when they touched. "Just like this. Go slowly. Gently. You want to—"

She never got to finish that advice. A pair of warm, soft, familiar lips—the lips that featured so often in her dreams—pressed against hers. For a moment she froze as he moved into her, and she gave in to her heart's desire for him. Her hands found their way to his hips, and she held on to the tight muscles, wanting to pull him even closer. She breathed, her mouth opening and inviting him in. Her heart hammered. Yes, this was what she'd wanted. This wasn't just kissing a boy from high school. This was her kissing a man she now had feelings for, a man who kissed her like she'd always dreamed of being kissed—

But then, reality crashed back around her, and she shoved him away.

"Why did you do that?" she spluttered.

They were both out of breath, staring at each other with wild, wide eyes. When he spoke, he did so without an ounce of regret or hesitancy. "Because I wanted to."

"Joanna—"

"I went out with Joanna, yes, but she's in love with someone else."

She knew that there was a difference between the right thing and the easy thing. Between the thing you wanted and the thing everyone needed. This was one of those moments when she had to decide: be with Tom Riley now and damn the consequences, damn the past, and damn her guilt? Or send him away, break her own heart, and save him from ever having to be with a coward like her ever again?

Every day, her guilt and regret about what she'd done to him grew, a guilt she couldn't shake. How could she lure him back into her life after what she'd done?

How could she possibly think that she could have him when a beautiful, sweet, smart, kind woman was out there, waiting for him?

She couldn't. Even if Joanna was out of the picture, she knew there would be other women, others who loved and respected and deserved him.

May took a step back, away from the man she still very much loved.

"I'm sorry, Tom, but…I can't…" She chose a small speck in the tile flooring and refused to take her eyes off of it. He'd come here to finish what they'd started last night; he'd come here to kiss her. And once again, she was rejecting him. Looking him in the eye while she did it seemed an impossible task. "I can't do this."

Tom's shoes moved into her line of vision; she countered with another step back as he spoke. "May, look at me. Listen to me—"

"Look, later tonight I'll send you my notes about the rest of the festival stuff we need to get done. I really need to make sure these lozenges get over to the Chens soon."

It was as strong a dismissal as she could manage, but her voice cracked all the same. *This is for the best*, she reminded herself. *This is for the best. He deserves someone like Joanna, someone who'll never hurt him. Someone whole and wholesome and not stuck in the past.*

"Yeah. Okay, I get it, 'you can't do this,'" Tom said, his voice vibrating with anger. "Classic May. Every time something gets difficult, you run away. I should have known better than to think you'd changed. But you'd still rather hide in your safe little world that you've constructed than take a step out to listen to me or take a chance. I'll see you around, then."

As his footsteps retreated, and he left her alone like she'd asked, May couldn't help but feel like it wasn't for the best at all.

Chapter Sixteen

Tom

As the days passed after their kiss, Tom tried to bury his emotions as best he could and get on with his life. There was plenty of work to be done around the vineyard, plenty of tasks that needed sorting out for the festival, and plenty of distractions that he could indulge in rather than wallowing in what had transpired between him and May after that kiss.

The kiss. No matter how hard he worked his body and his mind, no matter how he tried to shove his hurt and his frustration down into a little box buried somewhere deep inside his heart, he couldn't get away from memories of that kiss. Her soft lips against his. Her hand pressing lightly into his chest. Her body moving against him. For a brief moment of that embrace, she'd responded to him, giving in to the sensations and kissing him back. His brain was stuck on it and on puzzling out the reality of her dismissal.

She'd wanted him. She'd wanted the kiss. And yet, she'd turned him away. Why?

He couldn't figure it out. But maybe, more importantly,

he didn't want to. He was sick of running around after May Anderson, letting her fear impact his life. Wasting time on figuring out her motives and motivations would have been close to sympathizing with her, and that wasn't something he was willing to do right now.

He'd put himself out there, put his heart on the line and their pasts behind them, and she'd just rejected him. The pain was too fresh. He was too angry—at her and at himself—to wade into the deep waters of compassion. Even if he was inclined to try it, all of his hurt would have just sunk him like a stone.

It was like a complete confirmation of everything about her that he thought had changed. But no, she was inconstant and persuadable; impossible to read and immovable in her judgments. It was clear to him now that, despite all of the hope he'd been collecting in the quiet, hidden parts of his heart, she still saw him as the boy she couldn't trust when she was eighteen, that he still wasn't good enough for her, even after all these years and everything that he'd thought had developed between them.

And the really painful bit? It made him question himself. Maybe he *was* the bad seed of Hillsboro. That was why he'd wanted to leave with May in the first place, right? To escape the crushing, constant fear that he was the bad kid everyone in Hillsboro thought he was. Maybe *that* was why May didn't love him. Why the entire town seemed to hate him. Maybe all of his effort and hard work at being a good guy was in vain. Maybe they were all right about him.

It was this mental and emotional turmoil that carried him through the quiet, May-less days that followed, until he found himself in the basement of the vineyard's crush facility. The spine-crushing labor of moving empty wine barrels for hours on end always helped him clear his mind; he hoped that the same would be true today. If only he could teach his mind and his heart to be as empty as these barrels.

But then he heard the quiet clicking of a sharp high heel against the poured concrete flooring of the basement, and he knew he wasn't about to get the respite he so desperately wanted.

"I don't want to talk about it, Annie," he called as he adjusted his gloves.

The clicking stopped. Then a hesitant, familiar voice called out, "How did you know it was me?"

"Who else do you know who would wear heels to a working crush facility?"

For all of the artistry of the winemaking business—and there was quite a bit—crush facilities were more like scientific laboratories and factories that doubled as an artist's workshop. The heavy machinery that helped them in making and aging their wine wasn't exactly the kind of thing you should be dancing around in stilettos. Tom reached for the nearest of the newly empty wine barrels.

Annie sniffed, apparently annoyed that he'd ruined her grand entrance. If there was one thing she loved, it was statement-making as she walked into a room. "And what is it, pray tell, that you don't want to talk about?"

He ignored her, mutinously. For a moment, as he lifted one of the barrels over his head and slid it securely in the rack, his new guest hesitated. And for good reason. Annie didn't really ever get called on her performances like this one. She was far more used to being such a force of nature that she was allowed to do and say whatever would get her what she wanted. Usually, Tom was happy to indulge her. She always had her heart in the right place, after all.

But not today. He wasn't in the mood to indulge anyone but himself today. Today was about sulking in the depths of the dark spiral he found himself in, not about trying to let someone pull him out of it.

"I leave you two alone for one weekend and you have already broken up?" Annie practically screeched, her heels snapping as she approached him from behind, outrage coloring her every syllable.

"We can't break up. We aren't dating," he reminded her, a fact that shot through him like a fresh arrow. God, he was feeling all of this about someone he hadn't actually been with for eight years. What a fool he'd been.

"I meant Joanna—"

Oh, right.

"Joanna wasn't interested in a relationship."

"Right! And neither of you are ever going to be interested if you don't quit being hung up on other people! Which brings me to your next problem. May. Joanna tells me you're still in love with her. Is that true?"

The muscles in Tom's shoulders coiled—and not from the strain of lifting a hundred pounds of metal and oak over his head. He'd never really welcomed Annie's meddling, but he always understood that she just wanted to try and help her friends and the people she loved.

But he was not in the mood to extend her any goodwill right now.

"I was over May Anderson. You forced us together with the bloody festival. You put us in an uncomfortable situation," he said, as diplomatically as he could despite the rage simmering beneath his surface.

"Technically, I *suggested* an uncomfortable situation," Annie said, though her voice betrayed her knowledge that she was skating on very thin ice here. "You two were the grown adults who agreed to the uncomfortable situation. Now, if you love the girl, what are you doing about it?"

Tom sighed heavily, he was just so tired of going over it. "She doesn't want me. No second chances. No do-overs. It's done. It's over. So, please don't try and push us back together or anything, okay?"

This time, he didn't lift the nearest wine barrel so much as he slammed it over his head and into its rack holster. The force of it shook the metal slats holding the oaken crates aloft. Even with his distractions, he could practically hear Annie fold her arms across her chest and pout.

"I don't believe that. And if you believe that, then you're a bigger fool than I thought. And you accepted a marriage proposal from *me,* so I already know you're a pretty big fool."

That got Tom's attention. Turning on his heel, he abandoned his mindless physical work and focused squarely on Annie. "What do you mean?"

Annie, dressed in a casual swath of cream-colored, angular clothes that seemed peeled straight out of the pages of a high-fashion magazine, didn't shift or balk under his pointed glare. Instead, she tilted her chin and waved a painted finger in his face, scolding him as if *he* was the one who had done something wrong.

"I mean she is obviously still in love with you, but something is holding her back. These Anderson women are always tough nuts to crack. There's got to be, I don't know, some kind of problem—"

"Yeah, the problem is that she doesn't love me and she probably never has. Not enough at least. And you know what? I'm not going to push myself onto someone who doesn't want me. It hurts too much to love her. It hurts too much to love anyone."

Truth was, he agreed with her. He, too, couldn't help but think that May did love him, that she'd been opening up to him in the last few weeks like she had when they were younger. But something was holding her back from throwing herself headfirst into her feelings for him and he was done with being the only one who put it out on the line.

No. Believing that she was over him and that everything he ever feared about himself and about her was true...that was an easier pill to swallow. At least then, he didn't have to deal with disappointment.

Annie reared back; her face drew up in a shocked grimace of horror.

"How could you say something like that?" she spat.

"Because it's true." Tom returned to the business of tossing the wine barrels, letting the pain in his muscles detract from the pain in the center of his chest. "If she had really loved me, back when we were kids, do you think she wouldn't have come with me? You think true love can just shatter so easily? And now she's made it clear that her feelings haven't changed. That the man I've become still isn't good enough for her. She's made herself clear, and I can't keep pushing against it. I just can't take it."

For a while, there was nothing but the sounds of wood against metal as he lifted and returned barrel after barrel. Long enough passed that he'd begun to wonder if Annie was still there at all, a wonder that turned to certainty when a small hand touched the straining muscle in his left shoulder. The touch was tentative, hesitant, but her voice was sure. Pleading.

"Please, Tom. Don't give up on her."

Tom froze at the words. That's what everyone thought of him, wasn't it? That he was some kind of quitter who'd given up on May back then just like he was going to give up on her now. A wry, bitter laugh escaped his lips at the irony of it all.

"You know what, Annie? I guess I must have given up on her a long time ago."

"Tom—"

He spun on her then, too loose now to keep a tight lid on his feelings. He no longer had the emotional energy to keep them on lockdown.

"And why shouldn't I? She gave up on me first!"

As soon as the protest was out of his mouth, he regretted it. He'd always sworn that he wouldn't betray May's honor or his own by whining about the truth of what happened that night or by correcting the rumored record that followed them both like flies around a corpse. This was the closest he'd ever come to confessing what had actually transpired between them. Annie leaned forward, her interest piqued.

"What do you mean by that?"

"I mean..." He searched for an explanation, anything that would help him evade the truth. The painful, awful truth. "I just mean that it's not as simple as you think it is. What May and I have is complicated."

"Yeah, you keep saying that, but from where I stand it's pretty simple. The only thing standing in your way is you. You two are the ones complicating everything."

This time, he managed to swallow his wry laugh. Sweet, naive Annie. For someone who came from Los Angeles, the reality television and tabloid capital of the world, she really didn't seem to understand how damaging rumors and half-truths could be. If May didn't have this town, even the people who gossiped about her and manipulated her life with their whispers, she wouldn't have anybody. He knew that. Just like he knew that throwing in her lot with his would mean maybe ruining her livelihood forever, and that of her family.

They weren't complicating things. They were trying to survive in a complicated system. A system that was crushing them both.

"I wish that were true. But small-town life is really great

for making the easy stuff unimaginably hard." A note of bitterness entered his tone, against his better judgment. He couldn't help it. Annie had come to this town and swept in like a lovable thunderstorm; everyone who hated him loved her, sang her praises, and wouldn't dare snark at her in line at the grocery store or during her morning coffee runs. "We can't all be untouchable like you, Annie."

Her eyes widened with hurt. He regretted the way he'd spoken, but he couldn't take it back. Not when it was so true.

Annie protested. "I'm not—"

"You are." He softened his tone. When she'd first asked him out on a date what felt like a lifetime ago, he'd turned her down. He hadn't wanted her to be subject to the slings and arrows of outrageous small-town gossip. He still didn't want that for her, even if he was jealous of it. "And I'm glad you are. I wouldn't wish what's happened to me on my worst enemy."

Her eyes narrowed slightly; she clearly suspected something deeper than his literal meaning. "And what, exactly, has happened to you? I don't understand. You like the girl, she likes you, so chase after her. It's not rocket science!"

"You're right. It's worse. At least with rocket science, there's some logic."

With all of the barrels put away, there was nothing left to distract Tom from this conversation. Slowly, he pulled his gloves off and shoved them into his back pocket, then leveled his gaze at Annie. He had nothing more to say to her, no defenses of himself to offer and no more protests to make. This was the way it had to be. He and May Anderson didn't belong together, and life would be easier for everyone— Annie included—if they all just accepted that.

Annie waited for a long, tense moment for him to say anything else, and when he made it clear he wouldn't, she tugged her purse higher up her arm and tossed her head defiantly.

"You know what? If you're going to be this miserable, then you deserve it. You have a chance for something real and you're throwing it away on some stupid *feeling* you have? That's not honorable, Tom. It's sad."

She spun on her heel and made for the staircase leading out of the basement, but Tom called after her, unable to help himself.

"Maybe you should tell May the same thing."

"Oh, don't worry," Annie practically growled, her high heels colliding violently with the wood steps as she ascended the staircase. "I'm dealing with her next."

"Well, as long as you aren't meddling in my life anymore."

Without even turning around, Annie breezily replied as she hiked up the staircase.

"Tom, you wouldn't get anything done if I weren't meddling in your life. I already told May I'm planning the Festival Welcome Party, which both of you have been too busy to think about, and I'll be texting your gran later because she still doesn't have a date."

Half an hour later, with Annie well and truly gone, Tom found himself back in the tasting room, his body thoroughly spent by the physical labor but his mind and his heart not having gotten the message.

The problem with Annie's sudden visit was that it introduced a dangerous element into his life: hope. He'd been enduring too much of it lately. Life had been so, so much easier when he'd been bitter and closed off to the world, when he'd been resigned to the reality that he would never—and could never—have any chance at love and romance again. At least not in Hillsboro, and so not while his grandmother still needed him to be here.

"You know what I think the problem with you is, kid?"

Tom didn't even flinch when his grandmother appeared, speak of the devil and all that. She had a bad habit of doing that when he most needed and least wanted to hear from her. He just continued staring out the window, wondering if saving the old vineyard with this festival was going to be enough to sustain him.

It had to, right? He had to be able to live with a broken heart if it meant that he'd be saving his family's legacy, didn't he?

Rolling hills dotted with vines sprawled out before him, lush and green and golden in the summer sun. Out there, everything seemed so simple and full of beauty. He'd never been envious of a field before, but here he was, wishing he could just be a leaf on one of those vines, drinking in the sun and never knowing the true meaning of loss.

"No, Gran. What's my problem?"

He felt an arm wrap around him, and his grandmother laid her head on his shoulder. At least, with everything else, he hadn't lost her. He wasn't entirely alone. That little reminder brushed away any errant wishes of suddenly morphing into greenery.

Gran gave his shoulders a little squeeze. "You haven't realized yet that the smallest things in life, the most basic and fundamental, are actually the hardest to get."

"No, Gran. I think I have realized that. It's what makes this all so hard."

Annie was right. He loved the girl. It should have been so easy to run after her, sweep her into his arms, and fall madly, head-over-heels in love with her. If only it were that simple.

"She's going to come around, you know."

Tom wasn't so sure. But he couldn't let his grandmother know that his stores of hope were as close to empty as their bank account. Reaching around to loop one arm around her, he pulled her in tight for a hug. "Yeah. Maybe."

Chapter Seventeen

May

It was just another one of those days. Those days that May was having pretty often lately. Days where she could do nothing but put her head down, get through her work, and try not to think too hard.

Tom Riley had kissed her. Tom Riley had wanted to reconcile with her. Tom Riley had wanted to give her everything she'd been dreaming of getting back since the day he drove out of her life all of those years ago.

And she'd turned him down. She'd tried to be the bigger person, tried to give him a little short-term pain to save him a life of heartbreak and the love of someone who could never have the courage to live life the way he did. It was the right thing to do. She knew that.

But why did the right thing always have to feel so awful?

No, that wasn't fair. Doing the right thing *and* the wrong thing both felt awful. She'd been doing the wrong thing— letting everyone believe a lie—for a long, long time, and that felt awful. Letting Tom go so he would be free to love someone else and share a life with them *also* felt awful.

May Anderson couldn't win. She didn't know how. She'd never known how. Outside of her work, her personal life was one big, long trail of mistake after mistake that she had no hope of correcting. The best she could hope for was making someone else's life a little better, and the only way of doing that for Tom was this. Removing herself from his life completely.

So, she threw herself back into her work. She took on most of the festival planning alone, spent most of her time in the shop alone, and, like this morning, attended to her bees alone. The colony was doing well enough, but still, she fussed around the hives in her suit, attending to the queens, some of whom she'd eventually send off to other communities.

A sharp sting of jealousy pierced May's heart. These bees she was protecting, that she was nurturing, would go farther away from this small town than she ever would. They would get to go out and see the world, but she would be stuck here, trapped in the same cycles over and over again, wishing things were different but never being able to change them.

Maybe it was just the heat of the suit getting to her. She never let herself think like this.

Somewhere nearby, she heard the heavy crunch of boots against a twig. No prizes for guessing who would be following her now.

"Dad, you're lurking again."

A small chuckle confirmed her suspicions. He, at least, stayed a healthy distance away from her bees. "Was I? No, that can't be right. Can a man lurk around his own house?"

May didn't answer. She wasn't in the mood for guessing games. She'd had enough of those in real life; the last thing she needed was to get them from her father, too.

"Do you need something?"

"What have you got going on there?"

She swallowed, hard. Her parents had always been content to let May get about the world in her own way, asking some questions when it came to matters of money and space, but rare was the occasion when they actually showed any real interest in her. In fairness to them, it went both ways, and she knew that she could have been more helpful around the farm in recent years, since her dad's injuries had shifted him into a more managerial role and he'd given more control to Harper. Instead she had compensated for what was missing emotionally by funneling more money from her shop back to the family.

They were kind of like extensions of Hillsboro in that way. They loved her and protected her in their own way, but they weren't particularly keen to get to know her. May had been raising queen bees and sending them to different farms across the country for almost two years now, and this was the first time either of her parents had noticed, much less asked anything about it.

"It's nothing. Just a little project I do to help rehabilitate bee communities. That's all."

"That's all? That doesn't sound like nothing. That sounds like a pretty big something."

May shrugged and closed up the hive. "I started doing it a few years ago. I wanted to do something of value. Something important. But there's not a lot of important stuff to be done in Hillsboro." She winced, immediately regretting that. She couldn't imagine her father, one of the town's most venerated sons, would take too kindly to his youngest daughter saying something like that. She rushed to cover herself. "I'm sorry. I didn't mean that. Hillsboro has obviously been very good to me."

"Has it, Amelia?"

The hairs on the back of May's neck rose up as she

continued to close down the hive for the day. Was this some kind of trick? She stammered her answer, but she was also actually aware that she sounded more like she was convincing herself and repeating arguments she'd made internally a thousand times than convincing anyone else. "Of course it has. Everyone has really looked out for me, taken care of me. That's more than a lot of people can say in this life."

"True, but you know, one man's tight-knit community can be another man's cage."

Her father shrugged. She felt a flash of injustice rip through her. Why was he telling her this now? He'd been there for years, ignoring her as she slowly backed deeper and deeper into the iron bars of this community. Why hadn't he said anything then? Her voice went bitter. Not even the beautiful horizon, painted with color and the soft scent of nearby sweet pea flowers, could calm her down.

"Is that what you came out here for? To read me parables from the Curtis Anderson Gospel?"

"No, I came out here because I wanted to talk to my daughter. I'm getting worried that your mother and I haven't done that enough. And maybe it'll be too little, too late, but I figure I should try to start somewhere."

It was an admission, one she'd been desperate to hear from one of them for years, but it wasn't an apology. She bristled. She'd been fine without their help for some time. "I'm fine. I don't need to be *talked to*. I need to get to work."

Reaching for her cap, she was stopped by her father's calm, certain voice.

"Why do you breed these bees?"

"Because bee populations are necessary for a thriving ecosystem, and our current global warming crisis is killing them off in a circle of life spiral that might one day kill us all?"

"Uh..." Her father coughed, clearly caught off-guard by her deadpan reply. "That's a point. But also...isn't it a little bit to see a broken thing get better?"

"You're getting philosophical, Dad."

And too close to the mark. She was tired—so very tired—of being the destroyer. She'd destroyed her relationship with Tom. She'd destroyed her own life. She'd done nothing but bring ruin to everyone and everything she'd ever loved. These small creatures...they were capable of such big, great creation and healing. She wanted to help them get there, to be even a tiny part of the story that they could weave with nature.

But telling her dad that might seem to be agreeing with him or encouraging his presence here, and she really, really didn't want that right now.

"Then let me be as clear as I possibly can. You're more interested in healing broken things because you can't stand to face yourself in the mirror and see that you are the thing that needs fixing. That the man you love also needs fixing. And that your two worlds aren't going to get better until both of you do that together."

May raised an eyebrow and began removing her bee-keeping kit, making sure to step far enough away from the hive that she wouldn't even accidentally get stung. Well, at least so she wouldn't get stung by the bees. Her father, on the other hand, was a different story. His words pierced finer than any stinger. "And you thought the bee analogy was the best way to tell me that?"

"I'm not a poet. Just your dad."

"Well, thanks for trying, but I don't think that's going to happen."

"Why not?"

"Because he'd be better off if he just forgot I even existed."

"That's not true."

Heat flamed in May's cheeks, and it wasn't from the heat of her beekeeping uniform. "It is. Did you know that I'm the reason his family business is going under? No one in town will recommend the wine to the tourists. No one will sell it in the local restaurants. Since he's been back and been part of it, the place may as well not even exist. Everyone blames him for something—" May swallowed. She didn't want her dad to know the truth. Not the entire truth, anyway. For a moment, she carefully folded her jacket, then she corrected herself. Vague truths repeated in whispers were all she could afford. "Everyone blames him for something that isn't really his fault."

Her father's boots crunched unevenly across the pine-needle-strewn ground, signaling his every movement as he walked over toward a nearby patch of flowers. "Do you want to know a funny story?"

"Is it better than your bee analogy?"

"When Tom came and picked you up for your high school prom, he didn't have any flowers. He showed up at the door and told me that he didn't think he could take you because he didn't have enough money for flowers and was too embarrassed to ask for any from his parents. Money was tight a round here at the time. It was before the tourists found us, and we were all struggling. So, I took him out to the fields and said, *Kid, whatever you want, you can have.* And he picked these."

Until now, May had been clutching her uniform in her hand and waiting for the ground to swallow her up so she didn't have to listen to this story. Revisiting her past with Tom wasn't very fun for her. But she didn't need to look up to see where he was gesturing. Tom's bouquet had consisted of exactly one flower, and it was, incidentally, the patch closest to her now.

"Sweet peas," she muttered, the memory flooding back to her. "My favorite."

"Exactly. And I never thought anything of it. Not until recently."

"What changed?"

"You two started seeing each other again. And I saw the light come back to your eyes." May's heart stuttered. She hadn't thought...She'd always assumed her parents hadn't cared. That they'd been ignoring her because she was a difficult problem that they didn't want to bother fixing. Could it be that they actually did care but wanted to give her space? When she glanced up and met her father's gaze, it was soft and understanding. "You know what the sweet pea flower represents?"

May shook her head. Flower languages had always been Rose's thing. She much preferred the company of stinging insects to lush, petaled decorations. Besides, she was still hung up on that story. She remembered, clear as glass, that prom night. But it also reminded her of the way he'd approached her at the house just a few days ago, hat in his hand, ready to open his heart up to her.

"Forgiveness. Second chances. Fresh starts. *You* could have a fresh start. My dear, I cannot sit here and watch this town and your own heart keep you in prison forever. I don't know what happened between you and Tom. I don't pretend to. But I know that it's time for you to have your own Sweet Pea Summer. You have to let yourself start again. Give yourself a second chance. Or I worry you may lose yourself forever."

"I'm not going to lose myself," May whispered, but she knew she wasn't convincing either herself or her father.

The man approached her, and placed a gentle hand on her cheek. His expression wasn't fatherly now, but imploring, beseeching. "My dear, I'm afraid you already have. You used to be the girl who wanted adventures, who dreamed of the places outside the city limits, who craved new experiences and all the richness that life had to offer. But you're still here. And I see now that every day, you're losing more and more of the woman you could have become. Don't you want something more than this? More than hiding in this town and throwing away the key to your own prison?"

I can't, Dad. I just can't. There's too much you don't know, too much I could never say out loud. That was the answer she should have given. She should have squared her shoulders, spouted off some lie, and run off into the distance before he could ask any follow-up questions. But May couldn't make herself do it. Running off into the distance would have been hard with all the tears pooling in her eyes.

"Yes. Yes, I think I do."

"Then let yourself have it. At least let yourself try."

May couldn't remember the last time she'd fallen, crying, into her father's arms. She wasn't the crying type, and for most of her life, he hadn't been the comforting type, either. On the rare occasion she needed a good long sob, she usually went to her sisters for that. But when the old man offered her his arms, she couldn't help but collapse into them, giving over to the quiet hush of his breath and the comfort of his big hand stroking her hair.

"Your friend Annie called me, you know. And your mother. And both of your sisters. She's worried about you, too."

A tearful laugh bubbled forth. Of course Annie was the one who brought all of this up. "It's so weird, actually having friends."

"You could have more than that, if you open up your heart to it."

"Thanks, Dad."

After a moment, May couldn't help but ask, "Is that true? About the sweet peas? Is that really what they mean?"

Her father shrugged and smiled a secretive, fatherly smile. "I think one of the beautiful things about flowers is that they can mean whatever you want them to mean, my dear."

But hours later, when she finally crawled up to her bedroom in the soothing quiet of the evening, May couldn't be sure. Not sure about her fresh start. Not sure about whether she was ready for one. Tiptoeing so that no one would hear her rustling about this late, she went to the bottom drawer of her chest of drawers and began pulling out, piece by piece, all the bedroom decorations she'd retired so long ago. Her map of the world. Her travel books. Her photographs of Tom and the school friends she'd let slip away. Carefully, she laid them out in a circle around her and examined them.

They were relics of a person she'd been, of the person she'd tried to bury in order to protect herself.

Brave. Adventurous. A fighter and a lover to her core.

But the truth was, May didn't want to be the girl she'd been in high school anymore, just like she didn't want to be this thing she'd become in the years since then.

She wanted to be better. And that was why, with a dash of her pen across a photograph of her and Tom, she wrote a note and begged one of the late-working farmhands to deliver it straight to his house.

Now all she had to hope was that old May Anderson hadn't completely ruined everything for the new one.

Chapter Eighteen

Tom

If things haven't changed, if you still feel something for me, please meet me at our old spot. I'll be waiting there.

Tom read her note once. Then he put it in his pocket, got into his car, and drove like the road was disappearing behind him.

Chapter Nineteen

May

False Mountain hovered over the town of Hillsboro, a fixture of the skyline, but it rested just outside the official limits, meaning that once someone made the trek to the top, they could see the entire, sprawling countryside from up there. Facing north, the town laid itself out in all its sun-soaked glory; facing south, you'd see miles upon miles of tiny houses and farmland. Grapes. Flowers. Trees. The sweeping colors of sunset and the abstract collages of natural beauty collecting on an earthen canvas beneath it.

Life scattered itself out around the mountain, and with the lowering sun and the awakening stars the way they were this evening, May could see it all from up here. It was the ending of one day and the fresh start to a completely new evening.

Of all the places they could have met tonight, she was glad she'd picked this spot. Their spot. It leant her some much-needed perspective. In the last eight years she'd been living in Hillsboro without him, the town had become this monstrous monolith in her mind, a great and terrible impenetrability that she could neither ignore nor escape. Every person she met, every person who traded rumors about her or spread the thick molasses of gossip farther, they all loomed before her, larger than life, dominating her entire existence.

Up here? They were tiny specks. Rightfully small. Seeing them from far away reminded her of what they really were. Just people. People who had no right to control her life, her feelings, her heart, or her future.

All that mattered, all that *needed* to matter, was Tom Riley. And whether she was brave enough to start over with him at her side.

With every passing second, she reminded herself that it was totally possible he wouldn't come, that he was done with her now that she'd rejected him yet again. She accepted that. It was his right and it was probably for the best.

But with every passing second, it became less and less possible to deny the swell of want that grew and grew within her. Her father was right. She was trapped here. The only light she'd ever seen in this town was Tom. And if she didn't at least try to make things right with him, she'd never be able to see that light again.

Failure tonight was almost guaranteed. If he didn't show, she'd failed. If she didn't say the right thing, she'd fail. But at least, for once since that day when she'd let him leave her behind, she was actually trying something. If she failed with him, at least she would always know that she'd been brave enough—at least once—to try. And really, that wouldn't be a failure for her. At least she would have tried something, which was more than she had done for years now.

But then... There he was. Standing just at the rim of the hill, hands in his pockets, slightly out of breath and glowing in the sunset. *Think of something*, May thought. *Say something. You can't just sit here and not say anything.* With her heart in her throat and her hope catching her breath, though, she couldn't do much more than gesture to the picnic hamper at her side and say:

"I thought we could use a picnic."

Tom's smile was lopsided and easy. "Always."

"And I thought we needed to talk. Away from everything and everyone."

"I'm listening."

Oh, no. She'd backed herself into a corner there, hadn't she? Rats. Nowhere to escape. Nowhere to run. It was just her, Tom, and the truth. Staring down at her hands, she tried to fathom into existence some semblance of a coherent thought. When she opened her mouth to speak, only one thing came out.

"I'm sorry, Tom."

His smile slipped from his face. "Yeah. You should be."

Her fight-or-flight instincts told her to run, to hide herself away and never apologize or admit anything even remotely resembling a fault. But her heart knew better. There couldn't be love without forgiveness, especially not when she had so much to ask forgiveness for. "I'm so, so sorry for everything that I've done. For everything that I've been doing. And especially, for everything that I didn't do. You were right. I was a suggestible girl up for anyone's manipulations. And not much has changed. But I want it to."

Tom stayed silent, the intensity of his golden eyes focused entirely on her face. Waiting for her to speak again, to finish her rushed confession. May swallowed hard and tried to put into words the enormity of the mistakes making up the last eight years of her life.

"I was so afraid all those years ago of being wrong about you, of being truly vulnerable, and I took the first 'out' I could find. And ever since then, I've been more worried about my reputation and how people in town thought about me than the person I..."

She stopped herself short. Was she ready to tell him she loved him? Was she ready to make herself that vulnerable, when she hadn't even been forgiven yet?

"The person you what?" Tom prodded after a moment of silence. There was a desperate edge to his voice. He was giving her one more chance to be brave, and she had to make it count.

Somehow, from deep inside her, she found the strength to lift her guilt-leaden head up. Their eyes met. The thought of going through life without telling him how she felt almost stopped her heart, right then and there.

"Than the person I love. The person I still love. The person I never stopped loving."

Tom's face was a mixture of hope and fear. The exact same things currently warring for control over May. He breathed out heavily. "You love me? But you left me. You *keep* leaving me."

"I know. I've been so wrong to try to deny how I feel and to hide it from you. Back then, I was so afraid of what would happen when we left together that I let it keep me here, the one place I never wanted to be. And every day since, I've been so afraid to tell the truth, even to myself, that I've let it keep me from the one person I've always wanted. No more. I don't want to...I can't do it anymore."

She hadn't expected to cry again today, but the heat behind her eyes couldn't be ignored or blinked away. And when she searched the shadowed profile of Tom's handsome, hard face for any hint of understanding, they flowed even more quickly.

"But the town—"

"At some point, I can't keep hiding behind them. I can't keep letting them put me in this cage. I can't keep letting my fear of them hold me back from what I want. From you."

Carefully, oh-so carefully, she reached out her fingertips and brushed against the top of his hand. The touch was a question, a dream, and she hoped he would answer it, hoped he would made it real.

Tom turned to face her fully now, and removed his hand from beneath hers. For a moment, her heart sank and settled in the very depths of despair. But then...*then*, he raised that hand up and cupped her cheek, holding her like the most precious being in all of creation. His thumb brushed away one of the tears that had slipped down.

If she could figure out how to bottle that feeling and sell it, she'd be the richest woman in the world. But honestly, she'd have shared it for free. Everyone needed to feel so warm, so fulfilled, so beloved at least once in their lives. Her eyes slid closed as she nestled her cheek deeper into his touch.

"You want to be with me?" he asked, his voice breaking slightly.

"I want to try. I was wrong. About everything. I should have left with you all those years ago. I should have told everyone the truth about what happened. I should have been honest with myself about what I wanted. I should have kissed you last week. I should have kissed you the first moment I saw that you were back in town." Her eyes fluttered open, meeting his gaze. Could he hear her heartbeat over the rushing of the wind? Did he realize how close they had gotten?

His grin was contagious. Teasing. "You wanted to kiss me?"

"I've never wanted to stop."

The magnetic pull between them couldn't be denied. Not

friends, they looked him in the eye with friendly smiles
greeting nods of respect.

His gran on his arm, he walked into the ballroom with
head held high and a stomach full of butterflies that, this
e, had nothing to do with how the people of Hillsboro
him and everything to do with how many times he'd be
cing with May in his arms tonight.

"You look very dashing," Gran said, patting his arm as
y swanned through the entry arch and toward the dance
or. He'd bought a new suit for the occasion, a dark, tailored
ber that Annie had sent him the link to. He realized that
gran had to say things like that, but still, it made him
w his shoulders back a little. Confidence colored his
ks as he glanced down at her silver dress.

"And you look very beautiful, Gran. Should I escort
to—"

"Oh, no. That's quite all right. I already have a date."

"You do?"

At just that moment, a dapper gentleman in his fifties
Tom vaguely recognized as the clerk from the local
—wearing a black suit inlaid with silver pinstripes and
n that could have powered an entire electrical grid—
ned up and offered the older woman his arm.

"My lady, may I?"

lease do. Don't look so shocked, Thomas. He's a
of Annie's. Besides…" Gran glanced over her shoul-
ward the entrance to the hall with a knowing smirk.
e got your own fair lady to escort."

n followed her gaze, across the crowd of people, until
he saw her. Amelia Anderson, standing in the main
y, looking like heaven in a pair of black heels. A stun-
ess in a soft, summer pink wrapped around her body,
his heart beat faster as he drank in the sweet curves

for another heartbeat. Not for another breath. Doing what
she'd dreamed of doing since the horrible day she left him,
May leaned forward and captured Tom's lips with hers. His
fingers, still cupping her cheek, pulled her in closer as he
responded to the kiss, awakening every single one of her
senses.

It was as if she'd been sleeping for years, and now, all at
once, the world revealed itself to her again.

When they finally broke apart, neither of them moved
from the closeness. Instead, they held on to each other, fore-
heads resting together, as if they were afraid that letting go
now would mean losing this moment forever. "I've got to be
dreaming right now," he said.

"Why? Because you've finally gotten everything you
want?"

"No." A broad, toothy grin stretched across his face.
"Because May Anderson just admitted she was wrong about
something."

"Jerk!"

But even though she shoved him playfully, that didn't
stop her from letting him capture her lips once more in a
beautiful, heart-stopping kiss.

Chapter Twenty

Tom

The next few days passed in a flurried haze of kissing and preparations and dinners and long work hours when Tom didn't see May at all. But now it was all coming together, and he was so damn proud. As far as Tom could tell—though admittedly he was slightly biased—he and May were the only two people in Hillsboro who could have pulled this thing off. The chaos in the weeks leading up to the festival grew and grew, but together, Tom and May were the calm, collected center at the heart of it. He'd forgotten how they'd complemented one another, how they just seemed to *fit* in one another's company. When she got too stressed, he was able to keep his cool and work out a solution. When he grew agitated with faking his smile in front of townsfolk, she stepped in and charmed them until most people forgot all about the grudge they'd held against him for so long. They were a well-oiled, incandescently happy machine, and he wouldn't have traded those moments together for the entire world.

But on the night of the Festival's Welcome Party, he still found himself a nervous wreck. And not because a little too tight and the caterer had forgotten bread rolls they'd ordered or because there was, y town's worth of pressure upon his shoulders.

No. It was because everything else was going well. For the last few years, Tom had become use tinct cyclical pattern in his life, one where some marginally good would happen to him, follow immediately by some kind of unforeseeable, i disaster. He hated that about himself, but that reality of his existence. Any time something wa he held himself in silent fear as he waited for the to drop.

Being with May again was an unparalleled stuff that dreams were made of. Which meant got closer to what he'd come to think of as re-debut as a couple, he braced himself for an disaster to befall them all.

Even as he did so, though—loosening his he could breathe just a little bit easier—he co admire the old, rustic Crusher's Pavilion, an hall that had been standing on this spot, d storms, since the early 1800s. He'd given to get ready for the party, which meant tha vising Annie and all the staff and volunte in to make the place truly sparkle with world and new age elegance. Now, with in through the brick and wood beam arch the summer wind and the band set up at he could see all of the beauty and poten

And for the first time, when people as if they saw the same thing. When on their way to one of the staffed bar of her waist and hips. This wasn't like the last time he'd seen her across a dance floor, when he'd been all nerves and hard edges and dismissive indifference. Now he wanted her. He couldn't wait another second to get her on the dance floor, to sweep her into his arms and hold her there forever. The paste diamonds hanging from her ears danced in the light of her eyes as she looked for him.

They were searching for each other in this mixed-up world, in this overwhelming crowd of humanity, and when their eyes finally met and she smiled that smile of hers, it made all of that searching worth it.

Somehow, they found each other in the crowd, and he took her hands in his as they gazed deeply into each other's eyes. This was enchantment, wasn't it? This feeling of being under someone else's spell so completely that words and thoughts become secondary to that magnetic pull you feel to them. The best part, though, was that she was as much under his spell as he was under hers.

"Hi," she breathed, with a smile when she finally reached him.

"Hi," he agreed.

"You look…"

"*You* look…"

When neither of them could finish their thought, they laughed at the ridiculousness of it all. "Come on," May said, rolling her eyes with a self-conscious smile. "We are not teenagers anymore. This should be easy to—"

He couldn't handle it for another second. Dipping down, he captured her lips in his, not caring who was watching or what they might say. In that moment, all he wanted, all he cared about, was the taste of her and feeling her heartbeat against his chest as he pulled her in close.

When they finally pulled apart again, he raised one

sardonic eyebrow. "To be fair, the last time we went dancing, we were eighteen and a little bit drunk."

"Don't say that so loud," May said, barking a laugh as she allowed him to pull her into his side so they could survey the room. "I still haven't told my mom that we raided the wine cellar that night."

The party was starting to hit its upswing now, with guests moving along auction items and buffet stations, the dance floor and the bars. Decorations and lights hung over everything, giving it an almost otherworldly feel, one that several photographers stationed at various corners of the room captured. Tom noticed that Annie's photographer friend—the one who'd bullied May out into the woods in that ridiculous dress—hadn't shown up tonight, and he couldn't help but wonder if Annie had dismissed him once she realized that he and May were perfect for each other.

Despite Tom's worries, the room hummed with excitement and cheer as the townies mingled with the tourists, as the local shopkeepers in their department store finest rubbed elbows with the elites of San Francisco and New York who'd flown in for the occasion. A band of pride wound through him. They'd done it. They'd actually done it.

Electricity jolted through him as May took his proffered hand and he led her out onto the dance floor, where the band was playing the beginnings of a restrained, slow waltz. He didn't know the first thing about how to waltz properly, but May seemed as content to just lay her head on his shoulder and sway as he was to hold her.

"I think we did a pretty good job," May said, muttering against his lapel. Her breath tickled at his neck; he couldn't help but hold her closer. "If I do say so myself."

"You know, I have to agree with you. Even if Annie *did* do most of the work. Well, all of the work."

May shrugged against him. "It's what she does. And we did a very good job in letting her do it."

"She's *also* a matchmaker. A pretty terrible one, something we should be pretty grateful for."

Gradually, Tom became aware that the attention of the room had settled squarely on his shoulders, watching and whispering as he danced with the town's favorite girl. This could have bothered him. Maybe it should have. Yet holding May close was like a shield against the questioning glares and curious stares. They could think and feel how they liked. It didn't matter, not as long as he and May had each other.

He glanced to the far end of the dance floor, where Annie was currently dancing an actual waltz with Mr. Eiserloh, the town's ancient librarian, who'd just retired this year after almost sixty years of service to the town. The man was still happily married, which meant that Annie couldn't possibly set her matchmaking sights on him, but Tom couldn't imagine she'd step away from her favorite hobby for very long, not when she still had at least a few single friends to set up. "Who do you think she'll turn her attention to next?"

"Rose," May said, as easily as breathing and just as light. "It's got to be Rose. No question."

"I don't know. Maybe she should turn her efforts inward." Tom's smirk bubbled into a small, self-assured chuckle. Annie would certainly have an easier time of finding a match for the quiet, mild-mannered Anderson sister, but Tom liked Annie. He wanted her to be happy, especially given how lonely she'd been in the past. "After all, her ex-fiancé is now very much dating someone else. If he gets to be this happy, then so should she."

Lifting her face from his chest, May glanced up at him, open-mouthed, and was about to say something when a shadow from behind him crossed her face. Then he felt a pair of cold fingers tap his shoulders.

"Excuse me."

He turned, surprised at the voice. Of all the people he'd expected to be faced with tonight, Harper Anderson certainly wasn't one of them. Yet there she stood in a floral-print gown and a smile as fake and toxic as sugar substitute, waiting for their attention.

Tom stole a glance at May; she seemed as surprised as he was by the sudden interruption, but she recovered quickly as her sister addressed her.

"Do you think I could cut in?" Harper asked.

The party continued to swirl around them, and they both knew that there was no getting out of this without a scene.

"Sure," May said, shrugging and letting Tom go. He instantly missed her warmth. "I'll go grab us a drink."

In a flash, she disappeared into the crowd, leaving Tom and Harper to linger at the edges of the dance floor. No matter how he scanned the woman's face, he couldn't get a read on her. Was this going to be an awkward interrogation about his intentions? An apology for hating him for so long? A blessing of their new relationship? Or was it going to be one of those intimidation games that ended with a threat to stay away from her sister?

He didn't have the first clue. All he knew was that if he didn't start dancing with her soon, people were going to talk. The last thing he needed was more talk, especially on a night like tonight. Harper tucked herself into a stiff waltz position with him—way more formal and mechanical than the dance he'd just shared with May—and refused to look at him as he led her through an uncomfortable, stilted sway.

"So." She sniffed. *Ah, so it was going to be one of those intimidation games then.* His pulse quickened as she continued, her tone suddenly tense and not at all friendly, "Thomas Elizabeth Riley."

"Not my middle name."

The joke went ignored. Harper pressed on. She kept her feet rooted to the floor, which made any semblance of fluid movement impossible; their sway was awkward and reminded him of middle school socials. "What are you doing here?"

"It's a party, for the festival I planned," he said with a shrug and a good-natured smile, trying not to let anyone around them know that he was basically being held as an unwilling hostage in this dance. "I thought it would be good if, you know, I showed up."

Another joke flew right past Harper Anderson. He could hear a struggle in her tone, where she tried to keep herself kind and cordial while really wanting to lash out. "Listen. I don't know what you're trying to do with May, but I wanted you to know that if you hurt her again, then you're going to have some serious trouble from me. I don't want a repeat of the last time the two of you dated."

It doesn't matter what they think, he reminded himself, *as long as we have each other.* Raising one eyebrow in a cool, slightly condescending look that he wasn't exactly proud of, Tom glanced down at his current dance partner. His temper wanted to flare; rage pooled beneath his skin at the injustice of it all. But he had to keep his cool; he'd never win anyone's good opinion with outbursts.

"And what did I do, exactly, Harper?" he asked, still using that veneered, sickly sweet voice of his, the one he used when he wanted to prove to someone that he wasn't the monster they thought he was. Unfortunately, he still hadn't perfected it; Harper Anderson seemed capable of only seeing him as a beast.

"Be careful with her. That's all I'm saying."

"May is smart and strong and independent," Tom said,

leaning a little too hard on that last word. They'd both been guilty of letting other people control them through the years; it was time they both learned to let it go. "I'm sure she knows what's best for her. But I promise. She won't ever be hurt again. And neither will I."

The words were strong. A declaration. But just as he spoke them, Harper unwound herself from his grip, looked him in the eye, and spoke a declaration of her own. A sad, disappointed, uncertain declaration. One from a sister trying very hard to protect the people she loved most in the world.

"I just don't know if I can believe you."

A voice from over Tom's shoulder stopped him before he could respond. Not that he would have responded. Words had totally and completely failed him.

"Well, fortunately," May said, "he'll have a long time to prove you wrong."

"May—"

"It's okay," she replied, though it was clear to anyone with eyes and ears that things most certainly *weren't* okay. Her hands shook with the force it was taking to control her emotions. "I know you're just looking out for me."

Harper wasn't going to be shrugged off that easily. "Can we talk?"

"Sure." Without asking, May slipped into Tom's grip, where he was more than happy to keep her. "But I'm going to finish this dance with my boyfriend first, if that's okay?"

For a long stretch of pulsing music, Tom wasn't sure Harper would relent. But eventually, she nodded and retreated to the corner of the room, where Luke and her other sister waited for her, no doubt to recount what had just happened between them, leaving Tom and May alone.

"I'm sorry about all that," May muttered, rolling her eyes. "I left the bar as soon as I saw her turn on you like that.

I could practically see steam coming from her ears from across the room."

"It's okay," Tom said, his smile as weak as his lie.

"No, it's not. I'll talk to her."

For a few more bars of music, the pair of them danced, an easy swish back and forth moving their bodies like a heartbeat. Desperate for something to say to her—anything—he tried to shake off the last few minutes, only to find himself replaying that moment over and over again. *I just don't know if I can believe you.*

If Harper, May's sister, one of her only friends in the entire world, didn't trust him...If she was going back to a houseful of people who would try to dissuade her from being with him...

Unless May was willing to set the record straight for once, the town's enmity would always stand between them. And then what chance did they have?

The thought gnawed at him, until Tom felt a small, soft hand reach up and stroke his cheek. He glanced down at the woman in his arms, who watched him with sympathetic eyes. "Hey. I love you. I'm not going to let anything get in the way of that. I promise."

May smiled up at him, and for a split second—with the music and the lights and the warmth of her in his arms—he could almost pretend that he believed her.

But when he pressed his lips to hers, the kiss felt more like a goodbye than a promise.

Chapter Twenty-One

May

Post-party sleepovers had become something of a tradition with the "Anderson Sisters-plus-Annie" clan. Annie's disastrous party earlier this summer notwithstanding, evenings of dancing and wine and general merriment were usually punctuated by all the girls getting together at the Anderson house and chatting the night away as they wiped away their makeup and soaked up whatever alcohol they'd been drinking with a few pieces of sourdough bread and whatever kind of fresh cheese they could find in the fridge.

The Festival's Welcome Party was no exception to this rule, but the tone of the night was decidedly more muted, more awkward, than any of the ones that had come before it.

Usually, these nights were marked by late-night runs to favorite 24-hour taco trucks or oversized fast-food deliveries, movies from their childhood that would keep them up nearly until sunrise. Tonight, when they returned to the Anderson house, there was no eating ice cream directly out of the pint or trading pj's until they all looked like a mismatched set of shop mannequins.

There was quiet. Long, exchanged glances. The removal of makeup. And not much else.

And when Rose and Harper made it clear that they weren't going to do much more than that, retiring up to their bedrooms, Annie planted herself at the bottom of the steps, glued her hands to her hips, and tossed her chin in Harper's direction.

May, who waited on the first floor, watched the entire exchange with quiet, uncertain awe.

"All right, Harper, what did my knucklehead brother do to you?"

Rose and Harper stopped, halfway up the steps. Harper's brow somehow deepened even further than it had been before. "What?"

"It's just that despite the fact that this party went off without a hitch, thank you very much, you two are walking around like someone kicked Stella. What happened?"

Another layer of awkwardness piled onto the silence. Annie may not have known why everyone had chosen stilted conversation and early bedtimes, but the three sisters certainly did. May's stomach rolled as if she'd suddenly hit the top of a roller coaster.

Harper and Rose shared a look, one May wasn't sure she could read. Eventually, when it became clear that Harper wasn't going to field this one, Rose sighed, descended a handful of steps, and took it upon herself to speak.

"We actually wanted to talk to May about that."

Annie's brow furrowed, disturbing the soft pink sleep mask resting upon her forehead. She ripped it off and pocketed it. "Talk about what?"

"Nothing," May said, her tone flatlining. "There's nothing to talk about."

And in her estimation, that was true. She'd fought hard

to open her heart back up to Tom, to forget about what other people thought and embrace what she wanted with everything she had, damn the consequences. She was *not* about to let her sisters talk her out of that.

Because if there was anyone on this earth who could do it, it was them, the women she trusted more than anyone else.

As Harper leaned against the back wall of the staircase, arms folded and jaw set, Rose's face grayed. Her bottom lip trembled. Confrontation wasn't her strong suit, but when she spoke, conviction trembled the sound.

"We're worried about you, May."

Maintaining an air of civility—not to mention keeping her voice down so that their parents, sleeping upstairs, wouldn't suddenly wake up and check on the commotion down here—proved more difficult than May would have liked to admit. "I'm *not* listening to this. I'm finally happy, and you two want to step all over it."

Harper didn't move from her place on the wall when she snapped, "You *think* you're happy, but what happens when he leaves you again? Hm? You're not going to be so happy then, are you?"

Rose was wringing her hands now, caught in her own whirlpool of, "And what will people think? Do you want everyone thinking that you're some weak-kneed woman who will make the same mistakes over and over again?"

"I don't care what people think."

Harper snorted. "Really? When did that start?"

That stung. The unfiltered truth usually did. It took May a moment to recover.

"He loves me, and I love him, and right now that's all that matters."

"It's all that matters until he shatters you like he did the last time."

"There was no *last time*."

There it was. A confession. For a moment, as the truth landed and settled like the shrapnel after a landmine explosion, May couldn't breathe. She couldn't think. She couldn't *believe* they'd gotten deep enough under her skin to force that out of her.

The corners of her vision darkened as she realized what she'd just done. And worse, what was undoubtedly going to follow.

There was a reason she hadn't told the truth in all these years, not even to the people she loved and trusted above all others. It was because the truth was a threat, a terror, and now... it was one she couldn't take back.

Harper pushed away from the wall. Rose leaned against the bannister, as if she could no longer support her own weight. And Annie, for her part, couldn't seem to close her slackened jaw.

"What are you talking about?" Harper asked, her voice low and dangerous, humming like an oncoming tornado.

May tried to convince herself that it would be better this way, that telling them everything would only end in hugs and reconciliations and *I understand*s, but her heart knew better. Every word she spoke struck at her heart with the weight of an executioner's drum.

"I broke up with him, okay? I was afraid to leave Hillsboro. I was afraid I'd lose him. I was afraid of what everyone would say. I was afraid of failing, of being alone, and so I dumped him on graduation night. Everyone else *assumed* that he broke up with me, and I let them think that because I was so ashamed. Because I didn't want everyone to turn on me. I didn't think he'd be coming back. I didn't think it would matter. I thought it was harmless—"

"You..." Rose didn't meet her gaze. She stared at the

floor for answers, her brow knit in devastated confusion. May's heart ripped at the sight. "You let us believe a lie?"

"I didn't mean to. It just... It just sort of happened. And I'm sorry—"

That wasn't good enough for Harper. May should have known better than to think differently. Rage and hurt mingled in her screeching tone, apparently no longer caring if the whole state, much less their sleeping parents, heard about all this. "Sorry? *Sorry?* I convinced Annie to break up with Tom because of that story. You lied to us all—"

May didn't have time to register what she'd just been told about Annie and Tom. She wasn't a liar. She couldn't be a liar. "I *never* lied!"

"Maybe, but you were happy to live one!"

That came from Rose, whose lip now quivered as she tried to hold back unshed tears. May staggered back a step, almost as if she'd just been shot. Rose never raised her voice. May's betrayal had been enough to provoke the best of the Anderson sisters to lose the very thing that made her so special—her ability to love and forgive and show kindness to anyone.

May had never felt so small. Or so miserable. Defenses kept rising to her lips, even though she knew none of them were good enough to actually earn her their forgiveness or understanding.

"I didn't mean to—"

"You got up every day and decided not to tell the truth. Every day you made that decision. You did mean to. And just because you feel bad about it now doesn't mean—"

Through all of this—the revelations, the fighting, the insults, the bombshells—Annie had been noticeably quiet. She hung back, folding into herself until she nearly disappeared. But as Harper's tone rose nearer to screaming, she cut her off, heading straight for the door without a goodbye.

"I'm so sorry. I need to go," she choked.

May's heart ripped again, a feat she wasn't sure was even possible. She called after her friend as the full weight of what Harper had said earlier truly set in. Harper had told Annie the rumors of Tom and May's breakup as a way to break off their engagement. The end of Tom and Annie might have been all May's fault. "Annie!"

Her friend paused in the doorway. She turned slightly over her shoulder, eyes wet and brimming with tears. "May…" She trailed off, and for a moment, the woman in question held her breath, waiting for her to say something, anything, that would make all of this okay. That was what Annie did, after all. She fixed things. Nothing was ever beyond mending as far as Annie was concerned. Except, apparently, this, because when Annie did finish her thought, it was to say only, "I have to go."

And then she was gone. She let herself out, closing the door behind her and leaving May with her two sisters. The two sisters currently glowering down at her from the staircase.

She couldn't meet their eyes. Couldn't handle the thought of lifting her head up. She didn't know if she could stand watching another person she loved walk out of her life, and she could feel Harper's desire to storm out pulsing through the air.

It was one thing to lose a friend. Losing a sister? Unthinkable.

"Yeah. I think I have to go, too," Harper said.

With that, she left, her slippers signaling her long retreat down the upstairs hallway…and out of May's life. A cavernous emptiness opened in May's heart, and she dragged her eyes up to where Rose still stood on the landing, looking down at her with a mixture of hatred and love, pity and hurt, in her eyes.

"Rose," May said, the name a prayer and a plea. "Rose, you have to believe me. You have to know how sorry—"

Slowly, Rose lifted one of her hands. May's voice died in her throat. Parts of her heart died with it.

"I know you are. Of course I know you're sorry. But I just think we're all going to need a little bit of time, okay?"

A watery smile lifted Rose's lips, and just as the tears were about to tip over onto her cheeks, she retreated up the stairs. May didn't find the strength to speak until she was alone.

So very alone.

"Yeah . . . okay."

Chapter Twenty-Two

Tom

When Annie had come over the morning after the dance, Tom assumed this was going to be another one of their little heart-to-hearts about May. Annie would antagonize him about moving too slow. He would assure her he knew what he was doing. She'd go on to meddle even more deeply in their lives. Et cetera. Et cetera. Et cetera. Around and around they would go in this dance until he and May were married—wow, he could barely believe that was a thought he could have now—and Annie could finally move on to some new victims.

His assumption turned out to be partly true. She was here to talk about May. It just wasn't anything he wanted to hear.

Now, almost an hour of Annie's nonstop talking later, Tom sat in the small living room of his loft apartment over their crush facility, stared at his hands, and wished desperately for that sweet, innocent time when he thought her constant meddling merely annoying instead of life-shattering.

"I'm sorry to tell you this. I just…" Annie's voice cracked. She collapsed into a nearby chair. Tom did not look up from a small knot in the floorboards near her feet. "I just thought you needed to know."

He ran over and over all this new information again. Then again. Then again. Trying not to see what was so clear to him now.

Not only was May suggestible and persuadable...She wanted to do the same to others. She wasn't just a victim, caught in the deadly maw of the small-town culture that had eaten both of them alive. She was also one of its sharp teeth, ensnaring others in the same way she'd been ensnared.

"So, she asked Harper to try and break off our engagement because...?"

"I don't know. I guess she couldn't stand to see us together. Our relationship was hurting her feelings."

It was clear to him that Annie wasn't upset by the actual breaking up—after all, Annie was the queen of meddling; it would have been wrong for her to question someone else interfering in her life—but rather, she was upset with the lie and projecting that hurt onto the manipulation.

He knew how lonely Annie had been when she moved to Hillsboro. He also knew how happy she was to finally have friends. This betrayal must have cut her more deeply than he could have imagined.

"We wouldn't have worked anyway," he said softly.

"I know that. Obviously, we wouldn't have worked. But...that doesn't make it hurt any less. What if we *had* been meant for each other and then, suddenly, Harper breaks us up based on a lie? I thought she was my friend. I thought you were my friend."

"I am your friend."

"But you lied, too. You didn't tell me what happened between you two."

"I didn't think it was my place to say."

"And look where it got you."

That landed like a blow to the center of Tom's chest. He'd never seen Annie this way. Annie, the one person in this entire world who perpetually saw the sunny side, now stood before him in a puddle of shadow, trying to convince him that the woman he loved, the woman he fought to forgive, maybe wasn't worthy of it.

"I love her, Annie," he said, the words practically a plea.

Annie's face contorted in something like sympathy as she crouched down onto the ottoman before him.

"And what happens when history repeats itself, hm?" Her eyes burned, passion blazing through her. Hell hath no fury like a heartbroken friend, it seemed. "You think someone who could be so easily swayed would go the rest of her life without it happening again?"

"That's bitterness talking. You're angry and you're hurt—"

"And you should be too!" she snapped, her voice rising to a shout.

"I am!" he shouted right back, then caught himself and drank in long, calming, deep breaths to try and wrestle his emotions under control. "Okay? I am. She didn't want me and she still interfered with my life. Of course it hurts me. But I have to trust her, right? She told me she'd never let people drive us apart again."

"Honestly, I don't know anymore, Tom. I'm worried about you; what if she does?"

Tom shook his head, but by now they both knew he was trying to convince himself more than he was trying to convince her. Deep down, he knew that she was right. Or more accurately, that she *could* be right. That spark of doubt spread through him faster than wildfire, until it consumed everything inside him and left his heart as little more than charred cinders. He had known, hadn't he, that his happiness couldn't last?

He wanted to delay the inevitable, but it wasn't possible. His body, weighed down by his aching heart, dragged him to the pavilion, where the cleanup from last night's party had begun in earnest. The limp decorations hung pathetically from the high, vaulted ceiling; trash littered the floor as the first volunteer—May—cleaned them up as she waited for the rest of her crew.

The moment he saw her, he wished he hadn't. She was unconscionably beautiful, an image of everything he'd ever wanted and everything he'd ever dreamed of. But everyone had to wake up from dreams sometime, didn't they? Today was his turn. He made a beeline straight for her.

"Tom!" she called, turning to face him with a broad smile, one that only faltered when she saw how quickly and seriously he was walking toward her. "Hey. Where's the fire?"

"No fire. Just"—he narrowed his eyes slightly as he searched her face for any sign of distress, for any hint that she knew why he was really here—"wanted to see how you were doing. Are you okay?"

Just as quickly as she'd turned to welcome him, she returned to her sweeping. Her voice pitched a little too high. "Mm-hm. Why wouldn't I be?"

"Maybe because Annie isn't speaking to you and your sisters are trying to break us up."

His throat constricted as he spoke, but he held firm, crossing his arms over his chest and trying to hold his heart in. For a brief moment, May faltered in her sweeping. She didn't bother looking back at him when she went back to it.

"You heard about that, did you?"

"Yeah. I heard about it. I'm just wondering why I didn't hear about it from you. Or about the reason why."

May shrugged, letting her broom carry her farther and farther away from him. Her voice strangled, she tried to sound casual, but he could see straight through it. Every syllable she spoke was another knife straight to his heart. "It's not a big deal. It's something I have to deal with."

"Not a big deal? You can't think that," he choked.

Please just say you're sorry. Apologize and maybe we can move on. We've all made mistakes. If you just show me that you're sorry for them, then we can turn a page on this whole thing and forget about it.

He mentally begged her to change, to be something different than the shadow of her he'd designed in the dark recesses of his mind, a master manipulator who all at once hadn't wanted to be with him but also couldn't stand the thought of someone else bringing him happiness.

"It's nothing you should concern yourself with, I mean," she practically chirped.

How was it possible that words spoken in such a light tone could sink him so hard and so fast?

"No. I'm concerned. I'm really concerned."

"What do you mean?"

"You know, maybe we were a bit hasty. Maybe...Maybe we shouldn't do this, you and I."

That was when she chose to turn, hitting him with the force of those wide, green eyes once again. She looked as if he'd struck her. He hated himself for that, but he couldn't hate himself for what he was about to do.

She'd broken his heart more times than he could count, and even now she couldn't say sorry for it. For the rest of his life, he would have to wear this stone around his neck. He'd know that the woman he loved was inconstant. How could you bank an entire life on someone you couldn't trust?

She'd lied to him just like she'd lied to everyone else. Just like she continued lying to everyone else. His own breathing grew harsh and ragged, as if his body was fighting what he was about to do.

"I don't understand," she said, blinking as if her vision were suddenly getting very blurry indeed. He tried not to notice the tears rising up in front of those emerald eyes.

"I'm breaking up with you," he said, in as calm and measured a voice as he could. A clean break. That's what they needed. To put this entire mistake as far behind them as they possibly could. "Is that clear enough? I can't do this. I can't spend the rest of my life looking over my shoulder, wondering if the person I love is telling me the whole truth. Are you?"

"What are you talking about? I am telling the truth," she protested, but it was a little weaker this time. A little less certain. She knew that he knew about Annie. About the truth. He waited for her to fill in the gaps, but it never came.

"For how long? What happens when the truth doesn't suit your whims anymore? What happens when you change your mind about me, again?"

"I won't."

There was nothing he wanted more than to go back to last night, when she was dancing in his arms through this very ballroom. When he thought that everything would turn out all right. But he couldn't keep fooling himself that it was possible.

"I don't think I can believe that anymore."

"Tom—"

Dropping the broom completely, she stepped toward him. He took a measured, cautious step back, unsure if he was strong enough to resist her touch. His own vision blurred. Tom blinked away unshed tears.

"I'll sort out my end of the festival duties. I think it would be best if we try to stay out of each other's way until this whole thing is over, okay?"

"Tom, I really don't understand—"

"Annie told me. She told me about your fight with your sisters, about the way you got Harper to break us up."

"Oh."

"And I could have handled that. I could have...but you still can't look me in the eyes and tell the truth, can you? You're still so worried about what people think that you can't even tell the one person you're supposed to care about the truth!"

"I didn't think it mattered," May said, staring at the floor as though she wanted to disappear into it. "It was something I needed to figure out and handle myself."

"But that's the thing, May. If you can't trust me to help you handle things, then you don't trust me at all. And if that's the case, then how can I put *my* faith in *you*?"

There it was, out there and unapologetic. His rough, harsh voice sent shockwaves through the air, and with every subsequent reverberation, May seemed to grow smaller and smaller before him.

"Okay," she finally muttered. "Yeah, maybe...maybe it's best that we just...yeah. Finish the festival on our own, then."

For a moment, he stood there, silently begging and pleading with her to say something, anything, to change his mind. But she didn't move. She didn't speak. She only raised the back of her wrist to her cheeks to wipe away some emotion that had gotten loose up there.

A wave of bitterness calcified his barely beating heart.

What had he expected? She was highly suggestible, easy to persuade. Of course she was going to let him talk her into breaking up.

She wasn't strong enough for anything else. And neither was he.

As he walked away, he felt the warm parts of him fall away too, leaving only sadness and ice to fill up his veins. Heartbreak was always worse the second time around.

Chapter Twenty-Three

May

Growing up on a flower farm, you learned to think and feel in colors. When you own your own shop and supply most of the products *for* that shop, then that learned behavior only gets reinforced, becoming more and more a part of you with every passing season.

Being with Tom was like the peonies, with their grand pink petals growing deeper and richer as they got closer to the heart of the bloom. The last few weeks, while they were rekindling their acquaintance, was the tentative blues of the young hydrangea, careful and cautious and safe.

Now? Now, she was gray as pulled, dying weeds, with their tangled root systems shriveling up in the sun.

The worst part of it all was that she hadn't just lost Tom. Losing him would have been bad enough, heartbreaking enough, all on its own. But in her lies and deceit and defensiveness, she'd also lost her friends and her family, the people who were more important to her than anything else in this world. Even worse, she felt so embarrassed, so ashamed of the way she acted. She hadn't just lost the people she cared about; she'd lost her pride, too.

She'd feared, for so long, that telling the truth about her breakup with Tom would land her squarely on the *out*side of Hillsboro's in-group. Turns out, lying was what earned her that distinction.

May Anderson was utterly, completely, and totally alone. A reality she could blame on no one but herself.

All morning, she'd been trying out her old tricks for distracting herself before the festival day started. She visited her bees. She tried her hand at making candy—a disaster. She didn't have even a hint of concentration and ended up burning it several times. She even tried yoga again, but it only reminded her of the Annie-shaped hole in her life.

There wasn't anywhere she could run to escape her loneliness and isolation. But life didn't stop. There was a festival going on this weekend, and they needed her help. Pulling the family's old truck to the top of the hill, May started toting boxes upon boxes of programs—all hand-folded by her in the wee hours of the morning, alone—down from her bedroom and into the back of the truck.

Maybe her screaming muscles would take her mind off things.

However, by the time she got the second box placed, a strangely familiar voice piped up behind her.

"Hey there, stranger."

May spun on her heel to spy the weathered, warm face of Tom's grandmother. That, in and of itself, would have been shocking. But when May's eyes wandered farther down the hill, she spotted her own mother trotting close behind.

But she wasn't alone. As the glare cleared, May discovered that there was another figure accompanying her mother, the three of them clambering up the hill toward her like a mismatched parade. May blinked.

"Mrs. Riley? Mom? *Dad?*"

She could understand the sudden appearance of her parents. But to have Mrs. Riley with them was unthinkable. May hadn't spoken to the woman since their awkward encounter at her house—the day that May and Tom had practiced what he would say to Joanna when he asked her out—and she hadn't wanted to. The shame was too much to bear.

Mrs. Riley had always been so kind to May. She hated knowing that she'd broken the heart of the person she loved more than anything in the world.

"We need to speak with you," her mother said, huffing up the hill and halting just beside Tom's grandmother. A knot formed in May's stomach.

"I'm really busy."

Mrs. Riley raised one caustic eyebrow at the two boxes waiting for their mates in the bed of the truck. "I can see that."

"I thought you said you were going to be nice about this," May's mother snapped.

"I *am* being nice. I'm also being direct, which is a quality I think May here appreciates, don't you, May?"

Her mind moved too fast for her mouth to catch up. Possibilities swung at her in every direction. Maybe they'd called a truce years ago and forgotten to tell everyone? Maybe they'd teamed up together when they saw May and Tom at the dance the other day. Maybe they'd come here to help her with festival prep.

All of them seemed unlikely, so she stumbled over a response.

"I would love some clarity about why you're here. Why all of you are here. And why the three of you are, you know, together."

Mrs. Riley shot her mother a *told you so* look and continued on. "We're all part of the same Wednesday poker game.

Your dad is killer in Hold 'Em," she said, as if it explained anything instead of rousing about ten thousand more questions in its place. "Do you love my grandson?"

May choked on her own breath. "*I beg your pardon?*"

"Yes," her father said, nodding his head solemnly. "She does love him."

Her mother gently prompted her, completely ignoring May's dropped jaw. "Answer the question, May, darling."

"Mom!"

"Do you love him, or don't you?" Mrs. Riley asked, as if it were the easiest question in the world to answer. In some ways, it was. May didn't need to dig deep inside herself for the answers; she'd known this all along... The problem wasn't whether she loved Tom or not, It was whether he had it in his heart to still love her. And whether she could prove to him that she was worth taking another risk on.

"Of course I do, but it's not that simple."

And she did. She loved him more than she ever knew it was possible to love someone. It was that love that made her want to protect him from her, that made her want to step away and keep his heart intact. She needed to protect everyone. It was all she had left. But her father looked down at her with warm, understanding eyes.

"Dear, we know the truth. And if we have to work a little harder against the gossips and liars in this town, then we'll do it. We just want you to be happy. That's all we've ever wanted."

May bit her bottom lip. She couldn't... She couldn't just...

Mrs. Riley adjusted her hands on her hips. "So, you love him. What are you doing to get him back? Because this doesn't look like getting him back. This looks an awful lot like sulking."

No, it looks like I'm trying to keep doing the job I agreed to do even though getting out of bed this morning felt more difficult than landing on the moon. May struggled to keep her cool in check.

"I'm not..." *Deep breaths, May. Deep breaths. And for God's sake, please don't cry.* "He doesn't want me back. And he's right not to."

"No." The twinkle in Mrs. Riley's eye turned to stone; her lips thinned into a hard line. "He's not. The two of you are stubborn and proud and hardheaded and absolutely perfect for each other, no matter what anyone else says. That's a love worth fighting for. I swear to you, it is."

May's eyes flickered between the three people before her. It wasn't fair, she wanted to scream. All of *them* had found the loves of their lives and had gotten many happy years with them. May just felt like a stupid kid who'd blown her chance through selfishness. Taking advice from them felt as concrete as taking advice from a fairy godmother. Or, more accurately, a trio of them.

"Maybe it wouldn't work. Maybe it's just not right for us," she said, her voice tearing. "Have you ever considered that?"

Her mother and Mrs. Riley shared a long, lingering look. May's father touched his wife on the shoulder. And when May's mother turned back to her, she couldn't believe the tenderness in the woman's eyes. She had never been the most touchy-feely of mothers, preferring the cold practicalities of numbers and the frosty reality of raising three daughters with a small business to run. For most of her life, in fact, May believed that her mother didn't really like her. But now, as their eyes met and her mother placed her hands on May's shoulders, she could feel her mother's love coming through the air, through her fingertips, through every word she spoke.

"We've spent the last eight years considering that, and in the last six weeks, you've both proved us wrong. Go after him, May. For your happiness and for your future. Please. You are never going to be happy unless you escape this town and unless you do it with him at your side."

No matter how hard May tried to tell herself not to cry, she still found herself tearing up as her mother pulled her tightly into her arms. It was only when she was released that Mrs. Riley continued, her matter-of-fact manner returning.

"He thinks you're inconstant and that you hide behind rumors and speculation."

May snapped her attention in her direction. "How did you know that?"

Her father shook his head, chuckling under his breath. "Everyone knows it by now, dear. You forget that Annie is the worst gossip out of us all."

"So show him you're not," Mrs. Riley encouraged. "Show him that his love is more important to you than anything."

"I wouldn't even know how to do that or what to say."

"Speak from the heart. That's all you can do."

The curtain behind the festival stage, which rested at the heart of Celia M. Hunter State Park, was a deep, rich, striking green, and as May stood pressed against it, waiting for her moment, she couldn't help but think it was the worst choice she could have made as far as decor was concerned. Her reasons for originally selecting it had been practical. Green was, according to several studies about repainting fire engines that she'd read during her three-in-the-morning festival prep, the color that the human eye could perceive the fastest, so people were naturally drawn to things made with or bedecked in that color. Now, when she looked at that forest-colored velvet, she could only think of what her mother used to say anytime one of the Anderson girls fell under the weather when they were little.

You look a little green, my dear.

May didn't know how she looked at this moment. She didn't *want* to know, actually. Imagining how she, with her sweaty forehead and shaking hands and trembling knees, must have looked to the random passerby was bad enough.

She also didn't need to know if she looked green because, in the depths of her, she *felt* green. As what she was about to do settled and solidified, a sickly slime filled her belly, threatening to upturn everything she'd managed to eat this morning.

Her mother, on the other hand, couldn't be accused of merely feeling green. Her emotions were written all across her face; she wrung her hands as if she were about to watch her daughter march up to a guillotine rather than give a speech in front of their small town.

"This is risky," her mother muttered, pacing back and forth.

May's lips pressed into a thin line. "Love is one big risk," she said, almost as a reminder to herself rather than to her mother.

Mrs. Riley glanced up from the foul-mouthed embroidery pattern she was bent over and raised one eyebrow. It wasn't so much a question as it was encouragement. A challenge. "You're really doing this, huh?"

"I have to," May said, with all the conviction she possessed. She didn't know how this would work out. She didn't know what would happen after she stepped beyond this curtain. She only knew one thing for certain, and it was the most important thing. "I love him."

"I know you do," her mother said, face contorting

uncomfortably. "I'm just hoping you're right about this whole thing."

"You're the one who told me to do this!"

"I'm the one who told you to go after him, not to do... *this*." She emphasized that last word as though it brought on a shudder to even think it.

The matriarch of the Anderson clan had always been obsessed with appearances and propriety and what people sat around and gossiped over all day. That was, in effect, one of the reasons May suspected her mother didn't like her as much as either of her two sisters—neither of them ever got into any gossip-worthy trouble. May seemed to attract it like flies to honey.

She should have known her mother wouldn't approve of this course of action. Still, she couldn't let it sway her.

"I lied to everyone, Mom. Or I let everyone believe a lie. And I did it because I wasn't secure enough in myself and my own feelings to actually, you know, be my own person. I can't just apologize to a few people or set the record straight for them. Everyone needs to hear this."

Her mother's eyes were wet and wide when she turned on her. "Even if it ruins your reputation?"

"Yeah." May nodded. "Even then."

"Well, here."

Her father, who had been sitting beside his wife, retrieved something from a small bag at his side that May had been too busy to notice. He pulled out a small boutonnière... One made entirely of sweet pea flowers. Carefully, he tacked it onto the lapel of May's dress and winked at her, lowering his voice so the other women backstage with them couldn't hear.

"For bravery. Go out and get your adventure, May. Have your second chance."

A round of clapping from behind the curtain alerted May

that their festival overlords were now in the midst of their speech to the assembled crowd. She tuned in, struggling to hear their calm, measured delivery over the thunderous throbbing of her own heart.

"After such a great first weekend of the festival, we wanted to call special attention to Miss Amelia Anderson and Mr. Thomas Riley, who were gracious enough to help take over the festival! Amelia has offered to say a few words of thanks and welcome of her own. Amelia, will you do the honors?"

Okay. No more delays now.

She had the rapturous attention of the entire town. She'd never get another opportunity like this, not if she lived for a thousand years.

If there was ever a day to tell the truth, this was it.

Carefully, she stepped out from behind the curtain, gave a small wave to the crowd, and shook the hands of the gentlemen who'd just retired the floor and the microphone. In a moment, they'd probably regret giving her this chance to speak, but May could only hope she didn't regret taking it.

A sea of familiar faces sprawled out before her, cheering her on as she adjusted the microphone and prepared to change—or maybe ruin—her entire life.

But also…maybe a little ruination was exactly what she needed right now.

"Yes. I would. Thank you. Um…hello. Some of you may know me already. I see lots of locals in the crowd today. My name is Amelia Anderson, but most people call me May. And I actually didn't take on this festival alone. I took it on with the help of Tom Riley."

She scanned the crowd. No sign of him. She tried not to let her stomach sink into the ground beneath her. When they'd divvied up responsibilities, he'd taken most of the behind-the-scenes stuff, so rationally she knew he probably wouldn't be here this morning.

Which was fine, of course. It had to be fine. Because this speech wasn't really about winning him back. It was about the truth. It was about doing what was right. It was about correcting a years-long wrong that she'd let these people carry on.

"Tom Riley is a good man. One of the best I've ever known. And we've all... Well, everyone in Hillsboro has been terribly cruel to him. Because, when I was eighteen, Tom and I broke up. And everyone thought it was his fault. But it wasn't. It was my fault. I let you all believe that Tom was a monster who'd left me, when, in reality, I was the monster. I used him as a shield because I couldn't bear to tell you all that I was too terrified to leave Hillsboro, too terrified that he would leave me and I would be alone."

Her voice trembled. She stared at a patch of grass between two people in the crowd, trying to force the right words to come out in the right order so that everyone here understood.

"I let you all believe that was true. Because it was easier for me. Safer. We all love each other deeply in this town, and because of that, when we feel like one of our own is threatened, we close ranks. By protecting me from this imaginary breakup, we hurt someone very deeply. We hurt Tom. And I'm ashamed that I let it go on for so long. Ashamed that I am the reason we hurt him. Tom is a good man who was so desperate to protect me and my reputation that he *let* everyone believe the lies. He bore a punishment for a crime he didn't commit so that you wouldn't put me on the outside of this community."

Her momentum built. So did her courage. She kept going, even as a few faces in the crowd contorted into masks of frustration and disgust.

"Well, today, I have to be honest. As much as I love you all, as much as I love Hillsboro, if being with Tom means being on the outside, then that's where I choose to be. I'm sorry I let you all believe a lie, but I'm not going to live that way anymore. I can't. I can't because... Well, because I love him. And that's more important than anything. That's worth the risk."

Chapter Twenty-Four

Tom

As Tom stood in the middle of the crowd, his head down and his heart on his sleeve, he couldn't believe that this wasn't a dream. But no matter how deeply he dug his fingernails into his palms, no matter how hard he bit into the inside of his cheek, he didn't wake up.

There she was, standing in front of the entire town—the community she'd let ostracize him for years, the one she was terrified of being excluded from—and telling them the truth.

All that mattered to her was her reputation, to holding on to her acceptance in their small town by even a fingernail, and still...she looked them in the eye and told them that they'd all been wrong.

His hands were shaking. Why were his hands shaking? Why did the back of his neck feel hot, as if someone—or many someones—were staring at him with repentant eyes?

Why did he want to run up on that stage and sweep her into his arms, kissing her like he'd never kissed her before? Why couldn't he hold on to his annoyance with her?

Oh, right. Because he loved her. And with every word she

spoke, apparently not realizing he was there in the crowd, hanging on to her every word, that love grew and grew until there wasn't any room in his heart for anything else.

Over the microphone, she sniffled. That sound, quiet and honest, lifted his head and finally, he saw her in all of her glory. Modestly attired in a sundress that made her look like sunshine itself, she clutched the microphone in her hand for dear life. Even at this distance, he could see tears welling up in her eyes, but she bravely blinked them away. Strength grew in her voice.

His heartbeat grew stronger and stronger with it.

"I love him. And I don't know if he still loves me, but I would be a liar if I stood here, in front of all of you, and pretended that I didn't. Tom Riley is the love of my life. No matter what anyone else says. No matter how anyone else feels about it. My heart has belonged, and always will belong, to him."

She didn't say anything for a long moment. Neither did anyone else. Shifting on the balls of her feet, she drank in a shaky breath, released on a self-deprecating laugh, and offered a small wave to the crowd.

"I think I've overstayed my welcome. Thank you all for listening."

For a moment, Tom felt as if he were watching a movie of this event. There he was, standing in the crowd. There May was, stepping politely down the steps as their festival overlords implored the band to cover up the awkwardness of May descending into the crowd. There the crowd was, standing between them.

Say something, you absolute barrel-head! he shouted at himself, screaming for him to wake up from the shock of what he'd just seen and heard enough to actually do something about it.

"May!"

The word, shouted from between his own lips, snapped him back into himself. He waved his arm over his head, calling it again. She stopped at the last step down from the stage, hovering slightly above the crowd and blinking in his direction, as if she wasn't sure if he was some kind of dream or if he was really there.

"Tom?"

Oh, he was there all right. And he'd heard every word.

Tom was vaguely aware that everyone who'd caught him screaming over the band was now staring at them, waiting for what would come next. The truth was, he didn't know what came next. All he knew was that, in this moment, he understood May Anderson as clearly as someone could understand another person in this mixed-up world.

That understanding meant that he could see her clearly now, and in seeing her clearly, he knew he'd never want to go back into the darkness again. Walking forward through the quickly parting crowd, he met her out in front of the stage, where they struggled to talk over the noise of the band.

"Hi," he said, swallowing back a wave of emotion.

"Hi," she said, clearly doing the same.

"That was…" No, the emotion wouldn't be contained. Now it was coming down from his eyes, one salty teardrop at a time. "That was some speech."

"Well, you know." She shrugged and shook her head, but there was no hiding her own tears…or her own smile, hesitant though it was. "It wouldn't be a May Anderson production without some kind of disaster. You remember when I starred in *Oklahoma!* in eleventh grade."

His heart slammed against his chest; it wanted to run straight into her arms. *He* wanted to run straight into her arms. But there was still one thing he needed to know. "Did you mean it?"

"Every word," she promised.

This time? He believed her.

"You know they're probably going to hate you, right?" he asked, glancing from side to side at the crowd and their oh-so subtle staring.

May nodded, emphatic. "Yeah. Probably. But I'd rather be hated for telling the truth than loved for being a liar. I didn't always feel that way, but, believe it or not, it feels pretty good to feel how I want to feel, not how anyone else tells me to feel."

The ring of truth rebounded in his ears.

"And that feeling is...?" He trailed off, stepping a little closer to her. His entire body craved the feeling of her lips against his.

"Being in love with you," she admitted.

"Then I have a confession to make."

"What's that?"

"I love you too."

Her eyes danced as she gazed up at him; they swam with all the hope and promise of a future he couldn't wait to begin.

"Really?"

"Always have," he promised, picking up one of her hands and kissing it, then repeating the action on the other. "Always will."

"And you aren't afraid I'll break your heart?"

"Of course I am. Less so now after that little display, but yeah." With her hands in his, it was easy to pull her in to him, where he could hold her as he wanted to do for the rest of his life. "The thing is, though, love is worth the risk."

She nodded, and the smile she offered him was too irresistible. "Love is worth the risk," she agreed.

Bending down, he captured her lips and tried to help her

feel everything he was promising now. His love. The future. Forever. No matter what lay ahead of them, no matter who hated them after this moment, he swore through that kiss that he would be right there at her side.

As the band quieted down, though, and the festival's formal presentation wound down, a familiar voice—repentant, hesitant, hopeful—broke them from their kiss. Tom and May turned to see Annie and May's two sisters standing there, their heads hung lower as they waited for their chance to make their peace.

"Excuse me, lovebirds," Annie said, her smile as blinding as ever, even as she wrung her hands and worriedly shifted her weight. "I think we have some apologizing of our own to do."

"So, I guess you heard everything," May said. "Can you forgive me?"

Just at that moment, Annie threw her arms around May's neck, pulling her in tight.

"You're my friend. Of course I was going to forgive you."

But the hugs didn't end there. Next, Harper and Rose joined the pile of embraces, all of them holding each other as tight as could be. Tom watched from the sidelines for a moment, until he felt Harper's strong arms drag him into the hug, too. He relished that feeling, that belonging. Hopefully, he'd have it forever.

"Thank you for telling the truth, May," Harper said.

"I'm just sorry it took me this long."

"Love you, little sister."

"Love you too. And thank you." The hug broke up, and May turned her attention to everyone in their small circle in turn. "Thank you all."

Annie, quick as ever, recovered the fastest out of any of them, and whipped a festival map from her purse, which she used as a prop to excitedly explain their next moves. "We were going to go to this booth where they freeze chocolate with liquid nitrogen. Do you want to come?"

May and Tom shared a look. Knowing that they weren't suddenly completely alone in the universe after this recent string of revelations was certainly a relief, but still, he wanted her to himself for just a few more minutes before rejoining the fold.

"Maybe in a bit," Tom offered.

"Okay, but you're missing out!"

Just like that, the sisters and Annie walked in the direction of their nitro-truffles, leaving Tom with someone infinitely sweeter. Tugging May back into his arms, he tried to memorize every inch of her, from the warmth of her skin against his to the handful of gray hairs already growing from the top of her head.

"So, what *do* you want to do now, Tom?" May asked, raising one curious and flirty eyebrow. "I would have thought frozen chocolates would be right up your alley."

Tom somehow managed to pull her even closer. The world around them dissolved as he did so. "I just think we should get started on our future, don't you?"

"Yeah," she agreed. "Much better than being stuck in the past."

"Oh, but before we go…"

"What?"

He lowered his lips until they were almost upon hers. "I'll be needing another kiss, please."

"Everyone is watching."

"I don't care. Do you?"

No, she didn't. By the way she threw herself into his arms and pressed her lips to his, he knew in the depths of his being that she didn't. And she never would again.

Epilogue

May

There is a certain kind of air that you can only find in Northern California, in those rare and beautiful places nestled between the mountains and the great ocean. In these small, imperfect places, full of beautiful, imperfect people, sometimes, that salty air from the sea and that earthy air from the mountains bow to each other, take hands, and dance—their movements certain and strong; their warmth and their chill perfectly blending into one smooth, fluid waltz.

On certain mornings, when the sunrise is perfectly painted along the horizon and the music of the songbirds and the trees is just perfectly harmonized, the air is crisp and clear. Like waking up to find that you can breathe in space. Like those dreams where everything is still and silent while also, somehow, containing the frenetic possibility of the entire universe.

And when May Anderson stepped out of her house that morning, her suitcases in hand and her heart more full than she could ever remember it being, she could swear it tasted like freedom. It felt like forever.

Even better, *she* felt like forever. Like every possibility and every hope and every silent, secret dream she'd ever had for herself was waiting out there for her, just beyond the horizon. Once before, she'd done this same thing. Back in high school, she'd come out here with her suitcases, and the possibilities had overwhelmed her.

Now there was no room in her heart for any fear. She could barely hold on to her heartbeat.

May Anderson and Tom Riley were finally getting out of this town. They didn't know what they were going to find out in the great, wide world. But all that mattered was that they were going together.

When she emerged from the house, she found her father sitting on the front porch, spectacles pulled down at the end of his nose and a steaming cup of coffee fogging up the lenses as he read his copy of the *Hillsboro Gazette*.

"Good morning, dear. Anything important to do today?" he asked, his cheeks growing mischievous dimples even as he continued reading. May couldn't help but smile. A watery smile, sure, but that's just because it was dusty out here. Probably.

"Nothing much. Just going on a little adventure."

He glanced up at her from over the lip of the paper; his eyes danced. "Well, don't come back until you have plenty of stories to tell."

"I promise."

Of course, the stillness and quiet of this morning couldn't last forever. Not in the Anderson house. No sooner had she made her vow than the front door *clanged* open on its hinges, practically rattling the house's foundations. Stella, first, darted out ahead of everyone, her hoof-sized paws rattling against the floor of the porch as she ran circles around May. Then the rest of the brigade followed.

Rose. Harper. Annie. Her mother. They all came in an excitable heap, carrying items and bags and fussing over her as though she were leaving for a trip to the underworld instead of a simple American road trip.

"All right," Rose sniffed, staring down at her socked feet as she handed over a *Muppets Show* lunch pail, one May remembered from their school days. "I packed you some sandwiches and some sodas. Don't want you two getting hungry once you hit that long patch in Kansas that I was reading about, where there's nothing for miles—"

Annie piped up, holding out a tin. "And I made cookies. You don't want your blood sugar to get too low out there. Emergency cookies. For emergencies."

"I appreciate the concern, but we're not going through Kansas, and I don't think either of us has low blood pressure." May stopped herself short. A smile tugged at her lips. After a lifetime of feeling like she didn't belong, like she was an outsider in her own family, here they were, showing her in their own small ways that they loved her. She pressed the small lunchbox to her chest. It had been Rose's favorite; she never let anyone else borrow it. Until now. "Thank you all."

Oh, it was no use. She wasn't going to pretend she wasn't emotional. Tossing her arms around her sisters, her friend, and her mother, she closed them in and tried to memorize every bit of them. The best thing about leaving home, her father had once told her, was knowing you get to come back to people who love you. May believed that now more than ever. The dust problem out here on the porch had only gotten worse, with its effects spreading to just about everyone— including May's father, who tried to hide the evidence with his newspaper. May tried to juggle all her packing pieces as she stepped out of the hug.

No matter what happened after she and Tom pulled out

of the driveway today, this old house and these people she loved would always be here for her. She hadn't been so sure of that back when she was eighteen. But now it was a knowledge written on her heart.

It was only a few moments later, after more tearful, joking goodbyes passed between them, that a familiar red pickup truck kicked up waves of dirt up the hill, and Tom Riley finally arrived. Hugs and kisses and threats about securing May's happiness were exchanged. Well-wishes followed soon after. And then Tom and May found themselves in the cab of Tom's truck. Alone for the first time.

"Good morning."

"Good morning to you," May replied, pressing her lips to his in a kiss before waving a hand at the picnic they'd packed for her. "I have enough provisions in here to last us all the way to England probably."

Tom clucked. "I don't think my truck can handle an Atlantic crossing."

"Not unless we want to end up like Jack and Rose."

"There was enough room on that door."

"Are you really going to start this road trip with an argument?"

"No. I'm going to start this road trip with a kiss. A real one."

Slowly, he lowered his lips to hers and cradled her face in his hands. She breathed him in, wanting to be closer and feel every bit of him.

He'd become a much better kisser in the years since they'd first dated. She was right. History was repeating itself. But with the wisdom of having failed before. Things were better now. So, so much better.

When they managed to break away, Tom readied himself at the steering wheel and glanced down at her. God, his smile. It could give her the courage to run across a battle-field. "Are you ready?"

She laced her fingers through his on the clutch, tether-ing herself to him. The golden hues of morning blossomed through the windows of the car, wrapping them both in the first rays of sunshine. She smiled up at him, wanting, in that moment, to do nothing else for the rest of her life.

"Yeah. I'm ready."

And with that they drove away, ready to find their futures. Together.

"Sweet as Honey" Pie

This is a Greek-inspired honey cheesecake pie with red wine sauce.

For the sauce:
- 1½ cups red wine (Pinot Noir recommended)
- ¾ cups sugar
- 1 teaspoon vanilla extract
- ½ lemon, juiced

For the pie:
- 1½ cups ricotta cheese
- 2 large eggs
- ½ cup honey
- 1½ teaspoons cinnamon

Before assembling your pie, you'll need to make your red wine sauce. In a large pan over medium heat, combine the red wine, sugar, vanilla extract, and lemon juice. Once a slight bubble begins, lower the heat to a simmer until the sauce is thickened—about twenty minutes.

While your sauce is thickening, preheat your oven to

325°F. Prepare a 6-inch springform pan, either by greasing it with butter or covering it in greaseproof paper.

In a mixing bowl, use a plastic spatula to combine the ricotta cheese, eggs, honey, and cinnamon until soft and fluffy. Pour into your springform tin, smoothing so the surface is level.

Bake for 45 to 50 minutes. Ensuring the pie is ready can be tricky—it should be brown on the top but still have the smallest bit of wobble. If the top browns too quickly, tent the top with tinfoil to keep from burning.

Once baked, allow the pie to cool to room temperature. Then slice and serve with a generous helping of red wine sauce!

Acknowledgments

Returning to Hillsboro in *Sweet Pea Summer* truly was such a gift, and I'm so grateful for the opportunity to have written May and Tom's story. First, I have to thank Emily and Kelsie, along with everyone else at Bookouture, who worked tirelessly to help me craft this into the book it is today. I can never thank them enough for all they did to help me as a writer, a storyteller, and as a person. I wrote this book during a particularly difficult time in my life, and knowing that I had two incredible people in my corner, rooting for me and this story, truly meant the world.

I want to acknowledge my stepfather, Derek Ponamsky, who won a National Championship this year. Geaux Tigers. You inspire me every day to chase my dreams and to never give up. I'm so glad I got to share that incredible journey with you.

Thank you to my sisters, who consistently remind me why I write these stories about the power of family and friendship. As I'm writing this, Elizabeth has gotten into MIT, Nia just got her black belt, and Lila is absolutely crushing it in everything she does. They are, as ever, the coolest people in the world, and I want to thank them for being my sisters and my friends.

Oh, and I have to thank Carrie Fisher. And Dolly Parton. And Queen Latifah. And my mom. And all the other strong, powerful women who, whether they know it or not, inspire me every day.

And, of course, as always, I have to thank Adam. This is a book about second chances and what-might-have-beens. I am so grateful that we took a chance on each other and on our love, so grateful that we have never had to fight for a second chance or wonder what might have been. Thank you for being my friend, my cheerleader, my "don't send that tweet" coach, my partner, and my husband. None of this would be possible without you. You have made my dreams come true.

About the Author

Alys Murray writes novels for the romantic in all of us. Born and raised in New Orleans, she received her BFA from New York University's Tisch School of the Arts and her master's in film studies from King's College London. She loves black-and-white movies and baseball games that go into extra innings.

You can learn more at:
AlysMurray.com
Twitter @WriterAlys
Facebook.com/AlysMurrayAuthor
Instagram @WriterAlys

Looking for more second chances and small towns?
Check out Forever's heartwarming
contemporary romances!

REUNITED ON
SUGAR MAPLE ROAD
by Debbie Mason

Ever since her fiancé's death over a year ago, Emma Scott's been sleep-walking through life, and her family is growing increasingly worried about her. Enter Josh Callahan, high school football coach and her brother's best friend. Though he may drive her crazy, his suggestion to fake-date is brilliant because there are no feelings involved. And his plan works... until Josh realizes that the feelings he has for Emma are all too real. But is Emma ready to share her heart again?

THE CORNER OF
HOLLY AND IVY
by Debbie Mason

Arianna Bell isn't expecting a holly jolly Christmas. That is, until her high school sweetheart, Connor Gallagher, returns to town. But just as she starts dreaming of kisses under the mistletoe, Connor announces that he will be her opponent in the upcoming mayoral race...even if it means running against the only woman he's ever loved. But with a little help from Harmony Harbor's matchmakers and a lot of holiday cheer, both may just get the happily-ever-after they deserve.

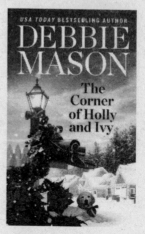

Connect with us at Facebook.com/ReadForeverPub

Discover bonus content and more on
read-forever.com

THE HOUSE ON FIREFLY BEACH
by Jenny Hale

Sydney Flynn can't wait to start fresh with her son at her sanctuary: Starlight Cottage at Firefly Beach. That is, until she spies her childhood sweetheart. Nate Henderson ended their relationship with no explanation and left town to become a successful songwriter—only now he wants to make amends. But when a new development threatens her beloved cottage, can Sydney forgive him and accept his help? Or will the town they adore, and the love they had for each other, be lost forever?

THE INN AT TANSY FALLS
by Cate Woods

When her best friend dies and sends her on a scavenger hunt from beyond the grave, Nell Swift finds herself setting off for a charming little Vermont town, where she's welcomed by friendly locals, including an adorable Labrador and a grumpy but attractive forester and his six-year-old son. Is Nell willing to start her life all over again and make this new town her forever home? Includes a reading group guide!

Meet your next favorite book with @ReadForeverPub on TikTok

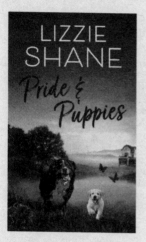

PRIDE & PUPPIES
by Lizzie Shane

After years of failing to find her own Mr. Darcy, Dr. Charlotte Rodriguez swears off dating in favor of her new puppy, Bingley. And there's no one better to give her pet advice than her neighbor and fellow dog owner George. When their friendly banter turns flirtatious, Charlotte finds herself catching *feelings*. But will Charlotte take one last chance with her heart before they miss out on happily-ever-after?

A CAT CAFE CHRISTMAS
by Codi Gary

In this laugh-out-loud, opposites-attract romance, veterinarian and animal lover Kara Ingalls needs a Christmas miracle. If Kara can't figure out some way to get her café out of the red, it won't last past the holidays. Marketing guru Ben Reese hatches a plan to put the café in the "green" by Christmas, but they will need to set aside their differences—and find homes for all the cats—to have their own *purr*-fect holiday... together.

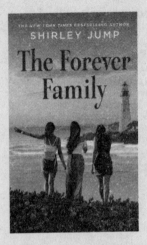

THE FOREVER FAMILY
by Shirley Jump

The youngest of three close-knit sisters, Emma Monroe is the family wild child. Maybe that's why a yoga retreat leads to a spur-of-the-moment decision to marry Luke Carter, a man she's met exactly three times. The next morning, Emma sneaks back home, where she should have nama-*stayed* in the first place. When her brand new husband arrives to convince her to give their marriage a chance, can she envision a future where her biggest adventures come not from running away but from staying?

SWEET PEA SUMMER
by Alys Murray

May Anderson made the biggest mistake of her life when she broke up with her high school sweetheart, Tom Riley. Now he's back in Hillsboro, California, to take over his family's winery—and wants nothing to do with her. But when they're forced to partner for the prestigious Northwest Food and Wine Festival, their plans to avoid each other fall apart. When working side by side causes old feelings to surface, can they find the courage to face the fears that once kept them apart?